You Before Me

by
Lindsay Paige

You Before Me
Copyright 2014 by Lindsay Paige

Printed in the United States of America.

ISBN-13: 978-1499571561
ISBN-10: 1499571569

Cover Designed by: Damonza
Edited by: K² Editing

Dedication

To my writing BFF, Mary Smith.
You are more amazing than words could ever describe.

Acknowledgements

Thank you, reader, for taking the time to read my book. Please consider leaving a review to let other readers know what you thought!

A huge thanks goes to my beta readers: Andrekia, Ariana, Heidi, Louise, Lucy, Michael, and Rachel. Thank you for your time and being such a help with Ryan and Gabe's story. I love you all!

Thank you, Damonza, for giving me a cover I love and tweaking it until I was absolutely happy with it.

Thank you, Kathy from K² Editing, for working with me. You're always a pleasure to work it and I'm happy you're my editor.

Thank you, Mary Smith, for listening to as I whined about this book. When I was close to chunking it and forgetting Ryan and Gabe existed, you listened to me and supported me. Because of that, I was able to finish their story and give them what they deserved.

Chapter One
Ryan

This is me on top of the world. I'm on my hands and knees while one of the frat boys, (Tim, maybe?), has my hips clutched tightly in his hands as he thrusts into me. It's ironic that the music in the background is about wanting to know my fantasy. This isn't it. He doesn't last much longer and he's already pulling away. Damn it. If I was a wee bit sober, I'd make him come back and finish me off too. No problem. I can do it myself. He left, who knows where, so I fall onto my back on the bed. My legs are spread open, and my hand reaches down to get the job done.

"Seriously, Ryan?" he says, entering the room just as I finish. Hey, at least he knows my name. More than I can say for myself about him.

"Should have done it for me," I slur, singing the last part a little. Satisfied and too drunk to hold my eyes open any longer, I pass out before he can say anything else.

When I wake up, I'm still naked and my head is pounding like there's a jackhammer grinding into my skull. Fuck, this sucks. I wipe my cruddy feeling eyes and have some sort of contentedness that I'm alone in frat-boy's room, if it's even his room to start with. My memory is hazy, so I still don't know who he is. The room doesn't have any obvious clues either. Oh well. My mouth tastes gross, and I'm immediately dying to brush my teeth. Ugh. I have to get back to my place first. Thank God for rich parents. At least they are good for something. I get to live off campus for free.

I begin a search around the room for my clothes, but all I find are my bra, thong, and shirt. After looking for a solid minute, I give up on my pants. I can drive home without them. While I was in high school, I became a pro at sneaking in and out of the house, and this will be no different. My parents weren't opposed to me going out, but being sneaky about it was so much more fun. There's a thrill that comes with it, and when they didn't care I was leaving, I decided to pretend the stakes were higher. So I would sneak in and out of my house like I would be in serious trouble if I got caught. I can easily do this. For one, it's my house. The tricky part will be that it's broad daylight, and I'm not wearing pants. No biggie. I got this.

With my shoulders squared and my head held high, I walk out of the frat house filled with more passed out bodies, my heels dangling from two of my fingers. My eyes squint once I open the door, and I groan. Fucking sun. I shield my eyes with my hand and spot my car parked by the curb. Thank you, sober Ryan. Looks like I was smart enough to park close to the building. I run to my car, open the little, square door to the gas cap, grab my keys, and then slide into the driver's seat.

See? Like a pro. I should be a pro by now, not because the amount of time I've been doing this, but for the number of times I've done this. I grab a scrunchie from my gear shift and throw my wavy, dark red hair up. Then I put on my sunglasses to help with that god-awful sunlight before finally pulling away to drive home. Now, I feel like I could conquer the world. Last night wasn't a good example of my normal Saturday nights, so I'm ready to get home, shower the filthiness away, and brush my damn teeth.

I hate Sunday mornings. Hate. Them. We're near a college town for God's sake. Why does everyone drive like old people who are loafing around on a lazy Sunday evening? Why? To piss me off probably. I've already given two people the finger as I passed them. I am so that driver that everyone hates and pisses people off. How it happened, I'm not sure. I still have a good fifteen minutes to go when the worst sound in the world begins.

Sirens. Blaring loudly to alert me of the unwanted presence behind me.

Fucking cop. Great. Just what I need this

morning.

I pull onto the side of the road and attempt to make my shirt cover more of my thighs, but it's useless. Well, let's hope this guy likes legs and then I can get away with a warning. He steps out of his car, so I roll my window down while he walks up to me.

Smiling my sexy grin, I sweetly say, "Good morning, Officer."

He's older than I am and very hot. His name tag simply reads: O'Connor. I can't see much of his hair, but I know it's brown as are his eyes and beard, which is a little thick. His eyes immediately land on my bare legs, and I swear he blushes. What kind of man blushes? This should easily be a warning, though. He quickly focuses on my face.

"License and registration, please."

"Yes, sir." I lean over, probably giving him a view of my bare ass, as I reach into the glove compartment for the registration. "My license is in my purse, which is in my backseat. One moment," I tell him, holding up my index finger once I've handed over his first request. If he didn't see my ass before, he certainly does now.

"Why," he clears his throat as he looks over the license I gave him, "aren't you dressed?"

My shoulders lift and fall in a shrug as if this isn't a big deal. "I stayed over at a friend's and misplaced my jeans. I got tired of looking. Aren't you a little young to be a cop?"

I'm half expecting that to piss him off, but he

just chuckles and gets back to business. "Do you know why I pulled you over?"

"I was obviously doing something I shouldn't have been doing. Are you going to give me a speeding ticket or something?" Intentionally, I pull the corner of my lower lip between my teeth. Guys love when I bite my lip. "Unless you have a better idea of what to do with me?" I question hopefully.

"Ma'am," he begins, a slight blush creeping onto his cheeks, but my big mouth decides to interrupt him.

"Ma'am? Am I over fifty?" My headache grows, and I decide to give in. "Just give me my ticket already. How fast was I going anyway?"

Apparently, that wasn't a good thing to say to him. His eyes narrow, his lips a flat line. "Seeing how you're already having a bad, pants-less morning, I was going to give you a warning. But since you are obviously hungover, even though you've yet to reach the legal drinking age, and since you asked for a ticket, I'll surely give it to you. Stay put." And then he walks back to his car.

What? Can this morning get any worse? Let's hope not. I wait rather patiently for Officer O'Connor to return with my ticket, a rock song about American boys playing quietly on the radio. When he does, he hands the piece of paper to me with a gleaming smile.

Bastard.

"Here you go, Ms. Kavanaugh. Stay out of trouble, will ya?"

I glare at him before looking at my ticket to see how fast I was going. 73 in a 55. "Can I go now?"

"Certainly. Have a good day."

"Whatever," I mumble as he walks back to his car.

With a sigh, I toss my violation into the seat and head home once and for all. The first thing I do is go to the bathroom for a shower. Stray pieces of my hair are sticking out, and I look terrible to say the least. No wonder he didn't let me off easy, even with a look at my ass. One measly ticket to tarnish my previously spotless driving record. I can deal. I'm sure once my parents find out, they'll add speeding maniac to my list of traits that further disappoint them.

I decide that I don't want a shower, but a bubble bath. I need to chill for a bit and not worry about anything else. While the tub is filling with water and bubbles begin to form, I plug my cell into my speaker system, open it to my playlist, and hit shuffle before undressing. The water is the perfect temperature as I submerge my body. This is what I need to cure my hangover, my bad morning, and fleeting memories of a hot cop who turned out to be an ass. Sundays are my lazy days, so this bath is the perfect way to re-start my morning. I'll just hang out here, rejuvenate, and I'll be ready for the new school week tomorrow.

I'm wrinkly and almost asleep to the sound of a deep voice singing about slow kisses when my best friend, Vivian, barges into my bathroom.

"Thank goodness you're in the tub," she says with relief as she puts the toilet seat down and sits on it.

"Why are you in my apartment and in my bathroom?" I close my eyes again, not caring in the least that she's in here right now.

"I need to talk to you. You gave me a key, so here I am. I know today is your alone day or whatever the hell you call it, but this is important."

"Well, it's not like my day has gone as planned so far. What's up?" I ask.

She jumps in to complain about her boyfriend. Viv suspects he's cheating, and she wants me to go with her to spy on him. She begins to tell me her elaborate plan of how we can do this. It makes me wonder how long she's thought he was cheating.

"So what do you say?"

I peek an eye open. Viv looks nervous, probably thinking I'm going to say no. "Why are you with him if you don't trust him? What's the point?"

Viv frowns. "It's not that I don't trust him. I'm a little insecure, I guess."

That makes me feel bad. "Sure, I'll go with you. Let me know when, and I'll be there."

"Thanks, Ryan. I better go. Catch ya later." She stands and leaves me be.

She's ruined my bath for me, though. I drain the water and then take a shower. The rest of my day is spent relaxing with a little homework mixed in. My mind wanders to my parents. They are probably at church doing holy activities. If I walked on the same side of the street in front of a church, I would probably catch on fire. Religion and I don't really get along. My parents have always tried to force it on me and being the little rebel that I am, I dug my heels in, full force. I rather leave that aspect of life alone until I want to deal with it and discover just what I do believe.

Back to my parents, I haven't talked to them in a month. They've called, but I haven't answered. College has freed me of them and the massive failure that I am every time they see me. But that's not what today is about. Today is for me to relax, and that's just what I'm going to do.

* * *

Viv meets me for our first class with my favorite drink, Sunkist. I don't question her kindness. As usual, I'm running behind. The orange drink fuels me, so I'm thankful for it, no matter why she brought it.

"Thanks," I say, holding up my bottle.

"Welcome. I asked him to go out Wednesday, but he gave me some lame excuse about needing to study. I figured that would be a good day to see what's really going on."

I nod, not able to say more because our professor walks in to begin his lecture. Part of me wants to tell her to confront him or break up with him already. She obviously doesn't trust him. Viv can say it's because she's insecure all she wants, but it can't all be her. What the hell do I know anyway? I'm the single, wild girl who sleeps with frat boys and gets a speeding ticket while pants-less. No wonder my parents think I'm a disappointment.

Later, during lunch, I tell Viv that I'm thinking about getting another tattoo.

"Are you trying to cover your entire body, Ryan?" She asks with a shake of her head.

"You sound like my mother." I don't know why I tell her these things, aside from the default that she's my best friend, but her frown irritates me. It's not her body; why does it bother her?

"Maybe she has a point. You already have three."

"Are you sure you're not an old lady hiding in a young girl's body? Because that's what you sound like. Besides, what's wrong with tattoos?" I love my tats. Getting them are addictive, and as long as they mean something to me, what's the harm? Each one has a story that I get to tell every time someone asks me about them.

"Nothing. *I* just don't like them. Are you going with me to the party this weekend?" She asks, changing the subject.

"Hell yeah, I'm going."

We talk about the party for a bit before going our separate ways for our next class. Later, when I'm on my way home, my mother calls. I groan before answering. It's time to stop ignoring them. Especially when they're going to pay for my ticket.

"Hello," I fake a cheery greeting.

"Ryan, hello. How are you?"

"I'm great. I was about to call you," I lie.

"I'm sure you were, dear. There's no sense in lying, you know. Anyway, I'm calling to check in and make sure that you aren't wasting our money. Have you picked a major yet?"

Of course. That's why she's calling. "No, I'm not wasting your precious money and no, I haven't picked a major yet. I still have time."

She goes on and on, telling me that I don't have time. That I need to decide as soon as possible. Blah, blah, blah. After about ten minutes of her ranting, I do the most mature thing I can think of.

"Mom, you're breaking up. We'll talk later. Bye." And I hang up.

This week really sucks so far. Hopefully, spying on Viv's boyfriend will be fun instead of another thing to add to my list of things that have gone wrong. However, my mother's words stick with me. I'm only nineteen and in my second year of college. I'm still taking general ed classes. I have no clue what I want to major in. That's a huge decision to make. I'll seal the fate of my future with that choice. How am I supposed to decide right now what I want to do with the rest of my life? It's intimidating, and I rather not think about it.

So I don't.

Chapter Two
Ryan

"What are you doing?" Viv asks, coming up behind me. She's entering my apartment yet again without even knocking.

I'm sitting on the couch with my laptop on my lap, searching for tattoo ideas with hopes of being inspired. "Looking for my next tattoo. Is it time to become stalkers?"

"Yep."

It's almost nine, and I'm already decked out in black jeans, a t-shirt, and a beanie. Viv looks similar minus the beanie. She's got her hair up though. I close my laptop and follow her out to her car.

"I feel like we should be wearing leather and high-heel boots. Instead, we look like bums hunting for our next fix."

Viv laughs. "Shut up. Do you want to know the plan or not?" She backs out of the complex's parking lot, and I tell her to go ahead. "He's

11

supposed to be home, so we're going there first. We'll do a drive by, and if he's home alone, we're trusting his word. If not, we're going to figure out who is there with him. That's as far as I've planned."

I rub my hands together evilly, knowing I want a good thrill to come from this. "We have to sneak around his house at least once. Otherwise, my outfit is pointless."

"Fine," she huffs, unhappy that I'm not taking this seriously.

We pull up to the curb, a few houses down from his house. There are two cars in the driveway. It's not looking good so far.

"Whose car is that?" I ask.

Viv eyebrows are pulled together as she frowns, heartbroken already. "I don't know. I've never seen it before."

"Let's go find out who's fucking your boyfriend." That was probably too blunt based on Viv's wince. She had to at least be somewhat prepared for this, though. She expected this was going on in the first place. I get out before she can object and she scurries to catch up.

"We're going to be damn good spies. I'll peek, and you be the look out. Got it?"

She nods. Crouching, we run up to his house, then walk with our backs against the side until we reach a window. I glance at Viv to make sure she's doing her part and then I put my fingers on the window sill, standing on my tiptoes to look in. I have the perfect view of the living room, even though sheer white curtains are in my way.

"What do you see?" Viv whispers.

"The living room. He's sitting on the couch alone." Just then, a girl walks into the room, completely naked. "Wait! There's a girl. Holy shit," I add when she straddles him, and they literally start to go at it. No foreplay whatsoever. He was sitting there watching TV, she walks in, and bam! Now they're taking his clothes off.

"What?" Viv nudges me, wanting to know what's happening, but not wanting to look for herself.

"They're about to fuck. I'm sorry," I add with some sympathy, but I don't look away. I can't. They are *animals*. Wow. She's riding him like there's no tomorrow, and he's playing with her breasts, squeezing them. Damn. I'm a peeping Tom! I'm a freaking perv!

"Shit," Viv mutters, dragging me away from the sex party inside with the sound of her voice and rustling leaves.

"What?" But when I look, she's sneaking off around the back of the house. Why is she going that way in such a hurry? "Vivian! Where are you going?" I whisper fiercely.

Suddenly, I see my shadow against the house thanks to a light shining on me from behind. I freeze. No fucking way Viv left me here to get caught!

"Ma'am? Is there a reason you're crouching

outside someone's window?"

I swivel, holding my hand over my face. The cop lowers his flashlight and comes closer. Ugh. Great. Officer O'Connor.

"Ryan Kavanaugh, right?"

"Yeah, you remembered." I wish I could say I feel less likely to get in trouble now, but I don't. I am surprised that he remembered my name though.

"Kind of hard to forget the half-naked girl with a boy's name. What are you doing?"

I cross my arms over my chest. He doesn't need to remind me about that. "*My* name isn't a boy's name because it's mine. Last I checked, I'm a girl. And I was out here because...well, you see." Damn it, I have nothing. "Look, my best friend's boyfriend lives here, and she thinks he's cheating on her. She talked me into spying on him with her to find out. Apparently, she saw you coming and left me here." Stupid bitch. She's so going to pay for this.

"Well, the neighbor saw you two and called it in. Come with me, please." He loosely takes my elbow and leads me towards his car.

"Are you going to arrest me because I can think of better use for your handcuffs."

He shakes his head at my comment. "No, I'm not arresting you. We're just going back to my car, so we both don't look like creepers."

"What's your first name?" I ask curiously, noticing that Viv's car is empty. She must still be hiding behind the house.

He glances at me, but then says, "Gabriel. Almost everyone calls me Gabe though."

Gabriel O'Connor. Gabe O'Connor. I like it. Someone speaks through the radio on the front of his shirt, and Gabe presses the button to answer back in police code. My phone begins to buzz in my back pocket, so I pull it out and see that it's Viv. I'm not even going to text her back. She left me to get caught by the cops!

"Is your friend still around?"

"I don't think so," I lie. "Could you give me a lift home? Cops are supposed to be nice, right?" I give him my sweet smile. There is no way I'm going to push him into arresting me like I pushed him into giving me a ticket. Officer O'Connor will only see nice Ryan today.

"Yes, sure. I can give you a ride. My shift is about to end anyway."

He opens the door for me, and I slide in. As I watch him walk around, I decide I don't want him to take me straight home. He's hot. Too hot to pass up after running into him for a second time even if he did write me a ticket. When he gets in, I make my move.

"Hey, since your shift is over, why don't you do whatever it is you need to do to get off work and then we grab a bite to eat or something? My treat."

Gabe glances over at me. "You're asking me out?" He pulls away from the curb and starts driving.

"Sure, why not? Aren't you hungry?"

"I guess, but-"

"Then it's settled. You take care of your business and then we'll go eat." I angle myself towards the window a little as a silent message that the discussion's over. My phone keeps vibrating, but I ignore it. If Viv wanted to know what's happening, then she shouldn't have left me.

Gabe seems a little anxious and for a second I wonder if he's gay and that's why he feels uncomfortable about going out with me. But then I remember how he looked at my legs that day, so I toss that idea aside. Maybe talking will relax him a little.

"So how old are you?" I ask.

He doesn't look over to answer me. "Twenty-five. You?"

"Nineteen. Almost twenty."

Gabe's jaw tenses. Is my age what's bothering him? Let's get away from that topic then. "Have you always wanted to be a cop?"

"Yeah. It runs in my family." We pull into the police station. He turns with a serious expression on his face. "Can I trust you in my car?"

"Of course. I can go inside if you want."

Gabe shakes his head. "Sit here and wait."

"Yes, sir." I smile.

Gabe leaves me to go inside the station and do whatever it is he needs to do. About thirty minutes later, he walks back out, dressed in jeans and a red button up shirt. He looks even bigger now than he did in his uniform. Without his hat, I can see that he has curly hair. Can he get any hotter?

"Where would you like to go?" He asks as soon as he's in the car.

I tell him about a twenty-four hour breakfast diner across town. The ride is silent once more, but that's cool. Gives me plenty of time to think of different things to talk about at the diner. After all, I know nothing about this guy. Gabe reaches for the door, just as I do, causing his hand to land over mine.

He cracks a smile. "I'll get it. You're a lady, so-"

"That means I can't open the door by myself?" I quip.

Gabe lets my comment fly right over his head. "No. It means I'm a gentleman and you don't have to."

Hm. Fine. I drop my hand, and he finally opens the door. We find a booth along the wall and take a seat. There aren't a lot of people in here. Two old men at the bar, an elderly lady and a young boy at a booth, and then a middle-aged couple. The waitress promptly comes to take our drink orders. Once she walks away, I'm about to ask him a question, but he beats me to it.

"How did you get your name?" He asks, looking over the menu.

I shrug like it's no big deal and like it never bothers me. It's not just a name though. It's an identity. And mine is tied to nothing I would consider good. I've even thought about changing my name, but deep down, I know it fits me. So I keep it. But I don't tell Gabe any of that. Instead, I say, "My parents wanted a boy and loved the name Ryan. Turns out I've never been able to meet their expectations. They decided to name me Ryan anyway. What about you? Any special significance to your name?"

"Not really. It was the only name my parents agreed on."

Better than what happened with me. "You said being in law enforcement runs in the family?"

Gabe nods. "Yeah. All the men and some of the women have been in law enforcement at some point in their lives. My dad and granddad are retired. My older brother actually works for the FBI. Being a police officer just fit."

"That's cool." With a small pause, I continue, "I guess I should apologize for my behavior the other day. I don't usually leave the house without pants. Pretty sure that's what led to me getting the ticket. Next time I'll know better."

Gabe laughs. "Oh, yeah. It was that part of your behavior that sealed the deal. Your attitude and actual violation had nothing to do with it. I feel kind of bad about it now that you're buying me a late night snack."

"I deserved it." I shrug.

The waitress returns to take our order. Gabe gets pancakes, and I order French toast. She keeps giving me sideways glances. What the hell is her problem? When she walks away, Gabe chuckles, shaking his head as he catches my attention.

"It's probably because of how you're dressed in all black. You look a little sketchy."

I look down at my clothes. "Well, I had to dress the part. That's half the fun."

"Yet you were still spotted. You're a terrible criminal." He laughs, and it's such a hearty laugh. It's adorable. "You're a college student, right? What's your major?"

Frowning, I say, "I'm undecided. You sound like you had it all figured out. Your career path was basically laid out for you, and you knew that you would be happy with that job. I'm assuming, anyway. I, on the other hand, don't have a fucking clue. You have a passion for it. I don't have any passions or anything that I'm so good at that I would want to do it for the rest of my life."

Well. I didn't intend to say all of that, but my big mouth has a mind of it's own. To avoid looking at this practical stranger, I stare into my glass as I take a sip.

Instead of giving me an inspirational speech that I wouldn't care two cents about, Gabe simply tells me, "You'll figure it out. Find something you like and run with it."

I don't bother telling him that nothing catches my interest enough to make a job out of it. Our waitress brings our food, and Gabe smiles at her good-naturedly. He gives me the vibe of a pure, one hundred percent good guy. Maybe it's that stupid girl in me, but it makes me a little wary. There has to be a kink in his shiny exterior. It's so the stupid girl talking, trying to rationalize it because guys can't simply be good.

"Was he cheating on her?"

"Huh?" I look up from my French toast, my mind still lost in my good guy debate.

"You were spying to see if your friend's boyfriend was a cheater. Was he?"

"Oh!" Nodding, I say, "Yeah. They were starting to go at it like animals right before you showed up." I shake my head with a guilty grin at the memory. "I should probably be consoling my friend, but she left me to get caught, so she'll be fine. Are you from around here?" I rather learn more about him than talk about Viv.

"Yeah, born and raised. You?"

"Nope. People are supposed go away for college, and since my parents wouldn't let me go out-of-state, I went across the state. This was as far as I could get. We used to come to a town not too far from here for beach vacations, though."

He nods as if he's considering something. "Why do you think people should go away for college?"

"Well, isn't college supposed to be a time of your life where you get away from what you know to really experience new things? To learn about yourself and who you are apart from your family? At least, that's why I wanted to leave home."

I have Gabe's full attention now.

"That makes sense to me, although I never went far from home," he says in response.

"Maybe you didn't have to. Maybe you already knew all those things," I tell him quietly, looking down at the table. Our plates are empty now, and the conversation isn't fun anymore. It's more personal than I care for. I clear my throat, smile, and add, "I'll be right back." I grab the bill from the edge of the table and begin to slide out of the booth.

"You don't have to. I'll pay," Gabe objects.

"My treat, remember?" I leave to take care of our tab before he can say anything else. This is why I always carry some cash in my pockets because I left my purse at my apartment. Gabe walks over to tell me he left a tip. It's time to go home now.

I let him open all the doors for me, wondering if he's the type to come inside for a little sex. Probably not. He opens doors for women and even called me a "lady." I don't think he's that kind of guy. Besides, he hasn't even been home yet, and he just got off work.

"Where do I need to take you?" He asks.

I give him directions to my apartment. We ride in silence the rest of the way. When we get to my place, I thank him for the ride and for allowing me to treat him to dinner before getting out. Gabe rolls the window down and calls out for me to wait. I lean down to see what he wants. Maybe he is that type after all.

21

"Here." He holds out a slip of paper. "You seem to find yourself in trouble quite often. If you ever need help, call me."

With a grin, I ask, "Is this your way of giving me a chance to ask you out again?"

Gabe chuckles, but ignores my question. "Have a good night, Ryan."

"You too."

When I get inside, I stare at his number. There's no time to think about him because Viv bursts into my apartment.

"Do you even know how to knock?"

"What the hell happened?" She throws her hands up like I'm the one who abandoned her.

"You tell me. You let me get caught! You didn't even warn me!"

Viv's shoulders sag. "Sorry. I panicked. You didn't get arrested, did you?"

"No. It was the same officer who pulled me over the other day. We went out to eat because his shift was over." Like a true winner, I hold up his phone number with a smirk.

Viv playfully shoves my arm with a laugh. "You bitch. Here I was worried I would have to bail you out of jail, and you went on a date!"

"What can I say? Troublemakers come out on top too."

* * *

Last night, Viv wanted to focus on Gabe

22

instead of her shitty boyfriend, so we talked about him while drinking rum. That was how she consoled herself. I knew better than to text while drunk, because we did get drunk and danced terribly to loud music that pissed my neighbors off, but today, I'm sober. The slip of paper with Gabe's number on it is burning a hole in my purse. I can't stop staring at the side as if I have x-ray vision and can see a glow around it, beckoning me.

While the professor is droning on, I decide I can't take it anymore. I dig for the number and grab my phone. Once he's added as a contact, I think for a moment on what to text him. Technically, he gave me this number in case I needed any help. But who cares about technicalities? Not me. My thumbs get to work, and I send him what I think is a cute, little message.

> Hey. It's Ryan. Thought you should have my number in case you wanted to call & ask me out. I went first. Now, it's your turn. :)

Five minutes pass, and I'm positive that had to be the stupidest message I've ever sent. There's no way that will earn me a response. Last night was pleasant, and I wouldn't mind another one, even though I rarely get second dates. Gabe's new, not a part of the college world, and really hot. Why not pursue him? Never know what could happen. Plus, the chase is part of the fun!

Damn it.

I sound like a guy. At least, what I think a guy would sound like. Maybe I *should* have been born a boy. Then some of my definitely-not-girl-suitable thoughts would fit, and my parents would have been happy with me. My phone vibrates and lights up with an incoming call. Holy fuckaroo! He's calling me right now! Grabbing only my purse, I scramble out of my seat, being extra thankful I picked one close to the door, and run out of the classroom.

"Hello?" I answer, slightly out of breath from the rush.

"Hey. Is this a bad time?" He asks.

"Oh, no. Not at all." I'm not skipping class or anything.

"Good. If Friday night works for you, I'd like to take you out on a date. A real one because the diner doesn't count." There's a hint of laughter in his voice, and I can't help but smile.

"Why wasn't mine real?" I question curiously.

Gabe chuckles. "Because it wasn't. What do you say to Friday? You aren't going to turn me down now, are you?" he teases. Gabe seems more carefree today. It's contagious.

"Not a chance."

"Great because you are an intriguing person, Ryan. I'll let you know the details soon."

"Okay, sweet. Talk to you later."

We end our conversation with that. I'm intriguing, though? What does that even mean?

Doesn't matter because now, I have a hot date. Mission accomplished.

Chapter Three
Gabe

Ryan Kavanaugh appears to be the personification of trouble. A pure dose of seductive trouble to be exact. I honestly don't know why I called her. When I first met her, I definitely wasn't expecting her to have so much skin showing. Those tan legs and ass are still haunting me. There was something about the way she carried herself with how confident she was with her body. She didn't care that I saw her. It was like, to her, having me see her like that didn't matter because she knew she looked good.

I liked that.

Too much.

And then, I found her snooping outside someone's house, dressed ridiculously in all black, but she looked damn good. Her wavy, dark red hair was a lovely contrast to her dark clothes. She wasn't happy to see me either. My comment about

26

her name pissed her off more than it should have. And then she had no problem making sexual comments. It's brazen. She conned me into going out with her, which turned out better than I would have expected. Between what she said about her parents and school, I was intrigued, just like I said.

I can't fathom my parents being disappointed in me. Ever. Maybe in some of my actions, but not as a person in my entirety. There's definitely something more to this girl. That last word reminds me of her age. She's young and in college. It seems odd that I would be asking her out. It almost goes against my good-natured ways. Her age, for me, walks that line. I honestly feel a little bad about giving her the ticket, which is one reason why I threw caution to the wind and called her.

Can't say that I regret it either.

Not yet anyway.

I have to think about what we're going to do on this date now. Movies and dinner seem so outdated, even for me. It's a classic, sure, but something tells me that Ryan would have more fun doing something else. What that is, I'm not sure yet. This is so hard to do without getting her input because I don't know a lot about her. She's either going to love it or hate it.

It's late afternoon when my phone rings, and I smile when I see it's my little brother. Who is only three years younger than Ryan. This is spelling out trouble over and over again. My family's opinion matters to me, and I can guarantee that Ryan's age would be of concern to them.

"Hey, Owen. How's it going?" I answer.

"Good. School sucks as usual, but things are good," he says.

"Still keeping up good grades?"

"Of course. I can't play football if I don't. That's why I was calling."

"Oh yeah?" I question, already having a feeling of where this is going.

"Yeah, we have a game tomorrow against our rivals. Mom and Dad have some dinner party thing, so they won't be there. Think you'll be able to come?" He sounds hopeful, and I can't blame him.

We're a close family, but work has kept me from going to most of his games. This is the first Friday I've had off in a while, and I feel guilty that I chose a girl before thinking about him. I wonder if Ryan would be up for a high school football game. We can always do something afterwards too. My parents won't be there, so I don't have to worry about my mother thinking I'm robbing the cradle. If Ryan doesn't want to go, then we'll reschedule. My family comes first. If Owen wants me there, that's what I'm going to do.

"I will be there," I confirm.

"Great. It starts at 7:30, but people usually get there early. As early as six, sometimes."

"I was once in high school too, you know. I played football. I know how it goes."

Owen laughs. "Yeah, but you're so old," he jokes. "I didn't know if you remembered."

"I'll see you tomorrow," I chuckle before hanging up.

Now to find out what Ryan thinks. I call her next.

"Twice in one day? I think someone is smitten with me already," she answers.

I laugh. "It's possible. I'm calling because something has sort of come up."

Her voice turns suspiciously curious. "Sort of?" She questions.

"Do you like football?" I ask instead of directly answering.

"That I do. I don't watch it religiously or have a favorite NFL team or anything, but I'm always up to watch a game."

"That is just want I wanted to hear. My baby brother plays with his high school, and I haven't been able to see many of his games this year. He called, asking if I would come watch. Does that sound okay to you? We can go out afterwards."

Silence is on the other end. Did I lose her? I pull my phone away from my ear, but she's still there. Just as I'm about to ask, she speaks.

"Sorry, I don't have a good excuse for that silence. My mind started thinking. Anyway," she drags, "that sounds fantastic. I'm excited. What time should I be ready?"

"Quarter to seven?"

"Can't wait! See you then, Gabe." I can hear the smile in her voice, which makes me excited too because she has a beautiful smile.

* * *

At precisely 6:45, I'm standing outside of Ryan's apartment door. She texted me earlier today to let me know which one was hers. I knock twice, faintly able to hear music playing. After the music stops, a moment passes before she answers the door, wearing dark blue jeans and a white strapless bra with a lace design over the cups, and she's currently brushing her teeth.

"Are you ever fully clothed?" I ask with a forced chuckle, trying my best to be a gentleman and not look at her cleavage.

"Sorry," she mumbles around her toothbrush. Ryan steps aside so I can come inside and runs to finish getting ready. I hear water running and then she calls out, "You shouldn't have had to see that. I should have warned you that I'm always late. Let me throw on a shirt and shoes, and I'll be ready."

While she does that, I subtly look around her apartment. Books, clothes, and empty bottles of Sunkist are scattered about. It's clean, though. Just a little messy.

"Okay," Ryan says entering the living room. "I'm ready."

I turn to see her. Brown boots are peeking from underneath her jeans and she's wearing a white sweater that displays a strong shoulder and collarbone.

"You look great."

She smiles. "Worth the wait?"

"Definitely."

Ryan walks over, takes my hand, and leads me out. She's very comfortable with me already. I like it. Her hair cascades around her face, and I can't see her features really well, but when I open the car door of my Dodge Charger for her, I do see a smile. Once I get in the car, Ryan angles herself towards me a little.

"You have a nice car."

"Thanks."

"What's your brother's name?" She asks.

"Owen. He's number 70."

Ryan nods, seeming to be thinking about something. "Will your parents be there?" She says after a moment, a hint of apprehension coating her voice.

"No."

"Whew. Good." Then she backtracks a bit. "I mean, I'm sure they are great, but I'm not really meet-the-parents material. Hell, I even messed that up when my parents first met me." She sounds slightly bitter, but then she changes the subject before I can question it. "Did you play football? You have the big, upper body of a football player." At this, she squeezes my bicep.

"Yes, I did, and I was pretty good too."

"Oh, I bet you were," she grins, reluctantly removing her hand from my arm.

"What about you? Did you play any sports?"

Ryan's kind of tall for a girl. She could have

31

been a basketball player.

"I played tennis," she says simply.

"Played?"

"It was fun to start with, but then my parents were pressuring me too much. I played through my senior year and then quit. I still play here and there if I can find a partner."

"Were you good?" I ask, picturing her in a white tennis dress, those long legs perfectly showing off how good they look.

"First seed, so yeah, I was. My coach was disappointed in me, but I couldn't handle it anymore."

I glance over at her as I turn into the parking lot. Boy, this place is packed! "Do your parents pressure you a lot?" I pry.

She laughs humorlessly, but her answer evades the question. "Everyone has expectations, including them. Oh! There's a spot." She points to the first empty space we've seen so far.

Ryan takes hold of my hand once more as we head to the main gate. I pay the fee for us to get in, and then we go hunting for seats. People are everywhere. Oh, yeah, I think as I remember what Owen said. Rival teams are playing tonight. That's why he told me about people getting here so early. I never really noticed this part when I played. I was always more focused on the game than the people watching.

There aren't many available seats on the bleachers. Ryan apparently finds some because she starts tugging me towards the middle section. She stops at one row about halfway up, but I don't see where she's expecting us to sit.

"You can sit on this one, and I'll sit right in front of you in that empty spot?"

Ryan wants to sit in front of me? How will that work for conversation?

"Sure," I say anyway.

She goes first, politely excusing us as we maneuver in front of the people. Then she steps downward to her seat, and I sit down on the row above her. Ryan reaches behind her and over that bare shoulder of hers, she says, "Open up," as she taps my leg. My knees come apart as she scoots backwards. Ah. Finally catching on, I move forward a little, and she leans into the space between my legs.

My hands start on her shoulders and then move down her arms as she turns her head to say something. We are truly relaxed around one another. It's surprising for this early on. I ignore it and focus on what she's about to say as three players go forward for the coin toss.

"Number 70, right?"

"Yep. That's him over there," I answer, my eyes landing on him amongst the group of players across the field waiting for their time to run through the banner the cheerleaders are setting up.

"How old is he?"

"Sixteen. Hey, do you have siblings?" I just realized she's never said.

Ryan shakes her head, my eyes drawn to her shoulder. It's only a shoulder, but her skin looks so smooth, and I wonder if it's as soft as her hands. My last relationship ended about six months ago, and my few dates since never made it to sex. This girl, especially with her body, has me thinking in fast forward. I'm not that guy though. Yet the fingers of my right hand dance up her arm, slowly dragging across shoulder, pushing hair out of my way as I go. When I reach her neck, I return to where I started to begin the process all over again.

Hoots, hollers, and applause starts as the announcers introduce our team. The players run through the banner to the music of Who Let the Dogs Out, as they are the Bulldogs. Ryan claps as well, and then I have to pull my fingers away from her lovely skin. It's time for the national anthem. We all stand and dutifully, Ryan places her hand over her heart when the music starts.

When it's over, my brother turns around, searching the crowd for me, his helmet in his hands. I stay standing, and he quickly spots me with a grin. I give him a thumbs up before he has to turn around for the start of the game, finally putting on his helmet.

"He's cute," Ryan tells me when I sit down and she scoots between my legs once more. She says it more as if he's a little kid and not a teenager. "It's obvious you're brothers. Y'all have the same curly brown hair." Without bumping into the people on either side of her, she turns to tug on one of my curls with a grin.

"Yeah, the men in my family all have an uncanny resemblance. However, my older brother doesn't have the curls because his hair is so short."

Ryan faces the field, but asks, "What's his name? How old is he?"

"Keith. He's thirty-three. Hey, do you want anything from the concession stand?" I can't believe I haven't asked yet.

"Maybe right before halftime? Unless you want something now then we don't have to wait?"

"No, I'm good."

As the game really gets underway, Ryan gets lost in it. She may watch it occasionally, but she still doesn't know much of what's happening. She'll tap my knee and ask me about something, so I explain it to her. If it happens again, I'll point it out to her to see if she caught it. A few times, she points it out to me before I can. She's really paying attention, and I like it.

Owen is doing great tonight too. Halfway through the second quarter, we're up by three touchdowns. Ryan makes a few comments about how well he's playing. She even mentions some of the plays I explained to her. There's a sliver of pride that runs through me that she's not only asking about what's happening, but she's absorbing it.

"Sorry you have to explain this to me, Gabe. I've never had anyone around who knew what they were talking about to do it. Honestly, when I watch, most of the time I'm checking out the players. I'm getting the hang of it though."

I laugh. "It doesn't bother me. I'm enjoying it actually."

At this, she turns to look at me, a playful smile on her lips. "You like teaching me things? What else would you like to teach me?"

Ahh! I've been doing well at keeping my mind out of the gutter since the national anthem played, and then she goes and says that. Before I can stop myself, I lean down to whisper into her ear, my lips brushing her earlobe. "There are many, many things." I feel her shiver from my touch, and I smile. I can't help the kiss I place on her neck before I go back to how I was sitting. "What would you like from the concession stand?"

Ryan asks for chili cheese nachos and a Sunkist, if they have it. If not, a bottle of water is preferred. I tell her to stay put to save our seats. I end up being gone longer than I wanted because I run into people I know from high school or people who know me through Owen. Plus, I get stopped on the way back to our seats by even more people thanks to it being halftime. At this rate, everything will be cold when I get back to Ryan.

"I was about to come look for you," she says as I take my seat behind her.

"Sorry. I kept getting hung up with people who wouldn't quit talking."

"It's okay. You can make it up to me later." She's not facing me, but I know by her tone that she's smiling.

Ryan eats her nachos, and I eat my hot dogs in silence while the band performs a pitiful halftime show. That hasn't gotten any better since I was in school that's for sure. Some high schools had fantastic bands. We had an okay one, and it doesn't seem to ever improve. Once we finish, I have just enough time to go throw our trash away before the third quarter starts.

The quarters pass quickly, especially when Ryan asks about little things here and there, and she's leaning into me with her arms resting on my legs as her fingers draw circles on my knees. Our team wins and people start getting up to leave. It's about ten thirty, but I'm hoping to see Owen for a quick second.

"Do you mind if we see my brother before we go?"

"No, that's fine."

She takes my hand as we walk down the steps of the bleachers before heading towards the field goal where the players are gathered. We stand along the sidelines with other parents while we wait for their coach to finish talking to them. Ryan leans into me, holding onto my arm. I move to wrap an arm around her waist. Owen catches sight of me, grinning wider when he sees Ryan. Their coach wraps things up, and Owen heads straight towards us. He's too cool for a hug around his friends, so I hold up a fist for him to bump.

"Good game, Owen. You may even be better than I was."

He grins. "Oh, I'm way better," he brags.

I roll my eyes and chuckle. "Owen, this is Ryan. Ryan, this is my cocky, baby brother, Owen."

Ryan shakes Owen's outstretched hand as he says, "Nice to meet you." He tilts his head at me. "I didn't know you were seeing someone."

"Don't worry, Owen. This is our first date, and somehow, I think I'll end up being Gabe's dirty, little secret." Ryan laughs, then changes the subject. "Congrats on winning. You played great."

"Thanks." He turns to me once more. "You brought her *here*? As a *date*? No wonder you're single." He laughs.

"I asked if it was okay, and she said yes. Besides, we're about to go somewhere else. Who's coming to pick you up?"

"I'm catching a ride with one of my friends." He looks over his shoulder, and someone waves him over. "I better go. Nice to meet you, Ryan."

"You too."

"I'll see you soon, Gabe?"

"Yeah. Let Mom know I'll be home for supper Sunday," I tell him.

"Will do. Later!"

He turns and jogs towards his friend. Ryan steps to stand in front of me, a sneaky smile on her lips as she loosely wraps her arms around my waist.

"Where to next, Officer?"

"Do you like cake?" I question.

She giggles, a ridiculously girly giggle. "Of

course I do."

"Then allow me to lead the way." Once she hooks her arm around my elbow and we start walking out of the stadium, I tell her where we're going. "There's a cafe not to far from here, and they have some of the best cakes I've ever had. I thought we could go there for something sweet to eat, and then walk around downtown or whatever you want to do."

"Sounds good to me."

At the cafe, Ryan gets a slice of German chocolate cake while I settle for a slice of upside down pineapple cake. She asks if they have any Sunkist, but they don't so she orders water instead. We're sitting at a little, high table, our knees touching.

"You really like Sunkist, don't you?"

Ryan just took a bite, so she only nods. After she swallows, she says, "It's that or water. I'm slightly addicted to it. Always have been."

"Mhm." I take a delicious bite myself, and then ask, "What's one of your favorite things to do?"

Without any hesitation whatsoever, the words fly out of her mouth. "Have sex."

She catches me off guard with her answer, my fork pausing halfway to my mouth. Ryan's eyes widen as if she's just now realizing she said that.

"Shit. I mean, crap. Sorry. That's, um, not a good, ladylike thing to say." Her cheeks flush a light pink, her eyes focused on her cake. Something tells me this is the first and last time I'll ever see her blush because it doesn't seem like something she does often. "I don't really have a favorite thing. If it's fun or if there's some sort of thrill to it, then I'm happy. Kind of goes back to what I said about my major. Nothing sparks a passion in me. Even simple activities apparently because I can't even pick a favorite, *appropriate*, thing I like to do." Ryan's dark green eyes peek at me from underneath her lashes. "Sorry, I didn't mean to ramble."

"Ramble away. I don't mind." I give her a kind smile because it almost seems that her own answer threw her for a loop, and she's slightly uncomfortable now. It doesn't seem to fit her personality, but it does make her more real to me. "And you do have a passion of sorts. Liking things that thrill you, as you say. It sounds like you're an adventurous, daring type of person."

Ryan laughs. She's so sexy when she does. Whatever emotions she's dealing with disappears into simple, carefree joy when she laughs. "Hm. Not so sure about adventurous. Daring seems to fit me, I guess. What about you? What else in your life fuels you besides your job? That does fuel you, right?"

"Oh yeah, I love what I do. I also like to go out to one of my dad's pieces of land and shoot targets with some of the guys in my family. We get together at least one Saturday a month just for that."

She shakes her head slightly, her hair falling forward to cover that shoulder I'm dying to touch again. The hand in my lap gains a mind of its own as it moves to rest on her knee.

"What?" I ask, referring to her head shaking.

"I don't know if I could shoot a gun. The thought of them is intimidating in itself."

"Nah. It's fun to target practice and a really good way to relieve stress. You're daring. Maybe you should try it. As long as you know how to use a gun correctly, you'll be fine."

At this, Ryan smiles. I'm confused for a second until, with laughter in her voice, she says, "Already finding something new to teach me, huh? Maybe you should have been a teacher instead."

That makes me laugh. "I don't know about all that, but if you want to try it, let me know. You can come with me next time we all get together."

Ryan softly giggles. "You would let me around your family? I'm not sure if that's a good idea." There's so much more weight to her words than she's letting on. Why doesn't she think so? Ryan seems perfectly acceptable. Before I can analyze it too much, she adds with heated eyes, "Besides, wouldn't a private lesson be more fun?" Her eyes fall to my neck when I swallow hard, and I briefly wonder if she's watching my Adam's apple bobble.

"You may have a point there."

We continue to have small talk, and I learn that Ryan is a pretty well-rounded person for her age. She can play a couple different instruments, although she said that she doesn't regularly. She can speak Spanish fluently, but again, doesn't that often. There's a lot that she knows how to do, but it seems as if she doesn't actively do any of them. She was right. There's nothing that stands out enough for her to dedicate herself fully. I'm sure there is more to it than that, though. However, she has definitely attempted to find that passion she's always talking about based on what she's told me.

There are so many hidden secrets about Ryan. She goes back and forth between talking a tad bitterly about her childhood to acting as if it wasn't a big deal at all. Her tone mostly carries an air of factual, there's-nothing-I-can-do-about-it-so-why-worry type of attitude. The familiar urge to figure out the crooks and crannies of her bitterness and repair them rises within me. I always find women who are in some way broken, and I always want to put them back together. Somehow, I'm alone in the end. That's for another day though.

As our night dies down, and we head to back to her place, Ryan becomes a dangerously enticing woman, slowly luring me in. There are the simple touches like her hand high on my thigh as I drive with those fingers of hers trailing a carefree pattern. There's her laugh, which is ridiculously sexy. It's almost as if she knows just the exact laugh that will turn a guy on. And then the tempting, dirty words she seemingly casually throws out about what could come.

By the time we make it up the stairs and stand

outside Ryan's apartment door, I've been captured. My mind and body are capable of thinking of only one thing. She's lets go of my hand to unlock her door, but she doesn't push it open. Instead, she turns, leans against her door and tugs me towards her with a sexy, sly smile. My chest is flush against hers, my hands clutching her hips. A fog officially clouds my mind as my senses zone in on her lips and this killer body. I don't even get the opportunity to be the one to lean into her first because Ryan does it.

She watches me as she brings her face to mine, her lips brushing against mine lightly at first. They lift into a quick, small smile as if knowing I'm hooked before she presses them to my lips. Ryan brings her hands flat on my chest. The feel of her is *everywhere*, all over my body, demanding attention. When she opens her mouth, my tongue instinctively reaches for hers. Ryan has a bit of a sweet taste from the cake. She grips the back of my neck, deepening the kiss, drowning my senses with all of her. Nothing exists in this moment except her.

When she pulls away, my lips can't help but try to follow them, wanting to reconnect. Ryan giggles and smiles while lightly running her fingers back down my chest. In a breathy, seductive voice, she asks, "Would you like to come inside?"

I nod quickly before kissing her hungrily again. We head inside a moment later, my hands still firmly planted on her body. Ryan falls onto the couch and pulls me down with her. I easily get lost in her touch. With her heady kisses, it feels like she's pouring everything she has into them to make them as hot as possible. She expertly removes our clothes, revealing a tattoo on her hip of a dandelion with the white seeds floating away.

While kissing me, Ryan reaches down between us, wrapping her fingers around me for a moment before guiding me inside her. Ryan is a powerful seductress as she infuses every movement, sound, and touch with an almost primal need. It drives me crazy with need before I finally come undone with my release a minute after she shudders with pleasure beneath me.

That was hands down some of the best sex I've ever had. But afterwards, as I'm redressing, I see two more tattoos on her back as she disappears down the hall to change into pajamas. One a large, pink seahorse on the right side, and on the left, a black and blue lavishly drawn outline of a hummingbird. Her absence causes me to suddenly realize what has happened.

Me, the classic good guy, just had sex on the first date with a nineteen year old. Almost twenty. I nearly feel sleazy. So easily she was able to make me run past a line I normally don't even cross. Not to mention that based on the fact that she did ask me inside, she probably does this often. Sex on a first date is most likely normal for her. Without meaning to, I shake my head. This girl is already messing with me.

"You all right, Gabe?" Ryan questions with

just a touch of concern. She sits down on her couch, wearing girly pajamas. I've come to notice that most of her emotions are carefully, very subtly crafted into her voice when she speaks. Unless you're really listening, you'll miss it.

"Yeah. I should probably go." I stuff my hands into my pockets. Her long legs are on display for me, and my mind is already thinking about sex again.

No. I can't go there right now. I can't be drawn in again, no matter how easy that would be.

Ryan stands, walks over to me, and kisses my cheek innocently. "Thank you for tonight. I had a lot of fun."

How does she manage to look so pure when I feel so lousy? Ryan is watching me, waiting for me to speak. Clearing my throat, I say, "Thank *you*. We'll have to do something again."

Her eyes are full of doubt even while she agrees, "Yes, we will."

"G'night, Ryan."

And then I'm gone, wondering how tonight and Ryan fits with the kind of man I strive to be. Because tonight, after I left, I didn't particularly feel like an honorable man.

Chapter Four
Ryan

I stare at the door long after Gabe is gone. I've slept with plenty of guys before and never have any of them looked so...so *guilty* afterwards. At least, to me, that's kind of how he looked. With my parents, I'm used to negative emotions and not meeting their expectations. But with guys? I'm usually pretty good with them. Am I losing my touch or something? Why did he look like that?

Finally, I get tired of staring at the door, so I go lay in bed and stare at my ceiling instead. The ceiling is so much more interesting, you know. With a sigh, I wonder if maybe my disappointment streak is starting to expand to my entire life and not just with my parents. That list is a long one. First, they decided to let the gender of their child be a surprise, but they were praying for a boy. That obviously didn't happen. Then there's my long list of activities where I either wasn't good enough for them to keep paying for it or they pressured me too much and I quit. It never failed. Every time I found something I enjoyed, they over-compensated on pushing me to be my absolute best. And my absolute best was never good enough for them.

I guess since I wasn't a boy, they figure me to be helpless or something. My parents have such high expectations for me and over the years, I started rebelling against all of them. Some for the better, some for the worst. All I've heard about is how things would be so much easier had I been a boy, and I gave up trying to please them to a certain point. I am in college and my grades are fantastic, but to make them even a little proud of me? That is obviously never going to happen, which makes me think of my stupid comment to Gabe about me meeting his parents.

That would have been a disaster. I have dissatisfied my parents enough. I don't need to let down someone else's. And trust me, they would hate me. I'm too outspoken, too sexually-inclined, too everything-your-mother-warned-you-about. Not to mention that I'm a quitter and tattooed and nothing parents like in a girl as a person and especially not as their son's girlfriend. Hell, if I were a guy and I was dating me, I wouldn't bring me home to my parents either. I know myself better than anyone else does, so I'm positive this is true.

Maybe my intuition about Gabe being a one hundred percent good guy is true. Before he left, he must have realized that this, me, obviously won't end well on his behalf and that's what the look on his face was. My phone vibrates on my nightstand, but it's just Viv, and I don't want to talk to her right now. Unfortunately, my gut says that Gabe is going to be placed on my long list of inadequacies. Oh well, right? I'm not dating material anyway.

That's my last thought as I drift to sleep.

* * *

Viv and I are out shopping. She wants to know about last night, and I want a new outfit to wear to the party tonight. The autumn air is getting chilly, but it's not cold enough to cover up a lot of skin. I feel the want to flaunt my body at this party, so that's the kind of outfit I'm searching for.

"All right. I'm dying to know, Ryan. Tell me already!" Viv says once we walk into our first store of the day.

I roll my eyes at her. "It went well. We went to his little brother's football game and went to a little café for cake. Then we went back to my place for sex."

"Good guys don't fuck on the first date, so you must have been wrong about that," she comments.

"I don't know," I trail off. Viv may be my best friend, but there is still a lot I don't tell her. "He looked like he regretted it before he left. I doubt I'll be calling him if I ever get into trouble. That's probably the last we'll see of Gabe O'Connor." I had to say that last part. Saying it aloud makes it seem more real, and I'm almost positive that I'm right about this.

"Maybe not," she tries, sounding hopeful. After a moment, she says, "You go on a lot of first dates now that I think about it. Why don't you ever go on seconds?"

I keep my eyes on the clothes before me, knowing she's going to have something to say about this. "Because good girls don't fuck on the first date, Viv," I throw her words back at her. "Lucky for them, and me if you think about it, I'm not one of those girls. If I want to sleep with them at the end of the night, I'm not going to hold out for a few more dates. And after that, they see me only for sex. Besides, you know I'm not really a dater anyway. Obviously."

When I look up at Viv, her eyes are wide open. "You have sex on the first date? Always?" Oh, come on. She had to know this. We've been friends since freshman year. She hasn't figured this out yet? I figured I would get a lecture, but I guess she didn't know this fun fact about me.

"Almost always," I correct. Is it really that big of a deal? It's only sex. "Ooh, look at this top." I hold up a white, spaghetti-strapped shirt. It's a v-neck and a little airy, so it wouldn't be skin-tight. The material is super soft too. I have to buy it.

"It's cute. What would you wear it with?"

"A tight skirt of some sort."

So we start looking for one of those. But Viv is back to Gabe.

"Has he texted you or anything?"

"Nope."

"Well, how old is his brother?" She asks.

"He's sixteen, but he has an older one who is thirty-three."

"And how old is he again?"

I narrow my eyes at her from across the rack. Where is she going with this? "Twenty-five."

"Mhm," she nods. "So you're closer in age to his little brother than him."

Honestly, I hadn't thought of that. Does our age difference really matter? It's only six years, and I'm about to turn twenty next month. It's not a huge difference or anything. I'm sure my parents would expect me to date someone closer to my age, but it's my choice. Not theirs. They aren't dating him. I am. Finally, I say, "It doesn't matter either way. I really don't think I'll see him again. What did dumbass say when you broke up with him?" I change the subject because I'm tired of thinking about Gabe.

"He thinks I'm crazy for accusing him of cheating. When I pushed him about her car in the driveway, he wanted to know how I knew that, which means he admitted it. And he hasn't spoken to me since."

"Perfect timing for a party with an excuse to get wasted." I hold up the skirt I found. "What do you think?" It's a gold, sparkly mini-skirt, and it would look great paired with the shirt and the right shoes.

"Ooh, I love it. Might have to borrow that."

50

I laugh. "Of course. Do you see anything in here you want or are you ready to hop to the next store?"

"Nah, let's check out and move on."

Tonight's party is being hosted by the football team, so I've been trying to convince Viv that she could hook up with any of one of them. They're going to be looking to get laid tonight anyway. After the shitty boyfriend, she deserves some yummy football player to give her a good time. Viv says she's going to lay low for a while. I stop pestering her because if that's what she wants, then I'll leave her alone. Viv has more morals or higher standards, as some would say, than I do, and I will respect her wishes.

We shop all day, and I rack up some charges on the credit card my parents gave me. I'm sure I'll get a call at the end of the month about that bill. It never fails for them to say if I were a boy, I wouldn't waste so much money on clothes. Seriously, just get over it already! You got me. Stop complaining. Nineteen years worth should be enough for the rest of my life and theirs combined. Besides, they don't have to keep reminding me of how everything I do isn't good enough for them. Not to mention the clothes that I buy, they don't always approve of. It's too slutty and not very "ladylike." Whatever.

Once I get home, I turn on my love song playlist and draw myself a bubble bath. It's not Sunday, but I'm in dire need of some relaxation. I may have to make a massage appointment next week. I've been so strung up lately. Probably because of the looming deadline my parents have on me for declaring my major.

The suds and hot water temporarily erase those problems. I soak for entirely too long, and I know that if I don't get out soon, my body will still be wrinkly when I get to the party. Prune-y won't get me laid. While I'm eating Ramen noodles, a guilty pleasure of mine, and watching the old TV show *M*A*S*H*, my father calls. I ignore it as usual. If I talk to him before the party, I'll be in no mood to have sex. My dad, most of all and despite my straight-A history, doesn't believe I'll graduate from college. He wants me to graduate, that is what is expected of me, but he doesn't think I'll be able to do so. He thinks that like everything else I've done, I'll quit.

Ugh. No. Stop it right there, Ryan. Tonight is party night. There is no time to think about what I'll do next to disappoint my parents. Although, that kind of makes me wish I had a sibling, like Gabe, and then my parents would focus all their attention on him. But they stopped trying to have a boy after I was born because my mother had two miscarriages. After that, they didn't want to go through that type of loss again. Which left them, their hopes, and their dreams stuck with me.

I wonder what it would have been like to have siblings. Does Gabe like them or wish he was an only child? Oh, great. Now, I'm thinking about

Gabe. He's on my mind as I start getting ready, as I ride with Viv to the party, as I talk mindlessly with different people, and drinking a couple beers along the way. But then a football player spots me. I know his face and his number, 43, but I can't for the life of me remember his name. How is it that I can remember almost everything Gabe said last night, but I can't think of this guy's name *and* I've slept with him twice before?

"Hey, Ry," he greets. Ah, yes. That's why. Because he insists on shortening my name.

"Ryan," I correct. I may not always like my name, but it's mine, and I'm going to own it. "Hey."

"You looked like you needed another drink." He hands me a red cup, and I graciously take three swallows from it.

"Thanks."

Bass from the speakers set up all over this place thrums through my body with the alcohol. 43 is looking at me with desire as he pulls me to him. He slips his beer-free hand underneath my shirt, his clammy hand touching my bare back. 43 leans down to whisper into my ear, some sloppy, not all that hot and dirty things to convince me to head upstairs with him. But the more he talks and lowers his hand over my ass, the more I get turned off. I was probably too drunk in the past to remember or care about these features.

"I'm not feeling all that great. I think I'm going to find Viv and get her to take me home." I push him away with a little more force than I intended.

"I'll take you," he offers.

I agree, only because I'm hoping that once I get away from all these people, I'll be in a better mood to fuck. That's what I really want tonight. But if not, then Mr. 43 is going to be very disappointed. He follows me as I try to find Viv, but she's nowhere to be found.

"C'mon, Ry."

"Ryan," I insert.

"Let's go already. She'll figure it out." He starts tugging me out of the house, his grip too tight for me to fight him on this. Him taking control is kind of turning me on anyway, so I let him.

Once we get back to my place though, I regret it. I haven't even unlocked my door yet because I don't want him to come inside. 43 has me pressed against my door, his slobbery kisses all over my neck before he starts heading towards my chest, where, thanks to my bra and new shirt, there is quite a bit of cleavage showing for him to touch.

"I'm not feeling well," I repeat. "Thanks for the ride, but I'm going inside. Alone," I add.

His lips move up the left side of my neck, so I turn my head to the right by instinct. His hands grip my waist tighter as he puts more of his body weight on me. "Ry," he starts.

"Ryan." Seriously? How many times do I have to correct him? "You don't need to try to change my mind. The answer will still be no."

That makes him stop kissing me. His eyes turn dark as he stares at me, his hold stronger than ever.

"No? You didn't hesitate before, Ry. Everyone on campus knows that you're an easy lay and now you're telling me no?"

"I may be easy, but I'm not that easy for you tonight." I try to push him off me, but it's impossible. He's not budging. "Get off me." I attempt to make my voice as level as possible, but even I hear how it trembles a little.

"Is there a problem?"

At the sound of his voice, my head snaps to the stairwell. 43 isn't paying him any mind yet. Gabe is standing rigid with his arms by his side, hands in fists, and he is not looking happy at all in his police uniform. His deadly stare is trained on 43. What is he even doing here?

"Buddy, I don't think this is any of your business, so-" Finally, he looks, stopping mid-sentence when he sees that it's a cop. 43 takes a small step away from me.

Gabe looks at me. "Ma'am?" He questions, and I've never been so thankful to hear him say that.

"Um, everything is fine." I turn to 43, who looks a little pissed. "Catch you later." I quickly turn around, pull the house key from my bra, and go inside without another look back.

With my back against the door, I can hear feet shuffling away, but then some coming towards me. A knock sounds loudly, making me jump. I slowly open the door to peek, and once I see it's Gabe, I open it completely.

"Are you okay?" He asks.

"Yeah. What are you doing here?"

Gabe doesn't come in when I move aside. He stays just outside of my doorframe. "You apparently left your phone in your friend's car and left a party without telling her. She called me from your cell, worried, and said that wasn't like you at all. She thought you might be in some sort of trouble. I was patrolling nearby, so I told her I would stop by to see if you were here."

Suddenly, I wonder how long he was watching. Did he hear what we said about me being easy? Which he probably knew anyway thanks to our date, but it has to be a different story when he hears that I'm that way from a complete stranger. I want to ask him if he heard, but then decide I don't really want to know.

"Oh, well, I'll call her on my house phone and let her know I'm fine. Sorry to have bothered you while you're working."

He frowns. "It looked like I needed to be bothered. Are you sure you're fine? I don't need to go hunt him down?"

I laugh at his concern. "Yes, I'm sure. Thank you, though."

There's a lull, and it's like he just realized what I am wearing because his eyes slowly rake over my body. That action alone has me all hot and bothered. Gabe clears his throat with a slight shake of his head.

"I have to get back to work. Call your friend, because she was really worried."

"I will."

"Okay, see you later, Ryan."

"Later." I watch him turn and walk away before I close my door.

Without wasting any time, I call Viv. She's already on her way here with my phone and to check on me herself since she hadn't heard back yet. When she does get here, I convince her that I just wasn't feeling well after explaining what happened. She leaves my phone and then goes on home, thankfully. Seeing Gabe completely threw me off, especially since he easily turned me on. I am dying to have sex now. I wonder if he would come over when he gets off.

But then I remember how he looked last night before he left. Inviting him over would be a bad idea. So I plop onto the couch, slip off my shoes, prop my feet onto the coffee table, and turn on Netflix to find a horror movie. I pick the first one it recommends, not really caring what I watch as long as it's horror. My phone buzzes next to me.

Gabe: I know it's late & rude to invite myself, but do you care if I come over after my shift?

He wants to come over? It's almost one in the morning. Maybe I misread his expression. After a quick debate, I text him back.

Only if you bring popcorn.

It's a little after half past one when there's a knock on my door. I pause the movie and go to the door to find a freshly showered Gabe wearing a t-shirt and jeans. He must have gone home first.

Gabe holds out the box of popcorn. "Here you go."

I giggle because part of me thought he wouldn't actually do it. "Thanks. Come on in."

He shuts the door and follows me into my kitchen where I put a bag of popcorn in the microwave. When I turn to face Gabe, I catch him admiring my legs. Guys go crazy over them because they are tan, toned, and long. They are easily my best asset. He smiles, looking a little embarrassed that I caught him. I hoist myself onto my counter to sit, leaning forward just a tad as my hands anchor myself on either side of me. We watch each other for a moment before Gabe walks over to lean against the counter next to me.

"You're probably wondering why I wanted to come over?" He says as he folds those big arms over his chest and crosses his ankles, looking completely relaxed in my kitchen.

"I figured you just really wanted to bring me popcorn."

Gabe laughs. "That's exactly why. Now that I'm here though, I feel underdressed."

I giggle softly, looking down at my top and sparkly skirt. "I haven't gotten around to changing yet." The popcorn begins to pop as I hop down from the counter. "Make sure it doesn't burn. I'm going to change and then you're watching a horror movie with me."

"You like scary movies?" He seems surprised.

"Hell yeah. I live for the thrill, remember?" I laugh and then leave him to popcorn duty.

When I get to my room, I'm not sure what to change into. It's late, and I want to be comfy, but not in pajamas. After quickly examining my closet, I decide the hell with it. I'm going to wear whatever the fuck I want. I pick a cute, dark gray pair of sweatpants that still manage to make my ass look good and a pink tank top. Upon my return to the living room, Gabe is sitting on the couch with the popcorn, the smell quickly overtaking my apartment. There are also two bottles of Sunkist on the coffee table. I faintly smile at how he thought that far ahead.

"What are you watching?" He asks when I sit down next to him, plucking the bag from his hands.

"I don't know. Netflix picked for me. It's halfway over. Want to pick a new one?"

Gabe shrugs. "Up to you."

I grab the remote and go to the second suggested movie and hit play. Out of the corner of my eye, I keep watch on when Gabe is out of popcorn. I'll tilt the bag his way so he can get more. The movie is terrible. Once I hit the forty-five minute mark and I'm still not interested, I bump Gabe's shoulder.

"Are you enjoying this?"

He shakes his head no. I get the remote and turn off the TV. Getting really comfortable, I turn a little to lay my legs over Gabe's.

"Why did you want to come see me so late at night?" I finally ask. He never offered to further tell me, but now I'm more curious.

Gabe puts his hands on my legs. One on my thigh and the other on my knee. He squeezes them a little before looking at me. "The truth?"

"Of course."

"I wanted to see you, especially after earlier with that guy." His brows come together with displeasure.

"You wanted to triple-check to make sure I was okay?" The thought is endearing. Gabe must have been worried about what happened.

He laughs at my question. "Yeah, pretty much."

"Well, that was my first incident like that. Your timing couldn't have been more perfect. Thank you. Although, I'm sure I would have been fine without you."

"You weren't scared at all?" he asks curiously. I shake my head in a lie. "What scares you then?"

Gabe's brown eyes watch me carefully as I think of an answer. I know what scares me, but that doesn't mean I want to share that with him. "What scares you, Gabe?" I ask instead. "I mean, you're a big, bad cop. There can't be a lot that scares you, right?"

He grins, knowing that I avoided his question, but he answers anyway. "Remember when I told you that going into law enforcement just fit?" I nod. "That's because it really does. I have always been on my best behavior. Part of that is because of my family being full of police officers, but mostly because I want to be able to look back on my life and know that I've been the best person I could be. I'm a good guy in almost every sense, and I want to help people as much as I can. I'm scared that I'll do something that will make me not-so-good, by my standards."

And sleeping with me on the first date fucked that up for him. It all makes sense now. For the first time ever, I feel guilty about sleeping with guys so quickly. He shouldn't have come over. I'm his mistake. Something that shouldn't have happened. It's time for Gabe to go because I'm not going to hinder the image he has of himself any more than I already have. I slowly remove my legs from under his hands and off his legs.

"That's, um, interesting." I have to say something, and I'm not about to let him know that I know I'm on his list of shouldn't haves. "It's late, Gabe. Probably time to go home."

Gabe looks a little confused, but then the light bulb goes off over his head. "Ryan, I didn't-"

"I don't know what you're talking about," I interrupt, stupidly outing that I do indeed know what he was going to say. "It's late, and I have a lot to do tomorrow. That's all I meant. Nothing more."

He reaches for my hands and holds it in his, running his thumb over my knuckles. "Tomorrow is a Sunday. What do you have to do?"

For some reason, his question makes me laugh. "Do you think I'm lying? I am many things, Gabe, but a liar isn't one of them."

Gabe focuses his brown eyes on me. "Then you would have no problem going on another date with me?"

He's challenging me. That's what his response is. A challenge. I narrow my eyes at him and remove my hand from his.

"Now, you're just hurting my feelings, Ryan," he jokes.

"No." I want to ask him why. Why does he want to go out with me again when he clearly felt so terrible about the first one? It doesn't even make sense!

"No?"

"No. I don't want another date." And to drive it home, I add, "I probably should have mentioned that I have a one date only track record that I'd like to keep." It's a dumb thing to say, but I want him gone, and I'm hoping that will help.

"One date only?" He questions.

Is he just going to repeat parts of what I said? "Yep. I have a long list of first dates and zero for second dates."

"And you want to keep that?" He says skeptically.

"Precisely."

Gabe seems to think about this for a moment. "Fine. Then you would have no problem hanging out with me again?"

"Why the hell would I do that?" It's out of my mouth before I can help myself. "I mean, no thanks. I wouldn't want to tarnish that shiny armor of yours." I smile sweetly. Then I get up and go to my door, opening it so there's no doubt of what I want.

Gabe runs his hands down his thighs and then stands. Finally! He walks over, coming to a stop in front of me. His head tilts as he looks at me like I'm a puzzle he can't solve. I think he's about to walk on out, but instead, he steps forward, cups my cheeks with his hands, and kisses me. Without meaning to, I relax into him as he gently parts my lips with his tongue. God, he's a fantastic kisser. Our mouths move slowly, like not a thing in the world exists more than savoring this moment.

And boy, is it worth savoring. For what seems like a lifetime, I'm lost in him with no hopes of ever being found again. But then Gabe pulls away after a final kiss. I can't find it in myself to open my eyes yet. My lips are buzzing from the lovin' they just got, as is the skin surrounding my mouth thanks to his facial hair, and my body is still paralyzed in place by his hands.

Gabe's breath fans out over my mouth as he softly says, "You look beautiful right now."

My eyes pop open immediately. The corners of his mouth lift in a smile. In a whisper, I become completely honest with him. "No one has ever said something like that to me."

"What? How you look after a kiss?"

I shake my head. "No. Well, yeah, that too, but I meant the beautiful part."

Gabe's smile falls. Oh, fuck. I shouldn't have said that. Stupid, stupid, stupid girl! He's probably going to think I'm weak or something because no one calls me beautiful. That is so not the case, and I need to make sure he understands that. Before I can recover, he kisses me softly just once.

"Well, they should because you are," he mumbles against my lips. He strong gaze bores into me. "Absolutely beautiful."

My muscles are tense, waiting for him to laugh and add that he was joking. I've never been told that I'm beautiful. Hot or sexy, sure. Beautiful? No. My grandmother used to tell me that I was, but that was a long time ago. She was old and probably thought all little girls were beautiful. That hardly counts. Gabe holds my eyes, letting me absorb what he said. For the first time in my life, I ask him to do something that doesn't include sex. The funny thing about it is that my question embarrasses me more than if I had of outright asked him to sleep with me.

"Would you like to spend the night?" I ask quietly. "No sex, though."

Gabe grins. I was really expecting a frown or a confused look, but I'll take a grin. "Only if I get a second date."

I laugh, finally able to release some of my

tension. "Okay, sure."

He drops his hands from my cheeks and removes my hand from the doorknob before closing and locking the door. Like the confident, sure-of-herself girl that I am, I take his hand and lead him to my bathroom first.

"There's an extra toothbrush and anything else you might need in the medicine cabinet. I'm going to go put my pajamas on."

While he's in there, I pick up the few clothes that were lying on the floor and toss them into my closet before changing into a cute pair of blue pajama shorts and taking off my bra. My tank top can stay on. Now that Gabe isn't right here with me, I'm a little tired, stifling a yawn when I hear the bathroom door open. Seconds later, Gabe appears at my bedroom door, still dressed.

"Just a second," I tell him, lifting a finger. I turn to my dresser, open a drawer, and start looking for what I know is in there. When I find them, I hold them up. "I have mens' basketball shorts and a shirt if you want to wear them. They drown on me, so they would probably fit you."

He raises an eyebrow at me. "You keep mens' clothing on hand?"

"They're mine. I bought them." His brows both rise higher. Why is he making me flustered? This is ridiculous. "Look, when I get sick, I wear these because they are the ultimate comfortable clothes. Do you want to wear the damn things or not?"

Gabe chuckles. "Sure."

I slam them into his chest as I walk past him to go to the bathroom myself, and I hear him chuckle again. Once I've washed my face, brushed my hair and teeth, and used the restroom, I go back to my room. I find him with his ass in the air because he's bending over to put his folded clothes on top of his shoes near my dresser. But when he turns around, I see that he's not wearing the shirt. Only the shorts.

Oh, he looks so hot. I would have never thought I would be a fan of chest hair, but it looks like heaven on him. Not to mention his happy trail and then those deep, V muscles. Fuck. It's going to be me who is resisting having sex. Not him! This is not fair.

"The shirt was too small," he explains.

Thank God. He doesn't need to cover up that body or those muscled legs. Before I have to wipe away drool, I manage a nod. "I'm so not sorry about that."

Gabe laughs. "Turn off the light and get in bed."

That's all I needed to hear.

Chapter Five
Gabe

I don't even know where to start with this girl. First, her friend calls, freaking out that something bad had happened to her. When I get to her apartment, that jackass had her pinned against the door, wanting to go inside. I overheard what he said about her being easy and her response. Yet I still texted her later about coming over. Ryan obviously noticed how I looked when I left the other day because she interpreted what I said about being scared into that. That wasn't how I meant it. And then she kept turning me down with outrageous excuses. When she got up and opened the door, I had every intention on leaving.

That was what she wanted after all. I, on the other hand, wanted to kiss her. So I did. Ryan looked beautiful afterwards, just like I said. Her eyelashes fanned over her cheeks, and she was as lost as I felt. I can't believe no one has ever said that to her. What do they tell her then? Anyway, she asked me to stay, and I wasn't about to turn her down.

Now, we're lying on our sides in her bed. Ryan had nothing but pure lust in her eyes when she came back from the bathroom, and it's still lingering there.

"You never told me what scares you," I say, knowing it's a risk to bring that up again.

She sighs. With a blink, her desire disappears. "Thanks for effectively making me not want to sleep with you anymore." She pauses. "Well, right now anyway."

I chuckle, but wait for her to answer me.

"If I tell you, do you promise not to bring it up ever again?"

"Sure." I'm expecting her to tell me something that isn't that big of a deal.

Ryan rolls to lay on her back and quietly speaks. "All my life, I've been trying to make up for not being what they wanted. I'm scared that it's a hopeless aspiration."

"Who?" I ask gently.

"My parents. I wasn't lying when I said I've been a disappointment since birth. Their expectations are entirely too high, and I can't ever meet any of them. That's all I'm willing to say. What are we going to do on our second date?" She turns her head to look at me.

I smile, even though my mind is floored with what she said. "We're having a private shooting lesson."

Ryan grins. "I'm kind of excited about that. A little scared, but a little excited too." She covers her mouth with her hand to yawn. Then she rolls over, gives me a quick kiss, and adds, "I'm getting sleepy. G'night, Gabe."

"Night, Ryan."

I close my eyes with her, but my mind is still thinking. Her parents are obviously a touchy subject, and I want to know more. Unfortunately, I promised never to bring it up again. Maybe Ryan will want to share that with me eventually.

In the meantime, I need to keep myself from swooping in like Prince Charming himself. That doesn't work. With every relationship and me doing just that, I've lost the girl. There's only so much I can spare to lose after having lost so many times. My gut tells me that if things ever get serious with Ryan, I won't just lose. I would be utterly defeated and completely depleted of love to give. There should be a guard around my heart, so I can most definitely stop being that guy who is too good, too eager to trust.

My body starts to relax as I open my eyes to see Ryan sleeping peacefully. The length of my night plus a long work day hits me hard and soon, I'm asleep.

* * *

A hand is tangled in my hair, slowly playing

with my curls, and my pillow is moving underneath me. As I start to wake up, I realize my head is lying on Ryan's breasts. At some point, she became my pillow, and I'm hugging her to me. I open my eyes and see that I'm correct. I lift my head to see a smile, and Ryan's gleaming green eyes, her hand sliding to the side, but still twirling a curl around her finger.

She giggles, making me smile. "You sleep like a girl. I couldn't even cuddle with you because you decided to use me as a pillow."

"Sorry," I say as I go to move away from her.

"Don't you dare, Gabe. Your hair is too soft, and I'm not done touching it. Lay back down, please." She gives me a sweet smile, so I do. Her fingers start moving once more, and it's kind of soothing.

"What time is it?"

Before she can answer, her bedroom door opens. A girl walks in, sees us, and starts backing out, obviously surprised to find me in here with Ryan.

"What the hell, Viv?" Ryan asks annoyed.

"Sorry!"

"I'll be right back." Ryan leaves me in bed and on her way out, she says, "This is the second Sunday in a row you've barged in on my Me Day. It's never anything that you couldn't text me about either."

Me Day? Ryan leaves the door halfway open, and I can still hear their conversation.

"Sorry!" she repeats. "I didn't know you had company. Who is that?"

"Why are you here? Do I need to get my key back?" Ryan's tone is slightly threatening.

"You weren't answering your phone. I wanted to make sure you were okay after last night, but I can see that you are more than okay."

I toss the covers aside and get up. There's no sense in me hiding in the bedroom. Ryan sees me first, her mouth parted for whatever she was about to say. The girl, Viv, turns around as I walk up to them. With her traveling eyes, I wish I had a shirt on. When I reach her, I hold out my hand.

"Hey, I'm Gabe. You're the friend who called me, right?"

"Yeah, that'd be me. Nice to finally meet you."

Ryan grabs her shoulders and starts pushing her towards the door. "Viv was just leaving." Ryan walks with her all the way to the door. "Stop coming over on Sundays, Vivian. I mean it."

"Bye," she calls over her shoulders before Ryan closes the door behind her.

"Sorry," Ryan says, coming back to me. She takes my hand and leads me back into her bedroom. "We'll pretend she was never here."

I laugh. "What's so special about Sundays? You said something about a Me Day?"

Ryan crawls into bed and pulls me on top of her. "On Sundays, I spend the day here all by myself. I mostly relax and sometimes take a bubble bath."

Grinning, I say, "So I must be special then, huh? To be here today?"

"Really special." Ryan leans forward with a smile and gives me a little kiss. "It's noon, by the way."

Noon? Wow. I haven't slept in that late since I was a teenager.

"Do you want to spend my lazy day with me? We can lay here all day." That seducing smile is back, her arms wrapping around my neck.

I dip my head and kiss her neck. "Mmm," I hum against her skin, "that is tempting."

"Please don't let there be a 'but'."

A chuckle escapes me. There were some things I wanted to do today before I headed to my parents for dinner, but most of the day is gone already. I could still get everything done, though. Lifting my head, I look at Ryan with a smile.

"You are too adorable and hot all at the same time. It's ridiculous, you know that, right?"

I laugh again. "That's good to know. And there's no 'but'. I just have to leave in a few hours to get to my parents in time for dinner."

Her stomach rumbles beneath me, and her eyes widen. "How about you tell me about your family while I fix breakfast?"

So we head into her kitchen. I lean against the counter near her, but far enough away that she can move freely without me getting in the way. She asks if I like omelets and when I say yes, she begins to fix two.

"Anything in particular you want to know?" I ask, but she shakes her head. Where to start? "Well, my mother is a stern, religious, old-fashioned woman who would like to have family dinners every Sunday to make sure that we'll still come around. My older brother, Keith, doesn't live around here, so it's kind of hard for him to make it. I go whenever I don't have to work. My father is strict, but he's more openminded than my mother. I think that would be the best word for it. He's more willing to bend rules than she is, which is ironic considering his job."

Ryan nods like that fits whatever image she had in her head. I can't see what she looks like because she's facing the stove. "What about Owen and Keith? What are they like? I mean, I know I met Owen, but that was only for a few minutes."

"Keith pretty much fits the bill of what you would think an FBI agent would be like. When he's home and away from work, he's much more relaxed and more like my brother. And Owen is a good kid. Good grades, great football player, and a kind person with lots of dreams."

"Does he want to go into law enforcement too?"

I shake my head, even though she can't see me. "No. Well, that's not his top pick anyway. All he can think about right now is making it to college to play football." Ryan's foot moves to rub against the back of her calf on her other leg, effectively distracting me from whatever I was about to say.

73

Her legs are amazing. They will be the death of me, I'm sure. Ryan says something, but I don't catch it. "What?" I ask, not taking my eyes off her legs until they turn around.

Ryan laughs, realizing why I didn't hear her the first time. "Gabe, I asked if you would get the drinks. I'm almost finished."

"Oh, okay." I push off the counter and go to the fridge. "Water or Sunkist?" I say, even though I already know the answer.

"Sunkist. The water is only in there for any guests who don't want my drink of choice."

I turn to face her with a raised eyebrow. "And you have guests over often?" There are only about three water bottles left, and I grab one.

Ryan narrows her eyes at me. "What are you implying, Gabe? But to answer your question, Viv hates Sunkist and as you saw, she's here a lot." She takes the plates and sets them on the kitchen table before walking away.

I put our drinks down, take a seat, and wait for her to return. She comes out of her bedroom with her phone and hooks it up to a speaker system.

Over her shoulder, she says, "I listen to music all the time, but especially on Sundays. Today, I'm in the mood for my Back in the Day playlist, if that's okay?"

"Sure."

I wonder what songs she would classify as "back in the day." The very first song is Stevie Wonder's "Superstition". Okay, I wasn't expecting that, especially for someone her age. The music plays as a soft background noise. Ryan comes to sit down with me, and we start to eat.

"What are the other men in your family like? You said that y'all get together every month to go shooting, right?"

"Yeah. We're simply a bunch of very competitive men with too much testosterone. I mean, it is a group of men shooting guns, talking smack, and throwing in a dirty joke every now and then."

Ryan laughs lightly. "That actually sounds really fun. With the things that come out of my mouth, it's easier to be around guys than girls sometimes."

"Build Me Up Buttercup" comes on, and I'm continuously surprised by what music is on her phone. "We're getting together this upcoming weekend. We can still get a private lesson in first. If you wanted to go, that is."

Ryan watches me while we eat silently. She's quiet for so long that Elvis' "Jailhouse Rock" starts playing before she answers. "Okay, sure. But even if I have fun when I'm with you, I don't know if I want to participate with your family."

"Fair enough. I think you'll like it though."

"What makes you say that?"

"Kind of hard not to enjoy it. You'll see."

Tina Turner starts singing some song I've never heard about the rain. When we finish eating, we put our plates in the dishwasher, and I excuse myself to the restroom, taking the opportunity to brush my teeth as well. I step out and hear The Temptations. Faintly, I hear Ryan singing "My Girl" as well. She has a pretty voice, but once she hears me coming, she stops.

"You didn't have to quit," I whisper in her ear when I come up behind her, grabbing her hips.

She giggles. "I didn't think you heard me."

"I did. You're good."

"Helps when I've taken singing lessons before. I'll be right back."

She disappears down the hall to the bathroom, and I sit on the couch, noticing she threw away the forgotten popcorn from last night. Chuck Berry starts singing "Roll Over Beethoven". I have to say I like her choices, and I'm impressed she has an entire playlist of songs like this. As I sit on her couch, I realize that I'm still shirtless in her apartment. That I slept here last night. I haven't figured out a lot about Ryan, but what I know so far has kept me coming back to her. Odd doesn't begin to cover my behavior, but I can think about that later.

Ryan comes back, but instead of sitting next to me, she straddles my lap, her hands resting flat on my chest. I instinctively hold her hips, trying not to let my hands wander down to her bare legs that are now seriously begging me to touch them.

"I've been thinking about something," she says. By that familiar look in her eyes, I know her mind is in the exact spot as mine.

"Oh yeah?" I question, my pulse already speeding up. I vaguely realize that "Let's Get It On" comes on.

Ryan realizes it because she laughs, clearly cracked up by the song. "I think my playlist is conspiring against us." I chuckle and she continues in a softer, no longer focused on the music, voice, "I've been thinking about these." Ryan lifts a hand and places the tip of her finger in the middle of my bottom lip. "And this," she says, moving her hands over my chest, up to my shoulders. Then she starts going down my arms, gently squeezing my biceps. "And these too." Ryan lets her hands go all the way to my own. She plucks them from her hips, my hands lifeless in hers, giving her complete control. She holds them up before intertwining them with hers. "Last, but definitely not least." Inch by inch, Ryan leans forward until she is close enough to press her lips against mine. "But mostly these."

She kisses me then, just as slow but even more intense then last night. There's too much sexual tension between us. I'm already turned on, and Ryan knows it because her lips lift a little against mine as she rests fully in my lap. These basketball shorts aren't hiding anything either. Ryan tastes minty, but the longer we kiss, the more I taste her. She lets go of my hands to hold onto my shoulders instead. My own don't even bother going back to her hips. They head straight for those toned thighs of hers that I want wrapped around my waist.

The silky smoothness of her skin disorients me

more than anything. I have just enough clarity to keep my hands from exploring because the moment they do, I'll be lost in her again. Ryan withdraws from my lips, kissing my jaw, before going to my neck. That beautiful shoulder is in front of me, so I start from the right, kissing and sucking my way to the crook of her neck while her lips travel to nibble on my ear.

"Gabe?" She breathes.

I hum against her shoulder in response.

"Let your hands move." I feel her hands over mine, lifting the fingers a little. "Your grip is too tight."

That clears some of the haze, and I pull away to see her giving me a small smile. "Sorry."

"It's fine." The moment clashes as Aretha starts singing about respect. Ryan sits upright, looking down at our hands, and I lean back into the couch. After a moment, she peers up at me from underneath those lashes, her red hair framing her face perfectly. "I'm sorry. I don't mean to keep putting you in situations where you feel the need to restrain yourself. I'm not exactly used to people holding back. Am I really that bad that you would feel guilty about me? Because that's how you felt after our date, isn't it? I don't understand why you keep coming back if I made you feel that way. I-"

"Ryan, stop talking." I intertwine our hands again. "*You* didn't make me feel guilty. *I* made myself-"

"Because of what you did with me," she

interrupts, her voice monotone. The next thing out of her mouth is full of emotion though. "What you're most scared of, Gabe? That's practically me. I'm not the kind of girl that guys show off to those who matter to them. I'm the You-Only-Need-One-Date girl, and before you even say something, I'm perfectly happy being that girl. My point is that you, your hopes, dreams, and personality are the complete opposite of the kind of girl I am. That's why I don't understand why you're here."

I think carefully about what she said before I respond. "I'm here because you are more than a type or kind of girl. There's always more to a person than that, and you aren't excluded. I know that there is more to you than sex and more than a personality that keeps you in a certain category."

"But you're concerned," she interrupts again. Softly, she curiously adds, "Can you tell me what about me has you worried?"

"You really want me to tell you?"

"Of course. It's good to be aware of my faults."

My brows come together, confused. "Your faults?"

"Just tell me, please."

"These things aren't your faults, Ryan. It's what makes you who you are, and I don't see anything wrong with that." She nods, but I can tell she doesn't believe me. "But if you really want to know, I'll tell you. All of these things scare me, sure, but I like these things about you too, okay?" Once she nods, I continue. "You're beautiful, and you have a very tempting and gorgeous body. It's almost too much considering your age. You know how to use this body very well and being pulled over when you're half naked doesn't bother you at all. Then there's how I'm six years older than you and that wouldn't sound so bad if your age didn't end with 'teen'.

"You're still in college while my lifestyle is way different than that. I'm done with that part of my life, and you're in the middle of that part for you. Ryan, sometimes, I have no clue how to handle your personality. But I like it. That's all that matters."

Ryan's green eyes study me, with "The Gambler" of all songs playing in the background. For a moment, I worry that I've said too much. "Okay," she finally says.

"Okay?"

"Yes. I can understand you better now, and that's really all I wanted to accomplish."

"Good." I lean forward to kiss her gently. She smiles, and my eyes catch sight of the clock on the wall behind her. I will have to leave in about two hours. "You said you take bubble baths?"

"Yeah?" She questions, not knowing where I'm going with this.

"I will have to leave soon, but I can go start the bath for you."

"Oh, thank you." Ryan slides off my lap and onto the couch.

I get up and go start our bath. Yes, I said our.

Never have I taken a bubble bath, but this feels like something I should do with Ryan. Thankfully, her tub is deep and wide enough for us both. At least, it looks that way. Once there is enough water and suds, I turn off the water and quickly undress. Just as I get comfortable, I hear "You Make Me Feel Like A Natural Woman" start playing.

"Gabe? Is everything-" Ryan walks into the bathroom, her eyes wide. "Okay?" She finishes, tilting her head to look at me.

"I've never had a bubble bath and these suds," I cup some in my hand as evidence, "looked like too much fun, so I thought I'd join you."

Ryan slowly smiles. "I'm not sure if there's enough room for us both."

"There is."

That's all the push she needs. Ryan bunches the hem of her shirt in her hands and slowly lifts it up and over her head, dropping it carelessly to the floor. Then she shimmies out of her bottoms, becoming completely and boldly naked in front of me. How she already has a body of a goddess, I'll never know. Even her tattoo on her hip seems meant to be there. Ryan steps into the tub across from me, lowering herself into the steamy water. Her hands find my knees and then travel up my thighs as she comes closer to me.

Her hair falls forward, the tips getting wet and sudsy. Ryan bites her lower lip before closing the distance between our lips to kiss me. It doesn't last nearly long enough, which is probably a good thing. She pulls away from me to turn around, her back tattoos partly on display. She slides back against me between my legs, our knees peeking through the bubbles. I'm already hard, and Ryan knows it.

"The point of this is to relax," she whispers, leaning her head backwards to rest on my left shoulder.

I let my lips brush her ear as I say, "Are you not relaxed?" My fingers are twitching to touch her and leave their current place on the sides of the tub. I move them to her shoulders, moving downwards under the water, deciding to stop once I've reached her hips.

Ryan's cheeks lift when she smiles, her eyes closed. "Not yet. Give me time. I was just telling you, Officer O'Connor. You seem kind of stiff," she bubbles out a laugh.

Smirking, I ignore her comment. My fingers begin to thrum on her hips, and I start moving them up her stomach. My thumbs just barely brush over the underside of her breasts. Ryan's eyes open.

"We're supposed to be relaxing," she mutters, turning to look at me.

I grin. "Isn't that what we're doing?"

"Nope. While you are very tempting, Gabe, I've decided I don't want to have sex with you."

My hands return to lay flat on her stomach. "Oh yeah?"

"Not today anyway. You've inspired me."

"I have?" What is she talking about?

Ryan grins. "Yep. I'm going to behave better. We'll see how long it lasts." Ryan frowns as a thought flits her mind.

"What is it?" I ask.

"Nothing. Time to relax."

She closes her eyes, leaning her head back on my shoulder once more. Her frown bothers me though. What is she thinking? I attempt to relax as well, even though that's still on my mind along with her body against mine. Twenty minutes pass in silence before I finally say something about it.

"Ryan?"

"Yeah?" She says without opening her eyes.

"Tell me why you frowned."

Ryan sighs and turns her head to look at me. "I was thinking about how when I stop trying to behave, stop trying to be someone I'm not, it will count as me quitting because I would be giving up. That it will be added to my long list of failures." Ryan sits up, moves forward, and then turns as she sits across from me in the tub. "Do you know that I've thought about changing my name? Countless times."

"Why?" I actually like her name. Sure, I thought it was odd at first, but it grows on you.

"My parents wanted a boy. They got me, and I've heard about it every day of my life. That name, *my* name, is tied to me being what they never wanted. That's why it pissed me off when you said it was a boy's name. Once I started college, though, I mostly stopped thinking about it and decided to

83

own up to it."

Since she brought it up, I decide to ask. "Why are your parents like that? Explain it to me. Why didn't they have another kid if they wanted a boy that badly?"

Ryan shakes her head. "Believe it or not, I'm their miracle child. I'm the only one of my mother's pregnancies that didn't end in miscarriage. That's why they didn't have another kid and they stopped trying. Everything they've ever wanted in a child rests on my shoulders now. They have empty hopes for me though because they don't think I can do any of it." Ryan cups some of the bubbles in her hands and glances at me. "You ruined my bath for me."

I take a moment to absorb what she just said. No wonder she doesn't think she's meet-the-parents material. Her own parents have made her feel like this. It's terrible. This is why she keeps using words like disappointment and failure. It makes sense now. Although, I'm sure there is more I'm still missing. More that I want to find out, which doesn't mean that I'm going to turn into a savior.

"I'm sorry." I move to lean towards her. "C'mere. I'll make up for it." All I want to do is make her feel better before I leave. Ryan looks a little skeptical, so I curve a finger under her chin and lead her to me. "Close your eyes," I softly order.

Ryan does, the corners of her mouth slightly

moving up and down as she tries not to smile. For a moment, I take in her features. She's beautiful. Without waiting any longer, I gently press my lips to hers. They part, already eager for more. I slip my tongue into her mouth to play with hers. Ryan releases a quiet sigh into my mouth as her fingers grasp my face. Her sigh is like a small billow of air that makes everything tumble within me.

I kiss her with unhurried passion, as if the clock has stopped and we have all the time in the world. But the water soon cools to bring back bits of my senses, and I pull away from Ryan. The bubbles have all but disappeared to leave our naked bodies almost completely visible. She hasn't opened her eyes yet, and her lips are barely pursed. That look on her face right now is one I will never tire of. Goosebumps dot her skin, her nipples at attention. Those dark green eyes finally stare at me, a smile rising on her lips.

"Thanks," she whispers.

"Any time."

Her gaze glances downward at me and my hard, aching body. It's probably time for me to leave, but all I want to do is get off. I don't know what Ryan wants, though. I don't think I should sleep with her again just yet. This needs to be done right, and I need to resist the lure before I do something I regret.

"I, uh-" I stop to clear my throat. "I need to get going." My eyes immediately snap to Ryan's moving hands underneath the water, coming towards me at a tortuously slow pace.

"Right now?" She questions.

I'm wound up too tightly for her to tease me today. Her hands land on my thighs, and I swallow hard, waiting for her to do something. My focus won't waver from her crawling hands, even when she speaks. I'm frozen by those slender fingers. She's paralyzed me.

"I would feel terrible knowing you left like this."

The tips of her fingers ever so slightly brush along my shaft. Oh my God. She's going to kill me. Suddenly, her hands are too far away from me, and water is sloshing as she stands. Helpless to Ryan, I take my time looking as I travel along her legs, her hips, her stomach, her breasts. I look at every droplet of water on my way up until I reach her sexy grin. She holds out her hand, palm up.

"C'mon. The clock is ticking."

I take her hand and stand, but wish more than anything I would have sex with her. I'm not going to do that though. She said herself she wanted to behave, and I should honor that for as long as possible. We step out of the tub, and I grab a towel off the rack, wrapping it around her shoulders. The corners of her mouth dip, her brows coming together in confusion.

"What are you doing?" She finally asks when I wrap one around my waist.

With a deep breath, I say, "You want to behave, remember?" Her frown deepens, and I swear she looks a bit disappointed. Then I add, "The next time I have sex with you, it won't be for the simple fact that I'm horny. There should be more than that, Ryan."

I don't know how I'm expecting her to react, but for her to roll her eyes and shake her head like I'm being impossible and silly wasn't it. She doesn't say she doesn't think it's possible or that she thinks that's ridiculous. In fact, she doesn't fight me about it at all because she only says, "Fine." Ryan doesn't budge when I go to walk past her, and I wish I could know what she's thinking. I kiss her temple before leaving her behind, going to her bedroom to get dressed.

The clock on her nightstand says I'll have enough time to go home, shower, and then go straight to my parents. I grab my almost dead phone from my stack of clothes, seeing a missed call from my mother. I'll call her once I leave here. As I'm walking out of the bedroom, the oldies music changes to rock, and the volume is louder than before. Is Ryan one of those people who listens to the music based on their mood, music that gives hints about them? Right now, "Bad Girlfriend" by Theory of a Deadman is playing.

Ryan has wrapped the towel around her chest and is leaning against the table where her sound system is. She lifts her head when she sees me, her face void of any emotions even with her small smile.

"Have fun with your family," she says.

"Thanks. I'll text ya later." I give her a kiss on the lips before I leave.

* * *

"Hey, Mom," I say as I kiss her cheek.

"Hey, Gabriel. It's about time you came over for Sunday supper," she teases.

"I know, I know." I take a seat at the table because I ran late and they are already seated. "Hey, Dad, Owen."

"Hey," they reply.

Without a word, we fall into our routine. I grab hold of Owen's hand since he is next to me, and also my father's. Owen and Dad take Mom's hands. We bow our heads, and my father says prayer.

"Amen," we say together when he finishes. Then we start piling food onto our plates.

"How's work been?" Dad asks.

"Good. I'm getting a partner apparently."

Dad chuckles, but Mom speaks first. "We're not talking about work at the table. You two know that," she chides.

My dad grins. "Is there anything other than work that you do, Gabriel?"

"He's dating someone," Owen chirps in next to me.

I slap his leg under the table, but it's too late. It's not that my family doesn't ever know of who I'm dating, but my mother is always the last to meet her. That's not by mistake either. She's the hardest to please, but she is always right with her opinion. After my last relationship and the apparent error of my ways, I don't want to make any more mistakes.

"Oh?" My mother's eyebrows shoot up.

"She's hot," Owen adds again.

"You've met her?" Even though Mom knows I save her opinion for last, she doesn't like it.

"Yes, he has," I say before Owen can say anything, but he still has to talk.

"How old is Ryan anyway?"

"Ryan?" My mother questions, confused by the name.

I sigh, glancing at my father who is smirking. He enjoys this too much. "That's her name, Mom."

"Why on earth would someone name their daughter with a boy's name? It's strange." She frowns, and I can already see her picking apart Ryan when she doesn't even know anything about her yet. With our family, our opinions matter. We try to be objective and look out for each other. Mom likes to take that to another level. She doesn't want any of us to get hurt and sometimes oversteps the boundaries. She means well, though.

To avoid saying anything just yet, I take a sip of my tea. "It's not strange, and I've only been on one date with her."

Mom nods. "How did you meet this Ryan then?"

"Might as well get it all out, Gabriel. She's going to keep asking until she knows everything,"

Dad inputs, telling the truth.

"All right. I pulled her over, gave her a ticket, and kept running into her. That's how I met her. She's something else, that's for sure."

Dad laughs. "You gave her a ticket?"

I nod, smiling at the memory. "She was going to get off with a warning, but she asked for it. Ryan has a fiery personality. So far, so good."

Owen nudges me with his elbow. "How old is she? She looked kind of young for you."

"Only a little younger than I am." If her age worries me a little, I don't know what my parents will say. "What about you? Where's your girl?"

Owen shrugs, the spotlight off me as my mother says, "He's focused on his schoolwork and football. Isn't that right, Owen?"

"Yes, ma'am."

Mom won't let us talk about work, but she will let us talk about football, and that's where the rest of our conversation goes. It feels good to be home for Sunday supper, but in the back of my mind, thoughts of Ryan linger.

Chapter Six
Ryan

After Gabe left, I showered and started cleaning up the apartment, jamming to my favorite rock bands. I'm not so sure what to make of Gabe and the past forty-eight hours. It seems best if I don't put much thought into any of it. Overthinking is part of my rambling problem, and I don't want to do either. Even though I am by myself, that doesn't mean my mind and inner dialogue won't ramble. Besides, if I start thinking too much, I might change my mind altogether about seeing Gabe again. It's been interesting to say the least. Nonetheless, these thoughts are shutting down indefinitely. I'm planning to focus on having fun and nothing more.

Even when "Better Than Me" by Hinder starts playing, I ignore it. There's still plenty to do around the place like vacuuming and washing clothes and homework. I have two papers due this week, and I haven't started either. Today is full of nothing but busy work. Once I knock out one of my papers, I decide to text Viv and see if she wants to come work on this paper with me since we both have to write one. She is seriously abusing having a key to my apartment though. I only gave it to her for emergencies or in case she needed to borrow some clothes and I wasn't here. Nowhere does it say she can barge in unannounced.

About thirty minutes pass before Viv arrives and the first thing she mentions is Gabe.

"Spill all the juicy details, Ryan," she says, sitting down next to me at the kitchen table with her laptop and textbook.

"Nothing juicy about it. He came over, spent the night, took a bubble bath with me, and left. No sex either."

Viv's eyebrows rise. "None?"

"Nope. I rather not talk about Gabe. Are we going to write these papers or not?"

She squints her eyes at me. "I've never known you not to want to talk about a guy."

"Always a first time for everything." My phone vibrates loudly on the table, so I pick it up.

"Is that him?" Viv says with too much excitement.

"That it is." I can't help but laugh when I read his message. Apparently, Owen thinks I'm hot. A hint of apprehension runs through me. Does this mean he talked about me with his parents too? Or just Owen? Owen, I can handle. I text him back.

Can't say I disagree with him, haha.

"Well?" Viv questions when I put my phone back down.

"He just said something about his brother. Time to get down to business, Viv."

And that's what we do. My phone goes off again, but I ignore it. I don't want to get too distracted. We work for about an hour in silence before we're done. I order a pizza online for us, and Viv leans back in her chair.

"I'm guessing that you'll be seeing Gabe again?"

"Looks that way. I know it's at the end of the month, but when are we going shopping for Halloween? You know there will be parties, and we have to celebrate my birthday somehow. Might as well do it by dressing up and going to a party." I don't know why she keeps bringing the conversation back to him or why I keep changing it when she does. But Halloween/my birthday is a legit question because it is coming up soon. I don't really celebrate my birthday, but it would seem odd if I told Viv that, so I keep it to myself.

"Whenever we know what we want to be. Do you know yet?" I shake my head. "Me either. What happened to you never going on second dates?"

I shrug. "I didn't intend to, and it's not like he's about to be my boyfriend. In fact, the more I think about it, the more I think I'm a phase of sorts for him." I'm not so sure that I believe the things Gabe said to me. There's a knock on the door, so I leave her to go answer. Once I've paid the pizza guy, he hands over our pizza and leaves. We eat it right out of the box and after Viv's first bite, she asks a question.

"What are you talking about, Ryan?"

"Gabe's a good guy, and I'm not the type of girl he would want to take home to his mother. I'm younger than him, still in college, and not good in any sense of the word. So wouldn't it make sense that he's just having a little fun with me for a bit? We need to stop talking about it. I'm overthinking it as it is, and I rather let failure take its natural course without any help from me. Besides, my mom told me I need to make a decision on my major in two weeks. Will you help me think of something?"

Viv doesn't know much about my parents because I never share much about them and she knows better than to ask. After she takes a sip of water, she nods. "Well, I'm going to major in linguistics, but the college has tons to choose from."

"Like what?" Okay, so I never looked at their academic programs when I was applying. I just wanted to get away from my parents. I didn't care what degrees they offered, so I don't know all of their programs.

Viv opens her computer again and pulls up the school website, reading off some of the programs, one from each letter. "Applied Physical Sciences, Biomedical Engineering, Communications Studies, Dermatology, Economics, Family Medicine, Genetics, blah, blah, blah. Ooh, Marine Science or Physics and Astronomy? What about Spanish? You speak that, right?"

I nod, but everything sounds boring, and I tell her so.

"Life isn't supposed to be fun 24/7, Ryan. You need boring moments too."

"Yeah, well, I don't want to be bored for the rest of my life. I'm good with math, but who wants to solve equations for a living? Genetics sounds interesting, but no thanks. If I *had*," I say it like it's a despicable thought, "to pick any that you mentioned, it would be Communications Studies or Spanish, since that can't be all that hard, and I know a lot already."

Viv nods, happy that I picked something. She clicks a few times and then counts. "There are one, two, three, four, five areas of study for Communications."

I groan as she tells me what they are. "Fine. Spanish. I pick Spanish. Those sounded horrible."

"Why are you settling if that's not what you want?"

"Because it doesn't really matter to me anyway. There's nothing I would love to do. Everything is just eh to me."

"What about Marine Science or even Dermatology?"

Sinking into my seat, I sigh. "Stop giving me choices, Viv. I'll change my mind and then we'll be back at square one. As long as I can get a job and make money, then I'm happy. Every single working person isn't working their dream job. Since I don't have a dream, anything will do." Maybe I should let my parents pick my major. I can't disappoint them if it's their decision. But then they would probably send me to medical school, and that's not going to work for me. Everyone in the medical field is amazing for what they do, but I can't do it. Viv shakes her head at me, apparently doing some thinking of her own. "What?"

"I can't believe that nothing appeals to you. At all."

"Believe it. The only thing that appeals to Ryan Kavanaugh is sex and men. I don't think my parents would be happy with a career as a hooker or sugar baby though."

Viv laughs. "You're crazy. You should work for Sunkist as much as you drink it." She nods to the bottle in my hand as I take a sip.

"I wonder if I would get free drinks for life. That might be worth looking into, Viv. Good idea."

She chuckles, shaking her head. "Well, I should go. There's some more work I have to do. See you in the morning."

"Bye."

Spanish wouldn't be my first choice, but let's face it. Nothing would be my first choice. Still, I feel accomplished. I've made a decision for my major. I pick up my phone to see what Gabe texted me back.

Gabe: I don't either. How's your lazy day going without me?

Me: Good. Homework is done & house is clean. Just need to wash clothes.

While I wait for his response, I put the rest of the pizza in the fridge and get started on those clothes. Panic clutches my stomach and rises like bile within me. I. Picked. A. Major. Spanish. That's what the rest of my life will involve. Is that what I want? What if I decide that I hate it? Or should I pick another language? It could be more fun and a challenge to learn a new language. There's French, Chinese, Japanese, or maybe Portuguese. Maybe I should do one of those instead.

Ugh.

I don't have a fucking clue!

Back to square one. I still don't understand how at nineteen, almost twenty, I'm supposed to choose what I want to do for the rest of my life. Sure, I could always come back to school and get a degree in something else, but that makes my first degree pretty much worthless and a waste of money. I can't make a decision like that! My parents can choose for me. They are older, supposedly wiser, so they can choose how I'll spend the rest of my life.

Yes, that's what I'll do.

Before Gabe can text me back, I text him.

Me: I envy you.

His response comes in seconds later.

Gabe: That doesn't sound like a lazy day.
And why?
Me: That stuff is kind of relaxing... Trying
to decide on major. Maybe I should be a
housewife since cleaning relaxes me. ha.
Gabe: hahaha. Dream big, Ryan. If you
could do ANYTHING, what would you
do?

To have sex with him again would be nice.
Can't believe he left with a boner! I was horny too,
but that's why I own a vibrator. I don't think that's
what he meant though. Five minutes pass, and I'm
still thinking.

Gabe: You're taking too long. There has to
be something you want to do. Just in
general. Not even as a job.
Me: Nope. I've got nothing.
Gabe: Don't think so much about it then.
Me: Easier said than done.

Gabe starts sending me texts with various
activities. Skydiving, surfing, rock climbing, riding

a motorcycle, learning a new sport, and so on. My answer to every single one is, sure, that sounds like fun. Then he sends me a message expressing his exasperation at my response. Everything does sound like fun though. I want to try everything, no one more than the other. For the rest of the evening, I try to think of a solution to my problem.

* * *

"Oh, no," Viv mumbles, her eyes catching sight of someone behind me.

I turn to look and see her ex-boyfriend coming straight for us. Standing tall, I act as her shield.

"Babe, why haven't you been answering my calls? I miss you," he starts, completely ignoring me.

"Oh, now you miss her? Maybe you should have appreciated her while you had her, you cheating bastard."

"Stay out of this, Ryan."

I shake my head. "Eh, I don't think so. Why don't you go find that girl you fucked on your couch? Viv is off limits to you now."

He glares at me. "This has nothing to do with you," he says, growing annoying.

"Actually, it does. Viv is my," I point to my chest, "best friend. She has no ties to you. If that girl won't walk around your house naked and sleep with you anymore, looks like you better get familiar with that hand of yours. Be careful or you'll get carpal tunnel. Might want to let them take turns." I turn, grab Viv's shoulder to swivel her and start walking away from him.

"That was great. His mouth was hanging open, like he couldn't believe what you said. If I didn't know you so well, I wouldn't have believed it. Thanks, Ryan."

"No problem. That's what friends are for."

We settle into our seats, and our professor starts teaching moments later. This is how Monday, Tuesday, and Wednesday go. Meeting Viv in the morning, going to class, doing schoolwork, and me worrying to death over picking a major. The idea of learning a new language sounds appealing. That thought itself is shocking. Something appeals to me that isn't sex or boys or partying. This is something that will carry into my life after college. It excites me.

Learning Spanish wasn't all that exciting because my parents forced me into that. It was easy, and I picked it up quickly, but it wasn't an interest. But what if I could learn French? It's such a lovely language, and I could be an interpreter or something like that. The possibilities could be endless. The idea that I've finally picked something for my future, finally made a decision that really matters, bubbles within me, rising and blissfully infecting every part of me.

I just left one of my classes, wondering what I'm going to do for lunch when a text comes in.

Gabe: Meet me for lunch?
Me: Of course!

We've been texting here and there, but I haven't seen him since last weekend. He hasn't said when we're going for our lesson, and I haven't asked. Gabe texts me the place, and I go to my car to head that way. I've never been there before, but it's downtown and I've walked passed it before when Viv and I have gone clubbing. When I arrive, Gabe is already sitting at a booth. He slides out when he sees me, giving me a kiss on the cheek once I've reached him.

"Hey, Ryan."

"Hey. How's your day been, Officer?" I smirk. Now that I'm not in any kind of trouble, he looks delicious in uniform. I can appreciate it so much more.

Gabe laughs, his large, wide torso rumbling from deep within his chest. "Smooth, considering that I get to take time to have lunch with you. I've been learning how to operate with a new partner. It's hard when you've been by yourself for a while. How's your day been?"

"Good. Just left my last class for today." I pause about to ask about his partner, as the waitress comes with our drinks. Looks like Gabe already ordered that for us. My grin is too big when the glass full of my favorite orange drink is placed in front of me. "You sure do know the way to my heart," I chuckle before taking a sip.

Gabe smiles. "I thought you would appreciate that."

"I do."

"Good. I'm happy I was able to see you today." For some reason, that makes me suspicious. I narrow my eyes at him, and he laughs, holding his hands up. "I mean, I have wanted to see you again."

"But," I insert for him.

"But I sort of have bad news about this weekend."

My shoulders sag, the pit of my stomach telling me that he's changed his mind about me meeting the men of his family. I can't say that I blame him. It's early, and I don't even know if we are dating or what we are exactly. There's something between us. Maybe.

"Stop thinking."

"What?" I ask, confused.

"You think too much, Ryan. It's nothing bad, I promise. It's just I'm not going to be able to work out our lesson as I originally hoped."

"What do you mean?"

His hands disappear underneath the table and by the motions of his arms, I know he's running his hands down his thighs. "We can still do it, but the new plan is that we go early, I teach you, and then you'll know the basics, even shoot for a good little bit by the time everyone else shows up. If it makes you uncomfortable or scares you too much or whatever and you want to go home, I'll still take you back. You could just hang out with us too. They won't mind."

To avoid speaking too soon, I skim over the menu, looking, but not paying attention. I was honest when I said that I was kind of excited about it, but it was a feeling full of nerves. It would be trying something new, and I have complete faith in Gabe.

"Will you quit looking at that menu? Just because you're avoiding my gaze, doesn't mean I'm not here anymore. Tell me what you want to do, Ryan," he says gently. "This is your decision, and we'll do it the way you want."

"That sounds dirty," I tell him. He chuckles, but waits for me to continue. I hate when he does that. It's hard to avoid answering when he's so obviously waiting for me to speak. "If you're certain about this and you're sure they won't mind, then yes. That's fine."

"I'm absolutely certain."

Scary pulses of anxiety move through me at both meeting people in his family and at what we'll be doing. These types of emotions, I'm not used to, so I shove them aside and focus on picking something for lunch as the waitress returns. We both order a sandwich, his a burger, mine chicken. I shift in my seat, trying to gain a sense of comfort somehow, and my knee brushes one of Gabe's. His eyes flick to me, and I smile.

"What time are we thinking for Saturday?" I ask.

"We get together around two, so we could be out there before one sometime? That gives us at least an hour to see how you do."

I nod. "What should I wear?" I don't know much about this, so I wouldn't know if anything special is required. My question sounds weird, even on my lips, but Gabe doesn't acknowledge it.

"Tennis shoes, jeans, shirt, bra, underwear, socks." He grins at his additional obvious answers, and the massive urge to kiss him runs me down like a freight train. He looks outrageously adorable right now, even with the badge and uniform. I wonder if I'll get a kiss before I leave.

Rolling my eyes, I laugh softly. "Who put you in such a good mood, Officer O'Connor?"

"You did," he says simply. So casually thrown into the air between us that my glass comes to a stop just as my elbow bends to bring it to my lips.

My face contorts into confusion. Me? As in Ryan? Don't get me wrong, I know there is a person, a *real* person underneath all of the boys, sex, and dirty comments that I like, but never have I *ever* considered that *anyone* would truly like her. I don't like her myself half the time. Why would anyone else? That girl feels too much, cares even more about my parents, and seems weak to me. Broken by the two people who are supposed to love her unconditionally. This girl that I am right now, hasn't made sexual advances towards Gabe, so he isn't talking about me as I am this moment. He's talking about *her*. The other me.

His lips part, but the waitress brings our lunch, interrupting him. When she walks away, neither of us touches our food. Gabe tilts his head, briefly waiting to see if I'll say something. I clear my throat first.

"I did?"

Gabe nods. "You."

Hmph. Isn't that interesting. He watches me carefully, but I've got nothing to say. My mind is in overdrive trying to process this. And honestly, that means my mind is spouting sentence after sentence in one long, rambling mumbo jumbo. Gabe slides out of his seat, motions with his hand for me to scoot over, and then he sits next to me, pulling his plate over to this side of the table.

"What are you doing?" My question sounds forced, clamped, like I'm barely breathing enough to talk.

"Sitting next to you." He shrugs before taking a bite out of his burger. His thigh is pushed against mine and when I haven't been able to stop looking at him in his new seat, he turns to say with a nod to my plate, "It's going to get cold, Ryan."

"Why are you sitting next to me?" His action is throwing me off, utterly confusing my already lost mind. It's ridiculous that he's stumped me with this one action.

"Do you want me to move back?" He asks, resting a hand on my thigh.

I glance down to it, shaking my head. "That's not what I said."

"What's the matter, Ryan?" he says softly. "You looked a little freaked out, so I wanted to sit with you. Plus, I can touch you this way." He flashes me a smile, squeezes my thigh, and I giggle.

"You...I just...never mind." I lean over to give him a little kiss. "Glad you're in a good mood."

I finally join him in eating and in between bites, we continue our conversation. He asks me if I'm any closer on choosing a major, and I excitedly tell him about my plans. It still sounds weird to me. Gabe smiles while he listens.

"I knew you'd find something you'd be interested in."

"Yeah, I just hope it sticks. Hey," I say, suddenly remembering I meant to ask him about his partner. "Why has it been so long since you've had a partner? Do you like this one?"

Gabe has finished eating, but I still have some left. While he talks, he angles towards me some more, his hand still planted on my thigh with his fingers moving lazily. "My previous partner transferred to Charlotte for a higher position, and they just hadn't refilled his position here until now. And yeah, he's okay. Fredrick doesn't have much experience, but I think it'll work out. He's at a coffee shop a couple stores down, eating."

Just as I take my last bite, Gabe looks down at his clock on his wrist. "Time to go?" I question.

"Yeah, just about. Be right back." He grabs the check off the end of the table and goes to pay. I watch him walk away, wanting nothing more than to undress him, before taking one more sip of my drink and following him. Once he's paid, he turns and takes my hand. "I'll walk you to your car."

"Thanks for lunch, Gabe."

"You're welcome. I'm glad I got to see you."

"I'm glad you got to see me too," I say with a grin, causing Gabe to laugh. My car is right outside, so it's not a long walk. I search in my purse for my keys and unlock my door with the press of a button. Gabe reaches around me to open the door, but I don't get in. Instead, I turn to him, stepping closer until there's less than an inch between us. "Do I get a kiss before I go?"

"Do you want one?" He answers, clutching my hips, curling his fingers into my back.

"Yes." There's no need for me to say more or anything other than that. Yes is the truth, and I don't see the point in saying otherwise.

Gabe smiles, looking dangerously sexy now as he eliminates the space between us. I've had plenty of kisses before, but none as addicting and consuming as Gabe's. His make me feel unhurried yet overwhelmed from the mere presence of his lips on mine. He's in control. The thought thrills me. Whenever I have sex, I'm usually the one in control and guys love it. But with Gabe, there's no mistake as to who is holding the power. He is.

My entire body slinks against him when he slips his tongue into my mouth. I grasp the back of his neck, half of my fingers diving into his hair. There's a tenderness, but a crazed hunger underneath as if he's trying to control himself. I pull his lower lip into my mouth, tugging it between my teeth, and his grip on my hips is iron-strong. My smile can't resist forming against his lips, breaking our kiss. His eyes open, those brown eyes examining carefully.

"See you Saturday?" It comes out as a question, my voice wavering slightly with an unbearable need to have him.

"Yes. I'll pick you up."

I slide into my seat then and Gabe shuts the door after saying goodbye.

* * *

I was actually ready when Gabe came to pick me up. He drove out of town to this field in the middle of freaking nowhere. There's a couple of picnic tables and an old, wooden barn, but then it's wide open with surrounding fields. We're away from the highway and completely alone.

The gun is large, scary, and intimidating in Gabe's hand. I gulp. Gabe lays it down on a picnic table along with a couple others and an array of ammunition, plus three cans of soda. He glances over at me where I'm standing a few feet away with my arms crossed over my chest.

"Are you doing okay, Ryan?" He asks carefully.

"Are you sure you know what you're doing?" I hate that I can hear my apprehension in my voice.

Gabe gives me a hearty laugh. "I'm a cop. Of course I know how to use a gun." He stops what he's doing and walks over to me, running his hands up and down my arms between my elbow and my shoulder. With his lips against my forehead, he soothingly adds, "If you don't want to, you don't have to." Gabe looks down at me, waiting to see if I'm going to bail or not.

"I'm just nervous. That's all. Let's do this." I have no confidence in myself at all, but I trust Gabe, especially with this.

He nods and leaves to go set up the target. There's a post about the height you would use for a fence, and he tapes it to a board that's nailed to the post. He also places two stacked cans of soda on top of it. Gabe walks back to me, grabs the shotgun, the largest of the guns on the table, and tells me to get the earmuffs.

My eyes widen, my jaw hanging down by my knees. "That's what you're starting me with? A shotgun? Are you sure?"

"Yes, stop questioning me." He doesn't snap at me like I was expecting. Instead, his words are gentle and sure.

I grab the protective earmuffs and follow him. He stands a couple yards from the target and points with the tip of his foot where he wants me to stand.

"You're going to want to stand like this." He has his left foot ahead of his right as if he's trying to use his legs to anchor his body better. It also tilts his body towards the right a little. Once I assume the same position, he continues, showing me as he explains it. He lifts the shotgun so it rests on his shoulder. "This is how you'll hold it, okay? This part will rest right here on your shoulder, and you'll use your left hand to hold it right here." I nod, my hands trembling slightly. "The earmuffs will help with the sound. Put those on. It's loaded, but the safety is on. I just want you to hold it, okay?"

I swallow hard again, but nod. Pushing my anxiety away, cramming it into a corner, I hold the gun like Gabe was. It's heavier than I expected. Gabe's voice is muffled as he tells me to hold it like I'm about to shoot it. He moves to stand behind me, his arm coming around to point at a green thing on the end of the barrel.

"You'll use that to aim. You want this to be a little lower than the spot you want to hit. I want you to aim at the cans. Are *you* sure?" He asks tenderly, reaching out to place his hand over my still shaking one on the barrel.

"Yep. Just let me focus for a second."

With a long, slow drag of air, I close my left eye and concentrate on the bottom can. The gun's weight doesn't seem too heavy, and my nerves are forgotten, but it's not comfortable on my shoulder.

"It feels kind of awkward."

"What do you mean?" He asks.

"On my shoulder, it feels weird, uncomfortable." Gabe comes around, looks and tells me to move it inward a little. "That's better. What now? I'm ready."

"Turn off the safety by pushing this in," he shows me where near the trigger it is, "then pull the trigger."

"That's it? You're not going to tell me what to expect?" I need to know, so I won't freak out when whatever happens happens.

"I'm going to be behind you because it's going to recoil into your shoulder. It's not bad, but you've never done it before, and I don't want it to scare you too much. This piece on the end will absorb most of it."

I nod, reposition the shotgun on my shoulder once more, turn off the safety, and aim. I don't notice that Gabe is standing behind me as I focus. For about thirty seconds, he waits until I finally pull the trigger, barely feeling the recoil. Adrenaline pumps through my veins hard and fast as the bottom can explodes.

Holy.

Shit.

I hit it! Before I can get too excited, Gabe tells me to pull a piece back, flinging the empty shell out, and push the safety button from the other side to turn it back on. He takes the gun from me and then I take off the earmuffs.

"Did you see that?" I ask excitedly. "I shot, and it exploded!"

Gabe chuckles. "I saw it. That was amazing. You took your time, which is the girl in you, and you nailed it." He holds up his hand, and I give him a high five with a laugh, the rush still running through me. "Let's go look at the damage." Gabe lays the gun back on the picnic table before taking my hand, leading me to the post.

The top can was knocked over, but is still intact. The can I aimed for, however, is destroyed. There are little holes all over what's left of it, and there's one huge gaping hole missing, causing the can to only be in tact from the back. Gabe points to one of the little holes.

"Inside the shell, there are a bunch of little pellets. When you shoot a shotgun, those pellets are released and fan out. That's why they are all over the place."

"I don't care about the technical stuff, Gabe. Sorry," I quickly add. "But can I do it again?" I rock on my heels from excitement.

Gabe laughs. "See, I told you that you would like it."

And boy, do I. Gabe puts the leftover can on top of the post, and we return to where we were standing. Just as before, I take my time to steady my excited, frayed nerves, aim, and then slowly pull the trigger back with my finger, the rush swirling and swooshing through me powerfully before it even goes off. It happens rapidly, but the can explodes just like before.

"Are you sure you've never done this before?" Gabe's faint voice rumbles through the earmuffs.

I laugh. "Positive. Can I try one of the other

ones?"

Gabe nods, takes the shotgun from me, and I pull off the earmuffs as I follow him to the table. Right now, stress – what it is, what it means, and how it feels – is completely foreign to me. My blood is still pumping swiftly with a buzzed elation. This is fun. So much more than I ever thought possible. I'm not comfortable holding it unless I'm about to shoot, so I let Gabe do that. He asks if I want to load this one, but I shake my head. That's for another day.

"This one doesn't have a safety," he tells me, glancing at my wide eyes. Gabe chuckles. "It's fine, Ryan. Don't freak out on me."

"I'm not." I rock on my heels. "This is amazing, but I don't feel comfortable holding it longer than it takes to aim and shoot."

Gabe nods, turning to walk back to where we were standing. "That makes sense, and I don't mind doing all the work for you." He flashes me a smile before getting back down to business. "Okay, this is a little different than the shotgun. This is how you're going to hold it." The curve of the handle is where the curve between my thumb and forefinger will rest. "You want to make sure this is how you hold it. When you're out of rounds, this is going to cock backwards, and if you're hand is there, it's going to hurt when it fires back at you. You're going to wrap your fingers around it, leaving your forefinger out straight until you're ready to shoot.

"Then you'll place your left hand over your other hand to steady it. This recoil is different than the shotgun. The gun itself is going to sort of fling back, like this." He moves his hands, the gun going from straight towards the target to upwards towards the sky. "You need to hold it tightly, and keep your arms steady. To aim, it's similar to the shotgun, but you have to line up these three squares." He points to two of them on the outer edge at the top of the gun, closest to me, and the other in the middle at the end of the barrel. "Once you line those up with your target, you're good to go. All you have to do is pull." After a moment, he adds, "The casings will eject automatically, so I'll be standing on your left to avoid them."

I nod, and he asks if I'm ready. I nod again, so he holds the gun out for me to take. This gun is so much smaller, which makes it feel so much more dangerous. Gabe senses my anxiety, I guess, because he stands behind me and places his hands over mine to hold the gun with me. To stall, I ask what kind it is, even though it means nothing to me.

"45 mag." His hands help steady me, the nerves fading as I match his breathing. His hands leave mine. "Here, you forgot these." Gabe moves the earmuffs from around my neck and over my ears.

"I'm good now," I tell him, and he takes a step backwards away from me. With long, slow intakes of air through my nose and breathing out my mouth, I find my calm. The gun is steady in my hands as I pull back the trigger. He was right, the recoil is different, but it happens so fast, I'm not sure I can describe what it does exactly. I aimed for the bullseye, of course, but the bullet hit the lower right corner in the white.

"You're hesitating right before you pull the trigger, and the gun dips a little. Try again. Take your time, but don't hesitate," Gabe says from my left. I nod and repeat the process, taking my time as instructed.

This time, I hit the black. On my third try, I make sure that my hands are still, almost to the point of locking my arms in place. I look at that little red circle, pulling the trigger back with my finger, a high taking over from the powerful force. My mouth parts when I see that I hit it. I lift the gun to do it again. Just to see if I can put another hole there. Holy fuckaroo. I did it. *Again.* And then, lost in this crazy high, I pull the trigger four more times rapidly.

The top of the gun pops back, just as Gabe said it would when it was out of bullets. Gabe's eyes are wide when I hand it back to him.

"Got a little trigger-happy, didn't you?"

Despite my trembling hands from the power that little thing holds, I grin. "Just a little." My entire body feels light from being overwhelmed by the force of the weapon. "I need a break." I hold my hand out, so he can see it shaking. He takes it in his, lacing our fingers together as he leads us back to the picnic table, setting the gun down before taking a seat with his back against the table.

I sit sideways in his lap, wrapping an arm around his broad shoulders once I've let the earmuffs hang from my neck again. He has one hand on my lower back and the other on my outer thigh so that his arm rests on my legs.

"So what do you think?" He asks.

"It's crazy," I breathe honestly, looking out at the target. "There's so much power in it, and it floods through me, trying to overrun me. It's addicting, but scary."

"Obviously considering your four back-to-back shots." His hands move up and down, one along my spine and the other along my leg, soothing me.

I almost feel faint, so I lean into him, resting my head on his shoulder. After about five minutes of silence and his hands gliding over me, I feel calmer. The rush is still there in the background, zipping back and forth in a little box, waiting to come out and drown me. I sit upright again, anxious to test out the other gun, but my eyes catch sight of a line of vehicles coming up the path at different intervals. Have we been out here long enough that it's time for his family to be here? Suddenly, nerves wash over me again, but these are different.

"Is that your family already?"

Gabe follows my gaze. "Yep. That'd be them." He turns to look at me again. "Don't be nervous,

Ryan."

I narrow my eyes. "What makes you think I'm nervous, Gabe?"

He laughs and picks up the hand I had resting on my knee, showing me that it's shaking a little again. I hit his shoulder and then remove myself from his lap as the first truck gets closer. He backs up near where we were standing earlier to shoot. Seconds later, another truck. Then a car and doors are starting to open and shut. Gabe stands, takes my hands, and leads me closer.

It's a huge relief when I see Owen get out of the truck that parked close to the shooting area. He grins at me and then his brother. All the men from five different vehicles look alike. It's scary, really. There is one, though, who sticks out like a sore thumb with his blonde hair.

"Who's that?" I can't resist asking.

"Charlie. He married into the family."

Ah. That makes sense then. They start towards the picnic tables with guns and bullets in hand. That's not scary at all. My eyes land on the man with Owen, though. That has to be their father. He has rough, rugged features and is seriously handsome to be what looks to be his late fifties. Each pair of eyes are focused on me, the intruder to their men's day. Never have I felt so intimidated as I do right now. Without meaning to, I show them my fear by taking a small step closer to Gabe.

He lets go of my hand to wrap an arm around my waist as the men set the guns down on the picnic tables. It's not until they've finished that they truly acknowledge me.

"Hey, Ryan," Owen says. "It's good to see you again." His eyes do a quick once-over of my body, and I remember what Gabe told me.

Before I can think about it, I say with one eyebrow perched, "Still as hot as you remember?"

Owen laughs, and a couple of the men chuckle. "Yep."

"Guys, this is Ryan Kavanaugh." As Gabe introduces the men, they step forward to shake my hand and say nice to meet you. "This is my father, Larry. My uncle Frank. His son-in-law, Charlie. His sons, Frank Jr. and Nolan. Owen, of course. And last, but not least, this is my grandfather, Billy."

His grandfather, with his hair salt and pepper, but again, good-looking for his age, clasps my hand between his worn ones. "It's nice to meet you, darlin'. Gabriel didn't tell us he was bringing a pretty, young thing to distract us. I may be retired, but I can out-shoot any of these boys any day. You'll see." He winks, and I laugh, but my stomach is a mess of angry bees. Gabe didn't tell them I was coming?

"Gramps, leave her alone." Gabe chuckles. "You all knew she would be here. Today is her first time shooting."

"Is that so?" Frank says with a smile.

I nod and Owen chirps, "Let's see what you got, girl."

"How about y'all go warm up first?" Gabe

saves me. I don't want to be the first person to shoot with them here.

Why I expected to have an ally in Gabe's father, I don't know, but he's not one because he locks eyes with me and says, "Owen's right. Ryan should go first." He's looking at me like I've done something wrong already. Have I?

Gabe looks at me. "Ready?" His eyes are an open question. I can back out if I want. I told him that I might.

But I'll be damned if these men, especially his father, will intimidate me.

"Yes."

Gabe reloads the shotgun, and all eyes are on me as we walk to where we were standing earlier. When I glance over my shoulder, the men are in a line, arms folded over their chests, watching from about ten feet away. All except Owen. He looks like he has faith in me.

Gabe's lips brush over my ear as he stands behind me. "Ignore them, Ryan. They're testing you, but you've got this." Gabe hands me the gun before walking to place another can on top of the post. I didn't even see him grab it. Gabe walks back to me, smiles, and puts my earmuffs back over my ears. He steps aside. This time, even though he's not as close as before, I know he's there.

I take a deep breath before lifting the gun into position. It doesn't feel right on my shoulder, so I adjust it until it's sitting at the right spot. There's no way I'm going to miss this, so I take my time. My hands, which were shaky, are now steady. I'm calmer than ever. I turn off the safety and move my finger, hovering near the trigger as I hear someone faintly laugh behind me.

Once I zone in on the middle of the can and feel sure of myself, I pull the trigger. My shot is dead on as the can bursts. A thrill runs through me. I cock the gun to toss the empty shell and push the safety back on before turning around to see seven stunned men and a grinning Gabe. My eyes briefly land on each man until I reach Larry, his father.

With a glare towards him, I ask, "Satisfied?"

The men burst into laughter, a faint smile on Larry's lips. Gabe walks over, takes the gun, and gives me a kiss as I remove the earmuffs.

"You're amazing," he whispers, before taking my hand to lead me over to the guys. "We were here only an hour before y'all, and she hit every can with the shotgun. I don't know how, but she's good with that one and the others." Pride seeps from his voice.

"I'm up," Owen declares, picking up a gun from one of the picnic tables and walking to take aim at the target on the board.

"You've never shot before?" Frank asks me.

"No. I've never been around guns before today."

Charlie, the son-in-law, comes over to shake my hand. "You did great. Don't worry about them. They made me do it when I first started coming too."

I give him a sweet smile. Larry still hasn't said anything, and he doesn't. Not until Owen returns and Gabe goes to put up a new target to shoot. How evil. He waited until Gabe wasn't around. Larry doesn't come over to me, he just speaks to me from the next picnic table over.

His eyes narrow, and the men turn away from watching Gabe when he asks, "If I may, how old are you, Ryan?"

Gulping, I glance at Gabe. He looks so hot and manly holding the gun in his hands. I turn my attention back to Larry. "Nineteen, but I turn twenty later this month."

"I knew it!" Owen says from next to me. He decided to come sit on the same bench as me. "I knew you were younger than Gabe, younger than he led on anyway."

My age has all the men's attention. Uh, oh. Is my age really a problem? That makes me the second youngest person here thanks to Owen.

"Gabriel is a little old for you, don't you think?" Larry asks.

"If I did, would I be here?" I see a hint of surprise flash before his eyes narrow at my words. Shit. I don't need to push him into hating me further. This was a bad idea. I shouldn't have come. My parents don't think I'm good enough. I shouldn't have thought that Gabe's would be any different. And his dad is supposed to be the open-minded of the two. His mother would definitely hate me. A shot sounds, but I barely hear it.

Frank clears his throat as if that would ease the tension I feel. "Are you from around here?"

"No. I'm originally from Asheville, but I came here for college. I'm a sophomore," I add as if that will help anything. It won't because I've already ruined what chances I had at making his father like me. My age, and most likely my smart mouth, stands in the way.

Gabe returns and mentions something about a skeet thrower, and that gets the guys excited. He looks at me, his smile quickly fading as he sees me attempting a fake smile. He lays the gun down, and all the guys over by Larry's truck now.

"Everything okay, Ryan?"

I shake my head. "I don't feel well. Could you take me home?" My voice shakes a little, and I hate myself for it. Maybe it's just older adults that hate me. Not just my parents, but all of them. Teachers didn't care for me, but couldn't deny that I was smart. My friends' parents always thought I was a bad influence. Maybe it's not my parents. Maybe it's *me*.

Gabe sits next to me. "What's wrong?" he asks, full of concern, but I don't look at him. I can't.

"Nothing," I sigh. "I want to go home. Please, Gabe?" My eyes were focused on the grooves of the wood making up the top of the picnic table, but Gabe hooks a finger underneath my chin to make me look at him.

"What happened?" When I shake my head, he repeats his question with a harder edge to his voice.

Quietly, I say, "I told you this wasn't a good idea." A shot goes off, momentarily distracting me as I see something orange fall apart in the sky. To keep Gabe from asking his question again, I explain. "You told me that my age scares you, and you didn't tell them. I don't see why it's a big deal, but that's just me. They care. *You* care. I don't want to cause any problems, Gabe."

"What are you talking about?"

"Your father asked how old I was, and I didn't lie. Then he asked if I thought you were too old for me, and I may have given him a smart ass answer. I told him if I did, I wouldn't be here. Pretty sure I pissed him off. Just take me home, please."

"Ignore my father, Ryan."

"But-"

"Hey, darlin'," Gabe's grandfather calls out. "You want to try a moving target?"

"We'll be there in a second," Gabe yells back without looking. He cups my cheeks in his hands, and I notice his father watching us. "Ryan," he says, waiting until I look at him again. "The girl you were the day I pulled you over, be her today. My father's respect has to be earned, and he's expecting that. Don't let him intimidate you because that's what he's trying to do."

"Well, he's a jerk for that." I try to laugh, but it sounds mangled.

"That's how he operates. C'mon. Let's go show 'em what you got."

Chapter Seven
Gabe

I'm angry that my father upset Ryan, but it reminds me of what I was worried about. What I think about when I'm not around her. The guys seem to like her, though. Except Dad, of course. He's being reserved today. But Ryan quickly shows the guys that she's a force to be reckoned with. It takes her a bit to get the hang of it, but as the orange clay targets are flung into the air, she starts hitting them. She giggles after each round with excitement. She's hooked on the thrill, the weight of the power, and the accomplishment she feels when she hits the marks each time. I love watching her and her confidence grow.

"I feel like a badass," she laughs, coming to stand next to me. "Well, just with the shooting part. Not the extra handling stuff."

"You should be proud of yourself. This is your first day, and you're doing better than everyone else."

"Except me," Gramps inserts, making Ryan giggle. I can already tell that he likes her.

"Yeah, except you."

Gramps walks over and puts an arm around her shoulders. "Darlin', you sure have surprised me. Lookin' sweet and innocent with your age, but you're a firecracker. Keepin' us all on our toes. I hope Gabriel keeps you around."

Ryan blushes, the second time I've ever seen her do that. "I hope so too, Mr. O'Connor."

"Might as well call me Gramps, darlin'."

"Gabe, you're up," Owen tells me, as my father prepares the skeet thrower.

In the background, I hear them talking. Owen, in particular.

"You know, it's totally possible that we could be dating too."

Ryan laughs. "You might be close to me in age, but you're still too young. You're cute though."

My brother groans. "Cute? That's a dude's worst nightmare."

I fire at the skeet, hitting it just in time to hear Ryan's response.

"You're cute as a button," she teases. "Shooting a gun like what we're doing makes you hotter though, if that helps."

Faintly, as I take my next shot, I wonder if she means that with me as well. "Don't tell my brother lies, Ryan," I say as I walk back over to them. "I'm the best looking man in the family."

Gramps laughs louder than everyone else. "If you were, you'd be married by now. You and Owen are the only ones left who aren't married. Owen's too young, so he doesn't count."

"Maybe he wants to play the field," Owen says. "Y'all are stuck with one chick for the rest of your lives. Maybe Gabe doesn't want to settle down yet. I wouldn't. Although, with the way Ryan looks, it wouldn't be too bad to have her for the rest of my life."

"Owen," I chide in disbelief, but Ryan laughs.

"Leave him alone, Gabe. That was a compliment. Suggestive for a sixteen year old, but still. Can you blame him?"

Before I can answer, Owen bursts, "You've already slept with her?"

God, what is wrong with him today? He's acting worse than usual. All eyes are on me, waiting for me to confirm or deny. Especially my father. He's been quiet, but he's been listening. Ryan watches me, waiting as well.

"Don't y'all know it's rude to talk about this in front of Ryan?"

"Better you say it in front of me than behind my back. Topic doesn't matter," she inputs.

"Yes, but we're supposed to be gentlemen."

Before anything else can be said, my father clears his throat. "Enough. We're out of ammo and skeets. Time to pack up. My wife is fixing supper as usual, if y'all want to head there."

That's my father's way of testing me. To see

how serious this thing is with Ryan and if I'm ready for her to meet my mother. "We already have plans. Thanks, though." Everyone here, regardless of if we have plans or not, knows what it means for me to decline. Including Ryan. I almost feel guilty, like I announced, not to just her, but to everyone that she isn't good enough. It isn't that though. With my mother, I want to be sure it's something serious before she meets the girl. Her opinion matters to me and if it isn't serious, there's no point in them meeting. Yet. Plus, I think Ryan has had enough of my family for one day.

Ryan is quiet as we all get everything together. Once that is done, we start saying our goodbyes, Ryan being polite with everyone. She seems to mean it when she says it was nice to meet them. With the exception of my father. I honestly wasn't expecting him to behave as he has, and I'll have to ask him about that later. Everyone starts getting in their vehicles and driving away. Ryan is leaning against the passenger door. I walk over to her.

"You know, you looked really hot earlier."

"And I don't now?"

She laughs. "Oh, you most certainly do. Thanks for today. I had fun, but next time, I think I rather it just be us the entire time."

"Okay. We can arrange that. Are you ready?"

She nods, so I open the door for her. We're going to make a stop by my place, so I can put the guns away. I realize that Ryan's never been there before, and I wonder if she'll like it. We pull into my driveway of my one story brick home. It's a simple two bedroom house, just big enough for me. Nothing special about it except it's mine. I ask Ryan to unlock the door for me as I gather everything. She holds the door open for me, and I go into the spare bedroom, where I store my guns. I'll have to clean them later.

I thought Ryan followed me, but when I turn around, she isn't in the room. Once I put everything safely back in it's place, I go looking for her. She's in the living room, running her fingers along the mantel over the fireplace, looking at the pictures. There are some of me from high school in my football uniform, some of me with family, and some from when I graduated. I lean against the frame of the wall and watch her. She picks up one, the one with my family, and runs her fingers over a figure.

There's a small smile on her face as she sets it back, perfectly in place. Ryan turns then, sees me, and jumps.

"Oh, I, uh, didn't know you were standing there. You have a nice house."

"Thank you."

She seems nervous for some reason. She clasps her hands in front of her, lightly rocking on her heels. Her eyes jump from me to down at her hands. "Do you," she starts, but stops abruptly. Her hands fidget and as if she realizes she looks nervous, she yanks them apart, stuffing them into her pockets. "Are you ready?" She finally asks.

"What were you going to say?" I'm curious as to what made her anxious.

Ryan narrows those green eyes, folding her arms over her chest defensively. "Nothing."

I push off the wall and walk over to her, resting my hands on her hips. "Tell me."

"No."

"Why?" My head tilts as I watch her fight herself over whatever it is.

"Because I changed my mind."

"About?"

"If I wanted to tell you, I would have done that already," she says exasperated.

"So you want me to take you home now?" C'mon, Ryan. Tell me what it was. She doesn't say anything right away, which I take as an opportunity. I swiftly pull her flush against me, causing her to inhale sharply with surprise. She keeps her arms crossed over her chest though. With my lips brushing against hers as I speak, I ask, "Sure you don't want to tell me? Ask me whatever it was?" My hands move to her lower back and down over her ass.

Ryan pushes me away, coming out of my hold. "Don't tease me if you aren't going to go through with it, Gabe. And we both know that won't happen." She's hostile towards me all of a sudden, and I don't understand why. Because last time I said I wouldn't sleep with her until it was more than just sex? It does make me feel bad that I tried to seduce it out of her.

"What's going on, Ryan?" I hesitantly ask.

She shakes her head. "Just take me home."

I would bet a thousand dollars that she's been thinking, and the girl thinks entirely too much. She's a rambler, verbally and mentally. Giving up, I hold my hands up in surrender.

"Let's go then."

She brushes past me and is out the door by the time I turn around. What in the world has her mind got her thinking now? I lock the door and get into the car. Once we're back on the road, I see Ryan turn towards me from the corner of my eye.

"You know what? I'll tell you. Not because you asked, but because I'm not the kind of girl to get *nervous* over a *guy*," she says it like it's the worst thing in the world. There is conviction and determination in her voice as she continues. "I refuse to behave any differently. I was going to ask you if you wanted to spend the night again, but I changed my mind. You are a good guy with a happy family, and that's awesome. I'm not that girl though. I want to have sex on first dates, if I choose. I want to have as much fun as possible before I finish college and officially have to grow up and morph into a more suitable person for society. You're wasting your time, Gabe, and I don't want you to do that.

"And I realize that I sound like a guy with all the sex talk, and I realize I probably should have more respect," she does air quotes, "for myself than to sleep with whoever I want. It's not about self-respect. It's about me being able to do anything a guy can do, even if that makes me a slut. Excuse me for liking sex. I mean, I haven't slept with anyone since you, and I'm not used to guys turning me down. That's part of my frustration. My point is that you're a nice, good guy, and it's not that I don't think I'm not good enough for somebody, because I am, but we're not a match. Even if you see more to me, I still don't understand it. Especially if we're not sleeping together. What's the point?"

Wow. Okay. I repeat what she said in my mind, trying to process everything because it was a *lot*. Without thinking, I ask, "Why are you so insecure about this?"

A glance at her shows me her wide eyes. I cringe when she responds, her voice too high for the inside of my car. "Insecure?! You think I'm insecure? I am *not* insecure. I am confident with who I am to myself. I like myself just fine, thank you very much. The problem is that *everyone* else *doesn't* like that person. Not enough to actually care anyway," she finishes as I pull into the parking lot. As soon as I park, she gets out and storms to the stairs.

"You do realize that means you're insecure?" I say despite my gut instinct when I reach her as she unlocks her door.

Her back is rigid, and I've definitely hit a nerve. I've never seen Ryan so tense. She swings open the door, sees something inside, her shoulders dropping. "Oh, for fuck's sake. What are you doing

131

here? How did you get inside?"

I peek around her shoulders to see an older woman with similar features.

"Your father and I pay for this place. Did you honestly think we wouldn't have a key? And watch your mouth, Ryan." Her mother smiles upon seeing me and adds, "Who is this?"

"This is Gabe," she says reluctantly. "Why are you here, Mom?" She repeats before anything can be said.

"Don't be rude, Ryan. Introduce me to your boyfriend."

Ryan steps inside, angrily tossing her house keys onto the table. "He's not my boyfriend, Mom. I'm too un-ladylike for a boyfriend, remember?"

Her mother ignores her and walks over to me, shaking my hand. "I'm Mrs. Kavanaugh, Ryan's mother. It's nice to meet you."

"Nice to meet you as well. I'll catch you later, Ryan?"

"Oh, no. Come on in."

"No!" Ryan yells, swiveling to face us. "Don't subject him to whatever it is you're here for."

"I insist," Mrs. Kavanaugh says, tugging me inside. "I won't be here long." Speaking to Ryan, she continues, "You weren't answering my phone calls, and I was nearby for business, so I figured I would come see you."

I'm forced to sit on the couch as Ryan paces, upset. "What the hell do you want, Mom?"

"Ryan," she chides calmly, sitting down in the

chair. "Language. I don't know why you're so upset. You should control your emotions better, dear." *This is so awkward.* "I'm here to check on your progress with choosing a major. I hope you've made a decision that we can be happy with." Them? What do they have to do with Ryan's future career?

Ryan hasn't relaxed in the least. "French. I want to major in French."

Mrs. Kavanaugh's lips dip into a frown. "French? Why on earth would you want to do that?"

Ryan throws her hands up. "I just do! Why? What's wrong with that decision?"

"We were expecting better," is all she says.

A harsh laugh falls from Ryan's mouth. "Better? You always want something better from me, but it's never good enough. What degree do you want me to have? Tell me! You decide! Because I'm too fucking incompetent to make that measly decision."

"You are not a boy, so quit talking with such vulgarity."

"You don't need to remind me, Mom," Ryan cuts her off.

The tension is so thick in here between them, that I'm almost choking on it. Nothing seems to affect her mother, though. She's just as poised as ever.

"All I'm saying is that you could at least behave as a lady. You seem so stressed, dear. Are you sure you want to stay here? You can drop out and come home if it's too much. We would understand if it's like everything else you do and you just can't commit to it."

What? She's encouraging Ryan to drop out of college?

"That would certainly please Dad, wouldn't it? Is there a particular date he has written down for when he thinks I'll fail at college too? I guess my 4.0 GPA means shit to y'all. College isn't stressing me out. *You* showing up here is stressing me out. *You* making Gabe sit here is stressing me out. Do I not stress out properly, Mom? Should I sit down, cross my legs, and act as if I'm not fucking stressed?" Ryan takes a deep breath, obviously trying to calm herself down. "Why don't you just leave, talk with Dad, pick a degree *you* would be happy with, and let me know. By phone."

"Ryan," her mother starts in what she's attempting to be a soothing voice.

"Stop talking to me like I don't have any sense!"

Mrs. Kavanaugh abruptly stands. "Enough, Ryan. Your outbursts are uncalled for. Is this what college has done to you? Are we paying for this?" She motions her hand, up and down at Ryan. "You come out here to tarnish your body with those god-awful, ridiculous tattoos. You waste money on clothes for parties. Based on the timestamp of charges on the credit card bill, you're out at all hours of the night. And now you're dating an older man," she flings her arm out to point at me, "and you pick a major in *French*? We had to force you to learn Spanish! What makes you think you want to learn and speak French? Pick something more respectable. At least appreciate all the money your father and I spend, so you don't have to work and go to college." Her voice turns deadly serious. "Do something worthwhile for a change, Ryan."

Ryan has stopped, frozen, her eyes glossy with unshed tears. "I'm fluent in Spanish," she says calmly. "My tattoos aren't awful or ridiculous because they mean something to me." Her voice cracks on the last word.

"What could they possibly mean?" Mrs. Kavanaugh interrupts. "A dandelion, a hummingbird, and a seahorse? Those things mean something to you?"

Ryan's lips part, and she looks like her mother just slapped her. Hurt is in every one of Ryan's features. Her lips quiver as she tries not to cry.

Adding another blow, Mrs. Kavanaugh says, "I'll discuss with your father what degrees are acceptable. This isn't like when you were a teenager and you can pick something, lose interest, and quit. We will not waste money for you to fail or quit or get more meaningless tattoos. Understood?"

Ryan nods. Her fight vanished the moment her mother said something about her tattoos.

"Good." She turns and leaves without another word.

The second the door closes, Ryan runs into her

room, a sob escaping. What in the world did I just witness? I can figure it out later. Right now, I'm going to comfort Ryan. She's lying on her stomach, her crying muffled by her pillow. I sit on the edge of her bed.

"Go away," she cries.

"No."

Despite her protest, I lay down next to her on my side and tug her against me. She doesn't fight me. Ryan comes easily, burying her face in the crook of my neck as her shoulders shake, her tears falling from her face onto me.

"Shh," I soothe, running a hand up and down her back.

It doesn't do any good. She cries for thirty minutes before sputtering to a stop. My shirt is bunched in her hands and with her grip, I wouldn't be surprised if her hands are cramping.

"I'm sorry I cried on you," she mumbles into my neck. "I'm fine now, though. You can go."

"Is that what you want?" I ask carefully. She nods, but doesn't answer. "Then why are you clinging to my shirt still? It's fine, Ryan. I'm not going anywhere and you don't have to pretend that you're all better."

She's quiet for a moment. Her voice cracks as she whispers, "I hate them. I hate them so much."

"I don't understand it, Ryan, but I don't want you to explain it to me. Not today. Unless you want to tell me."

"I don't." She pauses. "But I do." Ryan pulls

136

back to look at me, her eyes still glassy and her eyelashes wet. "I'm sorry you had to be here for that. No one has ever been around that before, and I don't know if I should explain or pretend it never happened."

"Who do you talk to about your parents? Vivian?"

Ryan shakes her head. "No. Not really anyway. I don't want her to know more than basics. I mean, why would I want to subject anyone else to that? My mother had no problem saying all of those things in front of you, and she's never met you before today." A tear spills over, and Ryan quickly wipes it away. "I'm sorry I yelled at you in the car. But do you see what I mean about everyone else not liking who I am? I disappoint *everyone* every single time. I'm never good enough. Do you understand now why I'm so damn confused?

"You're full of contradictions, Gabe. You're good, but you want me, the opposite. You like me, but you don't want to sleep with me again. You have a wonderful family, I don't. You're too old, I'm too young. And now you've seen how my mother is, and I don't want you here as a stupid knight in shining armor. I'm capable of saving myself and taking care of myself. I can do it. I don't need someone else to do it for me. I-"

"Stop talking, Ryan." She clamps her mouth shut. "Just because you can do something yourself, doesn't mean you shouldn't ask for or accept help."

She nods, seeming to accept what I said before

she returns to my earlier comment from the car ride over. "I'm truly not insecure. At least, not the way I see it. I like who I am." She sits up and folds her legs under herself, so I sit up to lean against the headboard. "Do I have low expectations about a lot of things? Probably so. I don't know if you overheard that night, but I am sort of easy. And I know that by sleeping with guys so quickly that they are less likely to stick around, which is fine. That really doesn't bother me. It makes things simple for me. Boys give me sex. Viv gives me friendship. College gives me an education. What more do I need right now?"

I can't help but chuckle at the seemingly absurdity of her words. "Sex, friendship, and education? That's all you need?"

She frowns. "Well, the material things in life too, but right now, yes."

Placing my hands behind my head to get more comfortable, I ask, "What's with your obsession with sex?" I've never seen a girl talk so much, so openly about it.

"Obsession? It's not an obsession. I love sex. And I'm not having nearly enough of it lately." She perks an eyebrow at me. "Might as well call it a passion of mine. Like you with your job and your guns. Besides, sex is one thing that I know I can do well."

"Uh, huh. I see."

Ryan narrows her eyes at me. "You see what, Gabe?"

I shrug. "Sex is your way of getting someone to tell you that you're good at something because you're parents are idiots who think you can't succeed at the things you do."

She rolls her eyes. "Please. Don't get all psychological on me, Gabe. I know my parents are idiots. I know it all too well. No one needs to tell me I'm a great lay or that I'm smart or that I can do anything I put my mind to. I know that already. It's not me who needs to be convinced. Sure, they messed me up with all their 'You're such a disappointment' speeches, but I know I'm more than what they see. What exactly that is, I don't know. That's one point of college, right? To find out who you are?"

"Yeah, I guess so. Who do you think you are, Ryan?"

Her shoulders droop. "I don't know." She clasps her hands, dropping her head to avoid looking at me. As she speaks, she glances up at me here and there. "For a lot of things, I feel really indecisive. Like when you asked me about my favorite thing to do or with my major or anything like that. I don't know what's me. I've been trying to do what I like while doing what my parents want me to do. It's not always possible for those things to coincide.

"When I was growing up, I dabbled in a bit of everything. I was really good at some of them, but by the time I could enjoy it, my parents moved me on to the next thing because my efforts weren't good enough for them to keep paying for it. Or like with tennis and I quit because it wasn't fun anymore. I overanalyze a lot of things and others not enough.

"Gabe, I can't tell you who I am because I'm not sure. But I can tell you who others think I am. That's the easy part. I don't agree with what they see, which only confuses me more most of the time. I mean, I'm not the greatest person in the world, but what they see as bad, doesn't always mean it is. And I was truly looking forward to majoring in French because that would be a challenge for me, and I would be learning something new. God, I'm rambling again, aren't I?"

I nod. "I think it's kind of cute." She rolls her eyes at me, but it makes her smile. "Do you know what I think you should do?" She shakes her head. "Make your own standards for yourself. Decide who *you* want to be and ignore everyone else." Sitting up, I stare into her green eyes, making her listen to me. "If people want to judge you, fine. That reflects more on who they are. Not you. Because, if you ask me, I'd say you're a tad bit on the crazy side and when you talk, you rattle on and on. You think entirely too much about every single thing. You're a girl trying to prove herself to people who will never be satisfied. I think you've been pulled in so many directions that you don't have a clue where you want to go. If you ask me, Ryan, I'd say that you just need someone to guide and support you. You're absolutely a beautiful, lost girl."

A tear wells and falls over onto her cheek. She lifts her hand, but I swipe it away with my thumb before she can reach it. Ryan gives me a half smile before leaning forward to kiss me softly. When she pulls away, she doesn't say anything at all.

"Why don't you sleep over at my place tonight? I'll cook you a good meal or two." I don't know why I invite her over other than the fact that I want her away from here for a little while, and I want to see her in my house again. "I'll even take you out tomorrow."

Ryan laughs. "You had me with your first question. You can't take the others back now, though. Do you want to go now? Want me to drive my car, so you don't have to bring me back here?"

"No, it's fine. Just pack your things, and we'll head there."

Ryan scurries off her bed, opens a messy closet, and looks for a bag. I watch as she moves around the room, tossing things into the pink bag. One thing that Ryan said, that bothers me the most, is what she said about not wanting me to be a knight in shining armor. I've been that guy in the past, and I always saved the girl, put her back together, and she either destroyed me in the end or left to find someone more suitable for her new self. With Ryan, I can't help but want to help. Maybe I don't have to save her, per se, but still be able to help get her through her issues.

My relationship before last, in particular, is the

one that stands out the most and is probably the one my mother thinks about when she worries about me. She was a little younger than me. I was twenty-four, and she had just turned twenty-one. She seemed like a good girl, a bit of a drinker already, but she managed to have a coy, very seemingly innocent personality about her. Truly, she was a deceiver, putting on whatever face she needed to get what she wanted.

When she needed to borrow some money, I loaned it to her. I trusted that she would pay me back, and we had been dating for about seven months or so. That was my last mistake. She liked to be taken care of, and I found myself wanting to take care of her. So I would buy her things here and there and before I knew it, I had spent a lot of money on this girl. After I loaned her three thousand dollars, she disappeared. Big, stupid mistake, I know. Not only was I out that money, but I was upset that I had fallen for it.

Mom shook her head at me when I told her what happened and brought up that I was too good and trusting for my own good. I decided to put it all behind me and move forward without another thought. So yeah, being that guy hasn't worked out for me. It doesn't make sense to me sometimes, so I'll have to go against what I would want to do naturally.

I won't swoop in and take care of Ryan's problems, like the "stupid knight" she spoke of. No. I'll simply be there to help her handle them herself. She can do it, just as she said. She needs a little guidance is all. Ryan leaves the room, heading to the bathroom, appearing minutes later. She sits the bag on the bed, walks to her nightstand, and unplugs her charger from the outlet. Once she puts it in her bag, she smiles at me.

"Ready."

On our way out, she grabs her keys and purse. Ryan seems more like herself as we ride to my house. She rests her hand on my leg as I drive, watching the scenery blur outside the window. The bottom falls right before we get there. I almost miss my driveway it's pouring so hard, and I can barely see.

"Great," I mumble, wishing more than ever I had a garage. At least my driveway comes right up to my side door, and there's an awning over it.

I rush to the door with Ryan's bag, only a couple feet away until I'm covered by the awning, and I still get soaked. I hate rain, hating getting wet, yet I don't own an umbrella. I can't really complain about it since I haven't done anything to prevent situations like this. Hurriedly, I unlock it and push it open, expecting Ryan to be right behind me. But when I turn to look, she's leaning with her back against the passenger door, her head tilted up to the sky. Her red hair turns even darker as it gets wet.

"What are you doing?" I yell over the loud rain.

Ryan faces me at the sound of my voice, and

she's grinning. The water drips down her face, clinging to her white t-shirt, revealing the skin underneath.

"C'mon," she hollers at me.

"It's raining, and it's cold!"

She laughs at my obvious response. "You won't melt, I promise."

Ryan walks around to the boot of my car, pulls herself up, and leans back against my window, her arms out. The rain pelts against her, and she seems to be loving it. What is she doing? Does she actually like rain? Reluctantly, I set her bag inside the door and go to her. Thunder booms loudly, but Ryan doesn't even flinch. Her grin is even more present now.

"You're drenched, Ryan, and you're going to get yourself killed or sick or something bad," I tell her, standing in front of her legs hanging off my car. My clothes stick to me uncomfortably, and I'm tempted to haul her over my shoulder to carry her inside without waiting for a response.

Ryan sits up. "Thunderstorms are one of the best things in the world. You have to enjoy them while they last."

Without permission, my eyes wander over her body. Oh, God. Her jeans are stuck to those legs I love so much, and her shirt isn't hiding anything, her nipples straining against her bra and t-shirt. Her lower lip trembles from the icy cold rain, proving she's freezing. Ryan's eyes do some roaming of their own as she absentmindedly licks her lips. Maybe rain isn't so bad. No thought occurs as I finally pick her up, hauling her over my shoulder, and head into the house. Ryan laughs.

"I said you wouldn't melt!"

Just as we step over the threshold, lightening strikes, sounding too close by for comfort. I bend over to set her back on her feet.

"I was about to come in, you know," she says with her hands propped on her hips, looking entirely too hot. "You didn't look like you would have gone for my idea of racing to the road and back. Running in the rain is a lot of fun, Gabe. Although, you throwing me over your shoulder was hot and so much more fun." She smiles wickedly.

That's it. I have to have her. There's no holding back anymore. She wants it, and good God if I don't. I don't answer. I can't. Nothing will come out. Oblivious to my turmoil, Ryan bends over to pick up her bag.

"Better go change."

I watch her hips swing as she walks away. My feet, knowing what I want, begin to follow her. She hangs her bag on the door to my bedroom and peels off her shirt first. Her back tattoos on display until Ryan turns to face me.

"Could I have a towel for my hair? I would just throw it up, but I forgot to bring a scrunchie."

"No."

"No?" She questions, confused as I continue to stalk towards her.

"No," I repeat, coming to a stop in front of her. I cup her cheeks and immediately kiss her briefly. "We're going to have sex. That okay with you?"

Ryan's surprise quickly fades, and she nods. I pull her lips back to me, finding her tongue, and sucking it into my mouth. There's a soft sound as her shirt falls from her hand and onto the floor. She bunches the hem of my shirt in her hands and lifts, breaking our kiss for a moment. My shirt slips from her fingers when I kiss her again. Grabbing her hips, I hoist her up, her legs wrapping around my waist, and walk to my bed to lay her down.

I lick and suck up all the remaining droplets of rain along her neck, across her shoulders. Ryan's body moves, and I realize she's removing her bra while I kiss her collarbone. Her breasts come free. Each one falls towards her arms a little from their weight. She's a pure seductress. I've never wanted anyone as much as I want her right now. My mouth descends on her breast, and I tug the nipple between my teeth, causing Ryan to shiver beneath me, her hands starting at my shoulders and running down my back.

I suck so hard when I pull away a *pop* sounds. As I kiss down and across to the other, I order, "Unbutton your pants."

Her fingers fumble with the button and zipper as I roll my tongue around her nipple, biting down gently. I grab her hands and hold them down on either side of her head as I hover over her. Lust is back full force in her eyes. She watches me, waiting for my next move, and I linger for a moment. With my hands gripping her possessively, I run them down her arms to her sides and then down her sides, kissing the dandelion on her hip.

Her breaths are soft pants of anticipation, mingling with the rain pounding on the house. I slip my fingers underneath the waistband of her jeans.

"Lift your hips."

She does, and I yank them down, the task extra hard thanks to them being wet. I'm seriously having to peel them off her. The air is sucked from my lungs when I see she isn't wearing any underwear. I glance at her as she sits up on her elbows to watch me, and she smirks. Her pants sit at her knees as I move off the bed to take off her shoes and socks before finally removing them completely. She's completely captivated me.

"There's a box of condoms in the drawer," I say with a nod to the small table next to my bed. "Get it."

While Ryan reaches over for that, I take off my pants and boxer briefs. She rips the packaging, holding the ultra-thin condom in her hand. Her eyes never leave my erection as I get back on the bed, lying down next to her. Without a word, I take her hand and pull it towards me. Knowing what I want, she straddles me.

"Put it on," I tell her.

She doesn't hesitate. Her touch nearly drives me over the edge as she rolls the condom down my shaft. Those green eyes flick up at me, waiting for me to tell her what to do next. I like being in control, but I would like for Ryan to think she's the one in control. I sit up, curl a finger under her chin, and pull her to me. I press my lips to hers, my hands reaching for the back of her thighs to tug her upwards just a little. That's all Ryan needs from me.

Her hand reaches down between us, taking my cock, and moving up and down twice before she guides my tip to enter her. Ryan lowers herself on me, a guttural groan erupting from her throat. God, she feels so good. Drops of water drip from the tips of her hair onto my chest, and she leans down to lick them off quickly. She braces her hands on my chest, moving her hips with the guidance of my hands. Ryan's slow at first, but once she finds a rhythm, she rides me hard and fast. Her breasts bounce, and I leave her hips to grasp them.

"Oh, fuck," she breathes. Her back arches as she tightens around me. Not yet, Ryan, I think with a sudden urge to see her back and those tattoos beneath me.

I grab her hips hard, so she can't move. She looks a little dazed as if she's lost in sex. I lift her off me, my hard cock swaying as I set her down next to me.

"Hands and knees, Ryan," I demand.

She falls forward onto her hands, her breasts swinging from the movement. She already has her knees apart and waiting. I get off the bed and walk to the end, reaching forward to grab her hips, and pull her back. A yelp of surprise escapes her. With my fingers at the base of my shaft, I tease her by pushing in with my tip, pulling out and slipping further past it. By the third time, she moans almost angrily.

Over her shoulder, she says, "You really are a damn tease, aren't you?"

I chuckle, my tip barely inside her when I swiftly push all the way in. The comforter bunches under her grip, and she cries out. Ryan constricts around me. My fingertips curl into her skin on her hips as I tightly hold her in place as I begin to thrust, pulling out slowly, but driving in hard. Her tattoos on her back look lovely, a perfect view. Ryan starts pushing backwards against my thrusts, causing us to crash into one another.

The pressure builds, and I lose control as I bury myself into her repeatedly. Ryan gets tighter and tighter before she screams out with her climax, pulsing around me, and I come. My energy drains in my legs as we fall forward onto the bed, utterly and happily spent.

Chapter Eight
Ryan

I can't believe we just had sex. It was even better than the first time, and I loved that he was in control most of the time. It's different than what I'm used to, but I really liked it. Gabe got up to throw away the condom awhile ago, and now we're still lying in bed. I'm on my stomach, and his fingertips gently glide over my back tattoos as if it's a road and he needs to go down each one. Then I feel his lips press a kiss to my shoulder blade, right where my hummingbird should be. I look over my shoulder at him to see that his eyes are completely captivated by the path his fingers are on. For some reason, that causes me to laugh softly.

"Gabe, you act like you've never seen a tattoo," I tease.

His eyes flick up to me, but then return to my back. "It's not that. I'm simply fascinated by yours, and I'm just now getting the chance to appreciate them."

"Why don't you get one?"

His hand stops and lies flat on my back as he places all of his attention on me. Gabe's eyes ever so slightly widen. He almost seems to be considering it, but then he shakes his head. "My mother would never let me in her house again."

I roll over, his hand coming to lay on my stomach now. He glances at my exposed breasts for a moment. "You're worried about your mother?" I question with laughter in my voice, lifting an eyebrow at him.

Those skillful lips fall in a frown. "I care about what she thinks, Ryan."

"So you're ready for her to meet me?"

Gabe looks at me with contempt, his lips in a stubborn line, which clearly tells me he isn't. I'm happy about that. After meeting his father, I rather not meet Gabe's mother. Before he can come up with an excuse, I continue.

"I think you should go with me to get my next one, and you should get one too."

"I don't want one."

"Really? You've never ever wanted to get a tattoo or are you hiding behind your mother's rules?"

"I'm twenty-five," he starts in rebuttal.

"And a goody-two shoes. C'mon, Gabe. Get a tattoo with me." The more I thought about it, the more I wanted him to have one. He would be even hotter with one.

His now dry curls shake with his head. "No. I don't want something on my body forever if you break my heart." Gabe smiles to soften his blow, but it doesn't bother me one bit.

"I don't want you to get anything related to me, Gabe. Jeesh. Tattoos are supposed to mean something to whoever gets it. All you would have to do is think of something that is so important to you that you want it to decorate your body."

"Are you saying my body needs to improve?" He smirks.

"Are you avoiding my question?"

"Roll back over, Ryan. I wasn't done."

I laugh at his disregard for my question, but I do as he wants. "There's more than those two, you know that, right?"

"Yes." He kisses the center of my back, his fingers moving over my skin once more. This time, he's touching the pink seahorse. Gabe adds, "But these are my favorite. Tell me why you got them."

For a moment, I hesitate. This is Gabe, though, and I trust him. I go over in my head what I want I want to say, trying to find words to fit what these tattoos mean to me. Memories swirl around me from the images inked onto my body. Feeling ready, I begin to tell Gabe the story behind each of them.

"They are all related to my grandmother, now that I really think about it. She was the only grandparent I'd ever known, and she was an amazing person. When I was little, she was the one to teach me how to make wishes on dandelions, and I loved it. She used to tell me that after I made the wish, the seeds blew away so my wish could be granted. I'll still do it if I see one.

"My grandmother took me to the aquarium once. I thought the seahorses looked a little odd compared to most of the other fish we saw. They were beautiful, though. Just different. When I told her, she laughed. I'll never forget what she said either. She told me that it's the differences between all life that makes it beautiful.

"And the hummingbird is in memory of her. She died when I was eleven and absolutely loved hummingbirds. She had little figurines and paintings all over her house, and a bunch of hummingbird feeders outside. That was my very first one. As you've seen, they piss my parents off, so that's a bonus."

And then reality comes crashing back down. His father hates me, and Gabe had to witness a public shaming by my mother. My mother who doesn't have a clue that my hummingbird is because of *her* mom, my grandmother. She doesn't know that they are all tied to my grandmother, but she should have at least known about the hummingbird. That should have been obvious. What she said about my tats today is probably why Gabe asked in the first place. I bury my face into the pillow, feeling Gabe shift next to me.

"Hey," he starts quietly, pulling some of my hair away in an attempt to see me. "Remember what I said. Ignore them."

I turn my head so only one eye is looking at him. He's so sweet.

"C'mon. You can help me make supper." Gabe kisses my temple, his beard scratching my skin, before getting out of bed. I roll over and watch his bare ass walk across the room to his dresser. He's too yummy with those strong legs, bubble butt, and broad, muscular back. Gabe's body is too perfect. A tattoo would tarnish it, I decide.

"You didn't say I would have to help," I tease.

He glances over his shoulder as he steps into a pair of gray pajama pants. "Did I forget to mention that part?"

"Yes, you did." I toss the sheets aside and walk over to where my bag is still hanging on the door. I can feel Gabe watching me, so I add, "Don't get distracted again, Officer. I'm starving."

He chuckles behind me. As I'm pulling out my pjs, he slaps me hard on the ass and then whispers huskily in my ear, "I won't. Hurry up." Then he walks passed me and down the hall like nothing just happened.

I shake my head and get dressed in a black and white striped cami with matching shorts. I pick our wet clothes up off the floor.

"Gabe?" I call out. "Does this door by the other bedroom lead to the washer and dryer? I'm going to toss our clothes in there."

"Yeah, but just put them in the hamper. I've got to wash clothes and I'll throw those in there too." He pauses, and as I open the door to do as he said, I hear, "By the time you get in here, I'll be halfway done."

"Shut up," I laugh. Once I toss the clothes into the hamper, I go into the kitchen. The rain has calmed down outside, but it's still coming down. Streaks of lightning can be seen from his kitchen window. Gabe is standing in front of his fridge with the door open. "What are we having anyway?"

"Well, let's see. You can get a salad going, and I'll start the pork chops." Gabe starts pulling things out of the fridge, and I take them from him, setting them on the counter.

"Sounds good. What else are we having with the pork chops?"

"How about..." He closes the fridge and walks over to his pantry, opening it up. "Mashed potatoes?" Gabe glances at me, and I nod.

We get things underway, him at the stove and me close to the sink, putting a salad together. I cut my eyes over at him, feeling a little odd to be in his kitchen, helping with supper. It's such a relaxed, couple type thing to do.

Tentatively, I ask, "Gabe?"

"Yeah?" He answers without looking at me.

I don't know why I'm thinking this, but I am. It's something I want to know, and I don't want a repeat. Of course, my big mouth is going to ask him anyway. "You do realize what just happened, right? You're not going to freak and kick me out halfway through our meal?"

He spins to face me. "What? Ryan, no. I-"

"You don't have to say anything, Gabe. I don't want to see that look again, and I don't want you to regret it, that's all."

Gabe walks over, placing his hands on my hips to make me turn my body towards him. "I didn't regret it the first time. I was disappointed in myself and-"

"We don't need to go over it again." I give him a quick kiss before changing the topic. "If you burn the food, I'll never forgive you."

He chuckles and turns back to the stove. As I cut up a cucumber, I think about what a crazy day it's been. I've always felt comfortable physically around Gabe, but now I'm not even worried about speaking my mind and asking him things I wouldn't normally ask. Just as I'm about to ask him about his father, there's a knock on the door. Our heads automatically turn towards the noise. My eyes widen when I recognize his mother, thanks to the pictures on his mantel. I'm not even wearing a bra! Gabe brushes his hand on my lower back as he passes me to open the door. If that's supposed to be a reassurance, it isn't.

Once again, I'm reminded of the differences in our families. These people love each other a lot. Enough that they share important things about their lives with one another and hold their opinions with a high regard. When I was looking at the photos earlier, I could see their happiness, their closeness, and the pride they had in each other. That's how a family should be. Not like the group of people I call my family. Even now, Gabe is a bit anxious over what his mother is thinking. I can hear it in his tone as he tries too hard to relax.

"Mom, hey. What are you doing here?" Gabe questions as she steps inside, little wet circles on her light blue shirt from the rain.

How does this look to her? Me in my skimpy pjs with no bra and Gabe shirtless in pajama pants at seven in the evening. My hair is still half wet and probably all messy from the rain and sex. Her lips are pursed as she gives me a once over. I focus on the cucumbers, so I don't have to look at her and see her immediate disdain for me. Maybe if I pretend she isn't here, then she'll magically disappear.

"I texted you to let you know I was coming, Gabriel. I thought it was odd that you didn't reply, but now I can see you were busy. Your father told me about today," she says as if that explains it all. Her Southern hospitality kicks in, and I hear her footsteps coming closer to me. Oh, God. "Hello." I turn to see her stick her hand out to me. "I'm Gabriel's mother, Camilla. You must be Ryan."

I set the knife down and reluctantly shake her hand. "Nice to meet you." Gabe looks as worried as I feel. "Gabe, I'm going to, uh, throw those clothes in the washing machine." Abandoning my task, I hurry out of the room, desperate to get away from her.

Faintly, I can hear their conversation because like the girl I am, I left the door opened a crack so I could listen.

"I'm sorry I didn't get your message, Mom," Gabe says. "What did Dad say?"

She doesn't answer right away. I toss some clothes into the washing machine. "Gabriel," she chides. "She's so young." Oh, fuck. Not that again. "When your father told me that, I wanted to come speak with you and see what's going on. You didn't bring her to the house today. By the cooking you're doing right now, y'all haven't even eaten yet." I hear Gabe shuffling around, probably keeping an eye on the food. I try to be as quiet as possible so I can hear everything. "I don't want you to make the same mistakes again. And she has tattoos, Gabriel."

Crap. She probably saw my tats when I walked away. See, this, us, we aren't a good thing.

"Mom, I love you, but stop, please. You know I never bring a girl to meet you until I'm sure. I haven't been seeing Ryan that long."

"And she's already spending the night? Already so comfortable in your house that she's doing load of laundry?" She interrupts.

"This is her first time here. Just listen to me for a second. Yeah, Ryan's a little young and has tattoos, but she's a good girl, Mom. I'm certain of that." Good? What the hell is he talking about? "I like her a lot. Once I finish getting to know her like I want, we'll all get together for dinner." Thanks for asking me about this, Gabe!

158

"Okay. I just don't want you to get hurt again, Gabriel. You're too good for your own benefit sometimes and miss some of the key indicators."

"I know, but don't judge her based on tonight or her age or whatever else. That's not right," he says gently. "When I'm ready and when Ryan is ready, you can officially meet her, learn about her, get to know her, and then you'll see that she's different. Until then, don't judge."

If I wasn't in here hiding and if his mother wasn't out there, I would run and hug him.

"All right then. I won't. Are you coming over tomorrow?"

The cabinet over the washing machine creaks as I open it to get the detergent. I cringe before I remember that's why I'm in here, so it doesn't matter if they hear me.

"No. I have to go in late afternoon."

"Maybe next week then. I best get going."

"Bye, Mom."

"Bye, Gabriel."

I hear fading footsteps, a door opening and closing, and then more footsteps coming closer. I press the buttons to start the cycle. The door opens, and Gabe stands on the other side. His lips part to speak, but I practically tackle hug him. His arms automatically go around me, even though he's confused.

"Sorry, I was eavesdropping, but thank you for what you said," I whisper into his neck.

He chuckles at my reaction, finally returning

my hug like he means it. "You're welcome." When I pull away, he adds, "C'mon. You need to finish your job because the food is about done."

As we're walking back into the kitchen, I ask him, "Did you become a cop so you could order people around?"

Gabe laughs. "No. That's just a perk." After we're back in our places, he says, "I don't like ordering people around. Not how you're thinking anyway."

I roll my eyes, ignoring him. Ten minutes later, we're sitting down at his table to eat. Absentmindedly, I run my foot up and down his leg, sometimes slipping underneath his pants to touch his skin directly. I realize that this will make my second Sunday spent with Gabe. Just as I'm about to mention that he must be lucky, his eyes snap from his fork to me.

"Ryan, you've got to stop that."

"What?" I ask, confused.

"Your foot. Stop."

My foot freezes, and I realize I was starting to go up his thigh. I bring my foot back to me. "Sorry, I wasn't really paying attention to that."

He laughs. "You barely knew what you were doing, and it was all I could think about." He shakes his head, taking another bite of food.

I can't resist smiling. After a moment, I compliment him on dinner and then finally bring up what I was going to say. "You're a lucky guy, you know."

"Oh yeah? Why's that?"

"We're spending a Sunday together again. You're turning my Me Day into an Us Day."

Gabe smiles. "I am pretty lucky then."

We eat the rest of our meal in relative silence. I help Gabe put things away and help him wash dishes. With a glance at the clock, I realize I might need to get up with Viv. It's been so hectic today that I forgot she's expecting me to go with her to a party tonight.

"Be right back," I tell Gabe. I grab his keys which are by the door and unlock his car. My purse is still in there because I was too busy getting wet to remember to grab it. The rain has momentarily stopped, so I run out to get my purse, wiping my feet on the mat when I come back. I lock his doors and shut the house door. "I forgot to text Viv," I explain when I see Gabe looking at me curiously.

"I'm going to check on the clothes," he says over his shoulder, already walking away.

I decide to call her quickly instead of texting. Sometimes, I just don't feel like bothering with a text. And with all the questions Viv might fire at me, verbally telling her is a lot quicker.

"Where are you? I was just at your place. Your car is here, but you aren't. Are you still with Gabe?"

"Yeah, sorry, I didn't call you sooner." I glance down the hallway, seeing that the door is still open a bit. "Things haven't exactly gone as planned today."

"What do you mean? Is everything okay?"

"Yes, everything is fine. I'll explain later, but I'm not going to the party tonight."

Viv sighs. "Ryan, it's a huge party! You know it always is when the frat boys throw one. I can't believe you aren't going."

"Why are you so upset over this one party?" I ask suspiciously.

Viv is quiet for a moment. "I needed you as backup because I was going to hang with this guy. You're my backup plan, you know that! Who am I going to make my excuse if things go South?"

"You really want to hang with this guy?" I question, looking at the door hiding Gabe and feeling guilty that I bailed.

"Yes, but don't leave for me, Ryan."

"No, it's fine. I did say that I would go with you." I regret every word that comes out of my mouth as Gabe exits the laundry room and starts walking over to me with purpose. "I'll get Gabe to take me home, and I'll get ready for the party." Gabe frowns slightly, but doesn't say anything as he grabs my hips, tugging me against him. God, he's hard again.

"No, Ryan, don't do that. How about this? You be on standby and if I need you, I'll text you. Then the officer can race you over here to save me."

"Who is this guy anyway?" I ask, wondering why she's extra worried. She names the leader of the frat boys. Someone I've slept with before, but she doesn't know that. If everyone I've slept with

162

was off limits to her, she would have to resort to the freshmen mostly. "You don't need to worry about him, Viv, but my phone will be on the highest volume, okay?" Gabe starts kissing my neck. What's got him so horny all of a sudden?

"All right. Have fun," she sings.

"Mhm. Bye."

His voice grumbles against my neck. "Do I need to take you home?"

"No," I breathe as his hands glide up my body, causing my shirt to rise as well.

"Good." His lips trail over my shoulder.

"What are we going to do for the rest of the night?" I ask as the rain starts to pour again.

Gabe lifts his head to look at me, a grin upon his lips. "What do you want to do, Ryan?"

I think about it for a moment before the light bulb goes off over my head. It's a bit of a gamble and I've never done anything truly like it before, but it's worth a shot. "I think we should be in the kitchen for a bit, then the living room, and then move to the spare bedroom." I let my fingers walk up his chest. "And maybe the laundry room? What about against that wall in the hallway too?"

Gabe tilts his head. "In every room of my house?"

Leaning in close to whisper in his ear, I say, "Yes, I want you to fuck me in every room of your house."

Gabe tenses, but then steps around me. I'm about to ask what he's doing, but he's just closing the blinds on the window of the door.

"On the table."

A thrill runs through me at his order. I move a chair out of the way and hop up to sit on the table. He disappears down the hall and into his bathroom but reappears moments later with a condom. Gabe walks over and pushes the napkins and salt and pepper shakers that are behind me out of the way before finally settling between my knees. He grabs my waist and scoots me forward so I'm on the edge of the table.

"Lift your hips."

With my hands on either side of me, I do. Gabe hooks his fingers in the waistband of my shorts and yanks them off. God, he's fucking hot when he gets like this. He's clearly thinking about only one thing, and that is what he's about to do to me. The condom is tossed onto the table before Gabe pulls the chair over, taking a seat.

"Lay down on the table, Ryan."

I lean back on the table as Gabe spreads my knees, muttering about how wet I am already. He kisses my inner thigh but switches to the other one before finally bringing his mouth down on me, his beard scratching my skin. Fuck. When I look, all I can see is a head full of curls between my legs. Gabe's mouth is hot as he sucks before piercing me with his tongue. My mind and body surrender completely to him right then and there. I'm lost in an ocean of scorching, never-ending pleasure.

When Gabe brings me to the brink, he pushes

me backwards, making me wait. He commands me to sit up and put the condom on him, my hands trembling with need. And then he fucks me on the kitchen table. My body is weak and shaking from the orgasm, but Gabe picks me up and we're off to the next room. After each powerful climax that makes me scream from the top of my lungs, I don't think I can do it again. I'm out of energy until Gabe tugs me to the next location and gets me all hot and wet to the point where I have to have him inside me again.

Once we've made our rounds, our clothes somewhere between his room and the kitchen, he plops onto the bed. Thank God. I didn't think his energy would ever run out. Unfortunately for him, we're not quite done yet. My mouth waters with what I want to do. His hooded eyes watch me as I crawl over him, my breasts brushing against his legs.

"Ryan," he starts as I wrap my fingers around his cock and swirl my tongue over the tip. He groans instantly, and I know he's extra sensitive. I lick and suck down his shaft, dragging noises from Gabe as I do so.

Slowly, I come back up and take him into my mouth. Gabe's hand goes to the base of my neck. I don't need him to guide me though. With a careful ease, I lower myself more and more until I can't without gagging. He's taut and salty in my mouth. When I suddenly suck in and Gabe curses, I've never felt so good about this in my entire life. I work him with my hand and mouth until a hot squirt hits the back of my throat, causing Gabe to mutter something incoherently. Watching him watch me, I pull away, lick my lips deliberately and lazily before swallowing.

He shakes his head slightly, but there's a faint smile on his lips. As I crawl to lay next to him, how spent I am hits me. Just as I get comfortable in his arms, my phone blares from the kitchen.

"Damn it," I whine. "I don't wanna get up."

Gabe chuckles. "I'll go get it."

He leaves, and I hear him answer it for me, returning seconds later with the phone held out to me. A glance at my screen tells me it's Viv.

"Hey, what's up?" I ask as Gabe gets back into bed.

"You've slept with him, Ryan?!" she yells and I flinch. I didn't think he'd remember, but I guess he did. Why would he mention that to her anyway? "Damn it, Ryan. How am I supposed to even get to know a guy if you've slept with half the men on campus?! I don't want him if you've had him."

"What are you trying to say, Viv? How did this even come up?"

"He was buzzed and made a comment about how he fucked you and how we should have a threesome!" She calms down as she takes a deep breath. "You're my friend, Ryan. All I meant is that I would feel a lot better about seeing or sleeping with a guy if I knew you hadn't have slept with them already."

"Sorry. Would you like a list?" I joke.

"No, just warn me next time, okay?"

"Okay."

We hang up, and I glance at Gabe who has fallen asleep. I turn my phone on silent, set it on his bedside table, and cuddle up to him. He immediately tugs me closer. Soon, I drift to sleep.

* * *

This time when I wake up, I'm on my side, facing the edge of the bed. An arm suddenly lands on me, and Gabe pulls me against his chest. I try not to move or let him know that I'm awake. I don't want to in turn wake him up. A couple minutes pass before Gabe nuzzles into my neck.

"You're awake, aren't you?" He mumbles.

"How'd you know?"

"You're too still."

I laugh. "Sorry. I was trying not to wake you up."

"It's time to get up anyway," he says, and I glance at the clock. It's seven thirty in the morning. "Are you going to let me take over your Me Day? There's some place I want to take you."

I roll over in his arms. "Where's that?"

Gabe shakes his head. "Not telling. You might not go if I tell you. So I'm making it a surprise."

A surprise? The kind where if I know beforehand, I wouldn't want to go. "Well, now I'm scared."

167

Gabe laughs, his smile a beautiful thing to see this morning. "Don't worry, Ryan. It's only going to be you and me. We'll have breakfast, showers, and then we'll head out."

That's just what we do too. Although, he should have just said shower because we took one together. It's around eleven thirty when we leave. Gabe takes me downtown, and I realize we're going to the art museum. This is where he wanted to take me? He glances at me, looking for a bad reaction, but I'm not going to give him one. If this is where he wanted to take me, then I'll have an open mind. Gabe reaches for my hand and leads me inside when I smile at him.

"Why did you want to bring me here?" I ask curiously.

"Honestly?"

"You can lie if you want," I laugh, bumping his shoulder. Gabe smiles. "I want to know, Gabe," I say seriously.

"I love seeing all the art. It's peaceful and there's just something fascinating about being able to see every stroke on the painting. You'll see what I mean."

I sure hope so because I don't want to disappoint him. There are a couple of people strolling around, and we come to the first painting hanging on the wall. It's an image during autumn by the colorful trees, and the sky is a bright blue dotted with clouds. Towards the right side, there is a log cabin nestled into the mountains. Gabe stands next to me, his head tilted as he examines it. I try to see what he sees.

No doubt it's a beautiful painting. Looking closer, I can see the texture along the surface from the different brush strokes. To think that each individual flourish of the brush made the image as a whole does seem fascinating like Gabe said. We move onto the next one which is a stormy ocean and a lighthouse. This one is stunning. I want to take it home and absorb it all. To take time to appreciate all the colors and details that went into making it look like this. I almost wish I had an artistic talent, so I could create something like that.

"Wow," I whisper.

"You like this one?" Gabe questions.

"Yeah, I do."

He squeezes my hand. "This is my favorite."

We move throughout the place, seeing all different pieces of art. But when we come across a large painting that has its own wall, I'm in awe. In a way, it's simple. A painting of fire. Orange, red, white, all mixed together on a black background. I can't even begin to absorb the magnificence of it. After five minutes of me not making a move to go to the next one, Gabe stands behind me, wrapping his arms around my waist, and rests his chin on my shoulder. As if by standing like this, he can see exactly what has me captivated. I'm trying to understand it myself.

The flames almost seem to be warring with themselves. Haphazardly going this way and that while stretching upwards. I see little flecks of white at the top of the wall, and I'm convinced that the fire is trying to reach for the sky. This one, huge inferno feels like it's battling itself while hoping to stretch to the sky. I wonder if the artist felt angry and lost at being pulled in so many different directions.

That's what I feel as my eyes rake over each stroke. The raging flames dance with the wind as it's forced to go in whichever different it's being push towards while struggling to rise up to reach its desired destination. It's so much like me. I want to go my own way, but I'm tangled with the coercion of my parents and their hopes for my life. And like the fire battling the unseen hands of the gusts of air, I struggle against my parents. While trying to find a middle ground, I end up fighting myself as well and destroying what's around me. I want to reach the sky. Or at least be a star. It's much calmer up there than down here with the fire.

I become overwhelmed with all there is, it's too much to take in. Faintly, I know I'll be back to see it again. It spoke to me, and I want to return later to examine it further. Maybe even find answers.

"This is my favorite. Hands down," I murmur, not wanting to speak too loudly. I want to tell him more, explain it to him, but I don't think I can. Instead, I turn in his arms to find those brown eyes. "Thank you for bringing me, Gabe."

He chuckles. "You're welcome. I'm so happy you've enjoyed yourself, but there's more to see, you know."

With a quick kiss, I reluctantly allow him to lead me to the rest of the art. It is relaxing, oddly enough. I never thought I would enjoy something like this. Boring is the first word that would come to mind. Not anymore. When we finish, we head outside and walk a little ways to an Italian restaurant for a late lunch.

"If you liked that, maybe we can make a trip to Raleigh. They have a large museum up there that I'd love to see," Gabe tells me with a hint of excitement. He really does love this stuff, and I never would have thought that.

"Yeah, sure. That sounds like fun."

After we've ordered, a seriousness settles over us. I don't particularly like it or want it to be this way. Not today anyhow. Gabe has one hand under the table, his fingers dancing over my knee.

"Are you still going to major in French?"

Withholding a groan, I shrug. "I'm not sure if I want to do that anymore. There's too many choices. It's impossible to decide, Gabe." He gives me a stern, disapproving look, and I feel the need to continue. "French was a rash decision anyway. I made it within a couple days. You would think that after a year of college, I would have more of an idea, but I don't."

"Ryan," Gabe interrupts before I keep going on and on. "Major in French." His tone is authoritative like when we're having sex.

"But what if I hate it? Or what if I'm terrible at

it?"

"You have to do it in order to know either of those things."

True. He has a point. "Why don't we talk about you?"

It slightly irritates me when he grins and says, "Let's talk away. What do you want to know or discuss?"

I narrow my eyes at him, taking a sip of my iced water because this place doesn't have any Sunkist. After thinking about it for a bit, I know just the thing. "Fine. Tell me what your mother was talking about last night when she said you overlook key signs that cause you to get hurt."

Gabe loses his smile, and I regret asking him before he even answers. The waiter brings us our dishes. It's not until we've started eating that Gabe tells me. "I sometimes have more faith in people than they deserve. I give them chances they shouldn't have. Because of that, I consequently ignore signs that show they will hurt me in the end. That's all."

He seems awfully vague, so I decide to let it go. "Did you play any other sports besides football when you were growing up?"

"Yeah, I played baseball too."

Mm. I could just picture him in a baseball uniform. It's even hotter than the football picture on his mantel. Wonder where that picture is because I want to see it. He's got the perfect ass for those pants.

"Do you ever wish you hadn't quit tennis?" He asks.

"No." I shake my head. "It was too much pressure."

"But what if the pressure wasn't there anymore? Would you play again?"

"I'm probably not that great now. It's been so long." Why is he asking me this? "I've done a little bit of everything, remember? Tennis, softball, gymnastics, track, swimming, piano, violin, choir, Spanish, dance, theater; you name it, I've probably tried it. Even took a kickboxing class once, but that was too boyish for my parents to handle."

Gabe's mouth hangs open slightly. "You weren't exaggerating. Wow." He sits back in his seat, simmering on what I said. "And you didn't love any of them?"

I shake my head. "Not really. They all had interesting tidbits that I enjoyed, but to say I loved it? Learning Spanish was probably the closest to that." Talking about this is bringing me down. All it's doing is making me realize how much I lack passion for any one thing in this world.

The waiter brings the check and once Gabe has paid, we leave. I brought my things with me, so Gabe could drop me off at home since he has to head into work. The ride is oddly silent, but Gabe speaks once we pull into the parking lot of my apartment complex.

"Don't worry so much about it, Ryan. You'll find that one thing that makes you tick. Promise."

I give him a half smile. "Thanks. I had fun, so thanks for that too."

"I'll see you sometime. I'm going to be working a lot the next couple weeks, especially with Halloween, so I'm not sure when I'll be able to see you again."

"Don't work too hard, Gabe. Later." I lean over the console, give him a lingering kiss, and then head up to my place.

I've got a lot of homework to do, and I need to make a decision on my Halloween costume.

Chapter Nine
Gabe

Work has been crazy and stressful. I've been working practically nonstop for two weeks, and tonight is going to be the craziest of all thanks to Halloween. However, I do have tomorrow off. Finally. And I haven't seen Ryan since the weekend she stayed at my house. I haven't really talked to her all that much either. Not that I haven't wanted to, but because of transfers and a recent firing, we're all working overtime to make up for being without a couple of people. I'll be ready when they hire someone.

Tonight, my partner, Fredrick, and I are patrolling downtown. Halloween brings out all the crazies. We're nearby for any fights or disturbances or anything that we may be called for. There are a couple others in the area as well. It's almost two in the morning, and we're parked along the street after getting some coffee.

The sidewalks are filled with people in costumes, most probably bouncing from club to club. Half of them are drunk. Just as I wonder what Ryan may be doing tonight, Fredrick says something inappropriate, which he does often.

"Holy shit. Look at her. What I would do to get with her. Man." He shakes his head at the pair of girls walking past us.

When I look, I see that it's Ryan. She's with Viv, who is dressed as a nurse, and it looks like she's some sort of sexy saloon girl from a western or something. There's a feather boa dangling from her neck to match her black and red outfit. The "dress" barely covers her ass or her breasts for that matter and she's wearing black stockings that stop mid thigh. They are stumbling down the sidewalk, laughing. She's obviously drunk even though she's underage. It shouldn't surprise me because when I first met her, she was hungover.

"Damn," he whistles as she tumbles forward, her ass showing, and Viv barely catches her.

"Shut up," I grit, suddenly feeling very possessive over Ryan. I do not want him to talk about her, especially not like this.

"What?" he asks, oblivious. "She's hot. They both are, but redheads are supposedly crazy in bed."

"Will you stop?" I mumble before getting out. I hear him asking why, but shutting the door cuts him off. He scrambles after me.

"Ryan," I call out before they get too far. Her

176

giggle is loud, but they turn.

"Gabe! Are you my birthday present?" she yells in one big slur. Birthday present? It's Halloween. How drunk is she?

"You know this chick?" Fredrick says as he finally catches up to me.

"Yeah, I'm dating her." I hear him say "oh" right before we reach the girls. "Woah, hey, Ryan." She clumsily wraps her arms around me.

"Best present ever!" she yells into my ear. Ryan sloppily kisses my neck. "You coming home with us?"

"Is that where you're going?"

"Yep! Well, we can't find my car, and we know we don't need to drive, so we were going to sleep there. See? Drunk but smart, Gabe!"

"Fredrick and I will take you home. Come on. Fredrick, help her please," I say, referring to Vivian.

"Should we be doing this?" He asks skeptically.

"Help her," I snap. He isn't about to question me right now. Ryan's hands start to wander down my chest as she mumbles something about missing me. "Ryan," I tell her softly, grabbing her hands. "We need to walk."

"Always a downer. Damn goody-good. Let's walk then!"

Once I wrap an arm tightly around her waist, it's like Ryan gives up. She leans into me completely and lets me lead her to the car. We get them both into the back seat, Ryan mumbling to Viv about her birthday. Surely, it's not her birthday. For one, she is drunk on Halloween, so maybe she's just wanting it to be her birthday. Wouldn't she have told me that today is her birthday? I could have tried harder to get off work to do something with her or bought her something had I known before right this second.

As we head to her apartment, the mumbles cease. I glance in my rearview mirror to see that they are leaning on each other, asleep. Great. It's going to be fun getting them up those stairs and into the apartment.

"I'm, uh, sorry about what I said," Fredrick tells me.

"Don't worry about it. Just help me get them up to her apartment when we get there, and I'll forget you ever said it."

When we get to the complex, I wonder what Ryan was talking about. Her car is here, so they didn't drive downtown. She wouldn't have ever found her car because it wasn't there. What trouble would they have gotten into if we hadn't have seen her?

Fredrick helps me wake them up enough to get them out of the car. He walks behind me with Viv as we go up to her place.

"So sweet," Ryan whispers.

"You owe me," I tell her, although she probably won't remember tomorrow. "Is today really your birthday?" I can't help but ask.

178

"Yes. That's what I said, Gabe." She laughs softly. "Funny, right? I was born on Halloween and I'm my parents' worst nightmare. How fitting." Ryan starts giggling like it's actually funny.

It kills me when she says things like that, but I know what she means. I've seen it firsthand. I want to ask her why she didn't tell me about her birthday. Instead, I ask where her key is as we reach her door. She reaches into her bra and I remember how she did that when that prick had her up against her door that one night.

"Safest place," she says, handing it to me.

I hold her against me and unlock the door. "Fredrick, we're just going to lay them in her bed and then we're leaving."

"Okay."

"You know," Ryan starts. "I could have fucked four different guys tonight. Four."

I clench my jaw as we get the girls into bed. "Oh yeah?"

"Yep. But I didn't," she sings, shaking a finger at me. "I'm supposed to be behaving, and I would have felt bad. Because of you, Gabe. Are you mad?"

We pull the covers over them. They look ridiculous in their costumes while they lay in bed. Viv has already passed out. Fredrick leaves wordlessly.

"No, I'm not mad," I answer.

"I didn't tell you about my birthday. Are you mad about that?" Ryan squints her eyes, pulling her brows together as she frowns, looking worried over the possibility that I might be upset with her.

I lean down and kiss her forehead. "No, not mad. I'll see you tomorrow, okay?"

She nods, already drifting to sleep. I set her key down on the coffee table and then lock her door from the inside before leaving. She said she didn't sleep with anyone, her four available guys, but it still bothers me. We haven't declared exclusivity to each other or anything. The simple thought of how she had been pursued by someone other than me tonight is irritating. And not just one person. Four people. I know her better than them, right? She talks to me, tells me about the more serious things in her life. That means something, doesn't it?

Or am I once again trusting a girl, expecting her to be one way, when she's really the opposite? No, I don't believe that. On some level, I think we both know she's mine. She said herself that she didn't sleep with those guys because of me. I still think that it's too soon for her to meet my mother, but I've hated that I haven't been around her much lately. I've missed her honestly. I wish she would have told me about her birthday. Is it because her parents ruined that for her as well? That doesn't explain why she wouldn't have told me, though. Maybe I've just been too busy, so she didn't mention it.

Ryan is on my mind for the rest of my shift. I'm so ready to see her tomorrow, especially after seeing her tonight.

* * *

It's three in the afternoon when I come to stand outside of Ryan's apartment, knocking on her door. Her hair is thrown up in a high ponytail, and she's wearing black sweats with a blue hoodie. She groans when she see me.

"Sorry, Gabe," she says when I raise an eyebrow at her. "But seeing you means I wasn't imagining last night. C'mon in." Ryan steps aside so I can walk inside.

"You remember?"

"Unfortunately." Ryan sits down on the couch, and I sit next to her. "Which are you most upset about? That I was so drunk I didn't even know we didn't take my car and that I shouldn't have been drinking because I'm underage? The four boys I could have slept with? That I didn't tell you about my birthday? Or what about the fact that I embarrassed you in front of your partner? All of the above?" She glances at me nervously.

Yeah, the boys irk me, but that isn't what bothers me the most. "Your birthday. Why didn't you tell me, Ryan?"

She shrugs. "It's just another day, Gabe."

I pick up her hand that's resting in her lap. "C'mere." Once I've tugged her into my lap with her sitting sideways, I continue. "It's not 'just another day'. It's *your birthday* and a big one too.

181

The great 2-0, no longer a teenager."

Ryan seems confused. "Why does it matter? You were working, so you wouldn't have been able to celebrate with me. Hell, I wasn't really celebrating by birthday anyway. I was dressed and partying because it was Halloween."

For a moment, all I can manage is a frown. Before I can speak, Ryan nudges her shoulder against mine.

"Shouldn't we be having hot sex right now? I haven't seen you in forever."

Just the mention of how long it's been since we've had sex, makes my dick hard, and Ryan grins. I shake my head to force those thoughts away. "No. We shouldn't." Ryan loses her smile. "What's wrong with your birthday, Ryan?"

She tenses, wrung tightly like that day her mother was here. Ryan gets up, walks to the door, and opens it, thoroughly confusing me. Her voice has no fight whatsoever in it. She sounds tired, really. "Just get the hell out. Please."

What am I missing? "Ryan," I start as I get up, but she cuts me off.

"Leave, Gabe. I was drunk and honestly, I wish I had never told you it was my birthday. Forget about it. Once you have, then you are more than welcome to come find me." She sweeps her arm dramatically to the outside, impatient that I haven't left yet. I'm stunned in place. "Gabe," she painfully whispers. "Please."

I search her eyes for clues, but she's closed off

more than ever. Ryan is nowhere to be found in those green depths. I don't know if I should leave or demand her to tell me what's going on. The seconds pass as I stand here, and I know that her fierce exterior is chipping away bit by bit.

"No, I'm not leaving," I finally manage.

Her jaw drops, but it quickly closes as she finds her words. "You have to. You're a fucking cop, Gabe! Surely, you know that if I ask you to leave, you have to go."

Ryan's anger doesn't scare me. I pluck her fingers off the doorknob and close the door. "You're letting all the cold air in." This time, it's her who is stunned speechless, so I lead her back to the couch, pulling her into my lap once more. Once my arms are securely around her, I say, "Now, tell me what's going on."

Her eyes search mine, much like I did earlier. I don't know what she's looking for, but she slowly starts to relax into me, resting her forehead on my shoulder, resigned. For a long time, Ryan doesn't say anything, and I don't push her. When she does speak, her voice is strained.

"I didn't even know what a birthday party was until I started school and a kid's parents brought cake to class for a party. I mean, I knew that there was a certain day of the year that I was born, but celebrating it was completely foreign to me. I never had a party or presents or anything like that. My grandmother would always take me out or we would go shopping around my birthday, though.

She would never say that was why we went. I think she wanted to, but she wasn't one to go against my parents even if she disagreed. She and my mother didn't have the best relationship, and she probably didn't want to make things worse.

"Anyway, it sort of makes sense because my parents bought me whatever I wanted throughout the year. They were always really busy with work too. Besides, sharing a birthday with Halloween meant I got to dress up and go trick or treating, so it worked out. Long story short, I didn't tell you because we don't celebrate birthdays. Not in a traditional sense. We give each other birthday cards with a bit of money inside, and that's it."

My heart tears for her. How fucked up is her family? I don't understand why they wouldn't do something for the day they were born. I kiss the top of her head, feeling a tear fall onto the bare skin between my neck and t-shirt.

"Are you satisfied now?" Her voice is monotone.

"That you talked to me? Yes." An idea forms, but I decide to change the subject. "Why did you pick a saloon girl costume?"

Ryan laughs, not expecting that. She sits up to look at me. With the pad of my thumbs, I wipe away her silent tears. "I love watching old TV shows like *Bonanza*, *The Rifleman*, *The Big Valley*. You get the gist. So that's what I wanted to be. How hot was I? Well, I was before I was wasted." She chuckles.

184

I make a show of looking at my watch on my wrist. "You're always hot, Ryan. I need to go."

She frowns. "Dinner with your family?"

"Yeah," I lie. Well, sort of. I'm supposed to go, but I'm going to cancel. "I'll text you when I leave, and you can spend the night at my place?"

"I have class tomorrow."

"I have work," I deadpan. C'mon, Ryan. Don't let me down. "Besides, I thought you wanted hot sex?" I smirk.

She laughs, playfully hitting me in the arm. "Fine. I guess I could come over. Better make it worth my while, Officer." Ryan gives me a swift kiss.

"I will."

After our goodbyes and a heady kiss, I leave for my secret mission. I run around town like a crazy person, searching for everything I want. Two and a half hours later, I examine my handiwork back at home. Ryan should be here any moment. Speak of the devil, I think as I hear a door shut outside. I walk out to greet her, so this can work just as I want.

"Hey, Gabe," she grins, hoisting her bag over her shoulder. Her hair is down, and she's changed since I saw her earlier. She's now wearing jeans, an orange v-neck sweater, and a scarf hangs loosely around her neck.

"Hey," I greet, taking her bag from her. "I have a surprise for you."

"You do?" She asks, confused.

"Yep. Close your eyes. I'll lead you inside."

Her eyes close instantly, but she says, "What have you done, Gabe?"

I place my hand over her eyes, just to be sure she doesn't peek. Her eyelashes tickle my palm. "Close your eyes," I repeat. When the fluttering stops, I place my free hand on the small of her back, leading her towards the door. "Two steps right in front of you," I tell her. She walks up the steps. "Reach for the door, please."

Ryan giggles and blindly sticks her hand out to find the doorknob. I instruct her until her fingers curl around the knob. She opens it and then steps inside.

"Ready?" I'm suddenly nervous of what her reaction will be.

"Yep."

My hand falls away. I step next to her to see what she thinks. Her lips part as she takes in her surroundings. My house has been transformed. There are streamers hanging from the ceiling from the kitchen into the living room, balloons floating everywhere. In the middle of the kitchen, a seahorse piñata, which took forever to find, is hanging. There's a cake sitting on my table with chips and Happy Birthday plates waiting to be used along with two of those cone hats kids wear sometimes. Ryan steps further into the house and towards the living room, seeing a game of Pin the Tail on the Donkey and more party favors. On my end table, there are bubbles waiting to be blown,

186

silly string, and even a mini pool set.

Ryan swivels to face me, awe written over her features. "What's this?" She asks softly, carefully.

I shrug nonchalantly. "I wanted to give you the birthday party you never had." This seems like such a dumb idea now. No way Ryan will go for this. But she slowly starts to smile.

"What do we do first?"

And that starts our journey of becoming kids again. Ryan wanted to do the piñata first and while she wore the blindfold, I gave her instructions on where to swing. She missed the first time, swinging entirely too low thanks to what I told her, and I sprayed her with silly string, causing her to giggle and squeal my name.

"So close. Just a bit higher," I lie.

She misses again, and I laugh, spraying her again. We do this a couple more times before I come behind her and help, breaking the seahorse in half. I hold Ryan by the waist and turn her away, so I can grab the candy for myself, causing more giggles to bubble out of her. We play all the games, blow bubbles, and engage in a silly string fight, making an absolute mess of my house. But it's tons of fun, and Ryan hasn't stopped smiling since she walked into the house.

"Okay! Okay!" she surrenders from behind my couch as I crouch behind the recliner. "You win! I want cake now." She peers over the couch, and I can see that she has the green silly string all tangled in her red hair. "Truce?" She questions.

"All right. Truce." As I stand up, Ryan runs for the kitchen, spraying me on her way, laughing. "Shame on you, Ryan," I chuckle, pulling it off my face. She slides into the chair, and I set my cans down. I was empty anyway.

"C'mon! Time for cake, Gabe."

I find a knife and two spoons and retrieve the ice cream, going ahead and taking off the lid. Ryan asks to cut the cake, so I let her. She cuts a large slice and puts it on the plate. I raise my eyebrows when she slides it over in front of me before getting up to squeeze between the table and me to straddle my lap.

"Do I get to make special requests?" She asks, running her hands down my chest.

"Of course. Whatever you want, Ryan."

She smiles, reaching behind her to slide the plate over further so she can access it better. Ryan gets a spoonful of cake and waits for me to open my mouth. I do, completely turned on by the fact that she's feeding me. Ryan watches me, seemingly fascinated before handing the spoon to me.

"Your turn."

I lean forward, pressing her between me and the table as I tug the ice cream closer. "Vanilla, chocolate, or strawberry?" I ask.

"All three."

Chuckling, I manage to get a small bit of all three onto the spoon, lifting it to her lips. She sucks the ice cream off the spoon with more force than necessary, and I shake my head at her, smiling. We keep going back and forth until the slice of cake is gone, and the ice cream has melted puddles around the edges of the container.

Ryan takes the spoon from me, setting it on the paper plate. "Thank you, Gabe. I don't even know what to think. Did you do this instead of going to your parents?" She wraps her arms around my neck, her fingers playing with some of my curls.

I rest my hands on her hips. "Yeah. Mom wasn't happy that I cancelled last minute, but she'll understand." I curl my fingers into her back. "I wanted to do this for you."

She rests her forehead on mine, her eyes closed. "Best birthday ever," she says quietly. When her eyes flash open, they are watery, causing me to notice her shallow, cautious breathing as if she's trying not to cry. "Gabe, I-" her voice falters, struggling with whatever she wants to say. Her mouth closes and opens several times, but nothing more comes out, so I decide to ease the tension.

"It may be your party, but you're going to have to clean this mess up because I'm not going to do it," I tell her, pulling a piece of silly string from her hair.

Ryan barks out a laugh just as I hoped. "That's so wrong."

"Just kidding." I pause. "Sort of." Ryan giggles, and I push her hair behind her ear. "Ready for your hot birthday sex now?"

Her eyes darken with desire, her laughing halts immediately, but she shakes her head.

"Maybe later." That is unusual for Ryan. With a blink of the eye, her desire is gone, and so many emotions take its place.

"Tell me what you're thinking."

Ryan takes a deep breath. "You really want to know?"

"Absolutely."

She almost looks nervous for a moment. It quickly disappears. I love that she looks directly at me, whether she's nervous or not. She's going to face it head on. Finally, she mutters, "I was thinking about us and how... how this, us, scares me a little."

For probably the first time ever, Ryan doesn't ramble on. She waits for me to say something. I wish she would babble endlessly to explain herself.

"You're going to have to give me more than that, Ryan. What do you mean?"

She shakes her head. "Nothing. Everything. I don't know. Thank you again for today," she repeats, changing the subject. "It means a lot that you did this for me."

I try to decide if I should press her or not, but her phone rings from across the room. Ryan makes no move to get it. Her eyes don't leave me. I wonder if she wants me to pry further. She doesn't give me a chance to make a decision.

"Can we go watch a movie?" She glances into the living room. "Maybe in your room, so we don't have to clean up yet?"

"Yeah, you're in charge, remember?"

Ryan stands, and I follow her into the bedroom after putting the ice cream away. I prop some pillows against the headboard before lying down with the remote, turning on the TV. Ryan cuddles up to me, resting her head on my chest as I search for a horror movie. Once I find one, I set the remote down next to me, idly running my hands through her hair, pulling out silly string along the way. Ryan becomes immersed in the movie, but my mind is elsewhere.

How do we scare her? What was she about to say before that? I'm full of unanswered questions. While I'm thinking, my hand leaves her hair and the tips of my fingers skim down her back, finding a sliver of bare skin from where her shirt rode up a bit. I'm so happy I decided to do this for her. It wouldn't have happened if I hadn't have made her told me though. She deserved to have a party, especially one like this that was full of child-play.

Ryan lifts her head to look at me, distracting me from my thoughts. Lust has taken over once more. She grabs the remote and turns off the movie, the end credits disappearing into blackness. Ryan straddles me, sitting upright. The hem of her shirt bunches in her fingers as she pulls it up and over her head. Ryan throws it aside, leaning down to kiss me.

"I'm ready for my hot birthday sex, Gabe," she whispers, kissing along my bearded jaw. Ryan grazes her teeth over my ear.

I roll us over, so I hover above her. Ryan's

gloriously red hair is splayed across my pillows. Right then, I decided that we're not going to have hot birthday sex. We're going to make slow, deliciously scorching love. With every ounce of emotion in me, I kiss her. Ryan sighs into my mouth. I run my tongue along her teeth, already lost. Ryan sucks on the tip of my tongue before swiping hers against it. My hands turn into fists on either side of her shoulders. Abandoning her mouth, I settle between her legs, grinding against her as I kiss her shoulder to her collarbone. Then I dip my head inward to kiss the swells of her breasts.

"Take off your pants," I murmur, lifting myself back off her. I hover as if I'm about to do a push up while Ryan quickly works underneath me to remove her pants. "Bra too." Once Ryan is completely naked, my eyes rake over her body. God, she's beautiful. I move so I'm only half laying on her, leaving part of her exposed.

Ryan hungrily brings my face back to hers so she can kiss me. I cup my hand over her between her legs. She inhales with surprise. My fingers brush over her, feeling how wet she is already. My middle finger runs between her folds before sinking lower, inserting into her. Ryan's leg between my legs moves, brushing against my erection and making me groan into her mouth. Leaving that behind, I travel to give special attention to her breasts, slowing moving my finger inside her.

Just as I take her nipple into mouth, I push in another finger. Ryan tightens around them, and I smile. I tug her nipple between my teeth and pull until it pops out, moving more vigorously inside her.

"Fuck, Gabe." She claws at my shirt, wanting to take it off. "I want you now."

Chuckling, I have no problem giving her what she wants. "Get the condom." I lift my chin towards the side table. She's got it in her hands, ripping the wrapper before I can unbutton my jeans. I take them off and I'm on my knees beside her. Ryan sits up and rolls the condom on me. She strokes me a few times. I love how I feel in her hand.

"Lay down, legs open wide."

I move in between her legs, quickly entering her. Ryan hooks her legs around my waist, lifting to have more of me. I put my hand low on her belly and push her back down. She lets out a low whimper, only the tip of me inside her now. Leaning down, I kiss her and begin to move deliberately slow. Ryan attempts to push me further and harder with her calves, but it doesn't work. The hand on her stomach moves lower to rub her clit.

"Good lord, Gabe," she breathes, her eyes tightly closed as I move slightly faster, kissing along her jaw. Ryan arches her back when my pace picks up even more, my thumb aggressively moving over her clit. She grabs onto my shoulders, squeezing. "Harder," she pleads.

That one word as she pulses around me, releases an animalistic vigor within me. I slam into her relentlessly, deeper and harder. When her hands reach down, the tips of her fingers digging into my ass as she tries to push me even further, I lose all control. I drive into her with everything I have, kissing her with all the passion I can muster.

She bites my lower lip, clenching around me, her legs tightening around my waist, and a throaty groan pushes its way out as she shudders beneath me with her climax. I don't stop, can't. Not until I find my own release. Ryan squeezes around my cock and I explode with a grunt, slowing down dramatically to prolong our orgasms. Her legs slip off my hips as I pull out and fall next to her.

I'm drained, so I go to the bathroom to clean myself up. When I come back, Ryan is snuggled underneath the covers, which are pulled all the way up to her neck. Her smile grows when she sees me. I crawl in next to her and she cuddles up to me.

"Today has been fantastic," she whispers. "Thank you."

"You're welcome," I answer, my eyes already starting to droop. It's been a long week, and I'm still trying to catch up on sleep. Twenty minutes later, I'm dozing when I faintly hear Ryan talking.

Her voice is soft and low with a hint of fear. "I think I'm in love with you." My heart stops, fully awake now, but I don't stir. "I don't know what the hell I'm supposed to do about that, Gabe. That's why I'm terrified. You hold a power over me and don't even know it." She wiggles to get closer to me and without thinking, I tug her tighter against me. Ryan sinks into me, oblivious that I'm not, in fact, sleeping. It's not until I feel her breathing even out that what she said hits me.

She's in love with me? Is that what she was on the verge of saying earlier? I almost don't know what to do about it either. This wasn't something I was expecting and especially not to hear it this way. I've learned so much about Ryan since we've started seeing each other. Her feelings kind of worry me. Only because I don't want to hurt or disappoint her. She deserves so much more than that, and I don't want to be one more person on her list of people not good enough for her.

I'm not about to let Ryan slip away from me, though. Like I was thinking earlier, she's mine. I don't want her going anywhere. I only want her where she is right now. In my arms. As I fall asleep, my last thought is that maybe it is time for Ryan to meet my mother.

Chapter Ten
Ryan

I wake up at four in the morning, my dreams terrible as I professed my love for Gabe, and he turned me down. Over and over. I didn't sleep well at all. You know, it's one thing to have your thoughts consumed with worry over a realization, but it's entirely another thing when you voice them. Even if it was barely a whisper, and Gabe was sound asleep. This massive piece of information has me completely clueless. What am I supposed to do about it? Wait until Gabe falls in love with me? What if that never happens? What if I disappoint him and he realizes I'm not good enough for him?

I remember Gabe saying something about how he thought I was intriguing when we first met, but that doesn't prove anything about him or his feelings for me. Maybe that means Gabe knew there was something about me the moment we met. Or it can mean nothing at all. It doesn't matter

196

because I know without a doubt, I've fallen in love with him. There have been bits and pieces about Gabe along that way that sunk me into this quicksand of love for him. We shared moments together that would make me slip and fall a little further for him. There were moments, like yesterday, when I didn't fall, but I tripped and rolled down a hill, building speed along the way, helpless to stop it.

With all these damn thoughts in my head, more sleep is a hopeless wish. Remembering that there's a mess out there waiting for us, I quietly get out of bed, slipping on the first thing I find, which is Gabe's t-shirt. I silently close the door behind me and walk to the end of the hallway. Looking at the balloons, the streamers, the broken seahorse, and the array of silly string everywhere, my heart swells again. He did all of this for me. The least I can do is clean it up, so he won't have to come home to it after work. Besides, cleaning can help me relax, and I'm on pins and needles.

It doesn't take but maybe an hour to throw away the trash, wash the few dishes, and put the games neatly on the kitchen table, which is my current task. Thankfully, this busy work has soothed me a bit.

"Ryan? What are you doing?"

I nearly jump out of my skin with a scream as I hear Gabe's gruff, sleepy voice. My heart pounds against my chest, wanting to break out and run away. Swiveling to face him, I see he's found a pair of pajama pants to wear. "God, you scared me," I say, my hand over my heart as if that would still it.

Gabe smiles slightly, his eyes still squinting as they try to adjust to the kitchen light. "What are you doing?" He repeats, looking around at his clean house.

"Oh, I woke up and couldn't sleep, so I picked up our mess."

He shakes his head, walks over, and takes my hand. "You didn't have to do that," he mumbles sternly, leading me back to the bedroom.

"I'm not tired," I object, knowing there has to be more to clean out here.

"Too bad. You're coming back to bed with me." He flips the switch to turn the light off and then we're in the bedroom. I lay on my back as Gabe slips underneath the covers next to me. Just like the first time we slept together, only this time he's awake and consciously doing this, he throws an arm over my waist and uses my chest as a pillow. "Now you can't go anywhere again," he says smugly. I laugh, twirling a curl from the top of his head around my finger. "Fall asleep with me, Ryan."

It's a simple request. One I would love more than anything. Not sure that it'll happen though.

"Okay," I answer, feeling the need to say something at least.

A few minutes pass, and I think that Gabe has drifted off, but his head lifts suddenly to look at me. I couldn't fake sleep if I wanted to. My eyes are wide with surprise at his movement.

"You're not even trying." He frowns.

"It's useless. I'm too awake."

Gabe thinks about something for a moment before scooting up to lay beside me on his side. He holds his arm out, lifting the covers as he does so. "C'mon." I move into his arms, one tugging me close as the other slips underneath my neck, working as my pillow the closer I get to him. Gabe intertwines our legs, and I'm cocooned in his warmth from head to toe. "Sleep, all right? We have to be up soon."

So I press my forehead to his chest, over his heart. I force my eyes to close and my mind to shut off, thinking only of how warm he is, his heart pulsing next to me. Gabe glides his hand up and down my back. Before I know it, I'm falling asleep with him.

All too soon, Gabe's voice cuts through my sleep as he says, "Ryan, it's time to get up."

"Mmm," I hum, not moving at all. Being nestled against him has me warm and toasty. No way in hell I'm getting up.

"You'll be late for class," he tries.

"Ugh, I don't want to go. It's terrible, dreary, and cold outside."

Gabe chuckles. "Have you been out there yet? How do you know?"

"I watched the weather yesterday," I tell him simply, dragging a laugh out of him. Lifting my head, I continue, "Can't we stay here today? As a birthday present?" Maybe that will work. Doubt it, but worth a shot.

His eyes widen. "Hold still. Don't move, okay?"

"What? Why?" I call after him, but he's already out of bed and out of the room. What did I say? Where is he going? Moments later, he comes back with a gift bag with Happy Birthday written all over it and white tissue paper sticking out the top. As I sit up, I'm practically dumbfounded as to what this is.

"I forgot about this yesterday," he says, sitting back down next to me. "It's not much because it was last minute, but I hope you like it." Gabe puts the bag in my lap.

I stare at it before looking at him. "You got me a present?" Sure, I've received presents before, but never an actual birthday present. One that wasn't just money. My throat constricts as tears threaten to fall.

Gabe nods. "Open it."

Wanting to take my time and remember everything about this moment, I gingerly pull the tissue paper out. I peer into the bag, pulling out the first thing I see which is a pair of black protective earmuffs.

"Now you have your own for next time," Gabe says.

"Thanks." I smile and then reach in, pulling out an orange gift card to the grocery store.

"It's orange because it's for you to support

your Sunkist addiction."

Laughing, I thank him again. The next thing I pull out is a gift card to the movie theaters.

"There's a horror movie coming out soon, and I thought you might want to go see it. Should be two more things in there." Left in the bag is a small square envelope and a larger one for a greeting card. "Open the little one first."

I slip my fingers underneath the piece of tape and open it. Inside is Gabe's business card and I flip it over to read his handwriting.

"One Get Out of Jail Free Card?" I burst into a fit of giggles, leaning on Gabe before I fall over.

"You've been behaving, but never know when you might need this. It's legit too. If you ever get in trouble, you can call me, and I'll come bail you out."

"I love it. Hope I never have to use it, though." Placing it next to me with everything else, I open the final envelope. Inside is a birthday card, and I silently begin to read it, my eyes drawing in on Gabe's handwriting first.

> You deserve to feel special every day of the year, but especially on your birthday. That's the day you came into this world, making it even more beautiful.
>
> You're a wonderful person, Ryan, and I'm thankful you were speeding that day. Hope I was able to make your birthday one to remember.

You Before Me

Happy Birthday, Ryan.

-Gabe

My eyes scan over the rest of the words printed on the card, even more sweet sentiments. I know Gabe is watching me, but I can't seem to look away from his scrawl. Finally, I look up, swallow hard, and throw my arms around his neck.

"Thank you, Gabe. Thank you so much."

"You're welcome." I pull away to kiss him, but he mumbles against my lips, "You need to get ready."

Jutting my lower lip out ever so slightly, I wish I didn't have to leave. "Sure we can't skip?" One last try won't hurt.

Gabe chuckles, finding my attempts amusing. "Not today, Ryan. Believe me, if I could, I most certainly would."

"Okay, fine. I have one last special request."

"Oh yeah? What's that?" Gabe smiles.

"Kiss me."

Gabe holds my head in place in between his hands. He leans forward, gently brushing his lips over mine as my eyes flutter to a close. My mouth parts in the slightest. Gabe sweeps his tongue over the entrance, and I open wider to let him in. I love these kisses from him. They're slow, delicate, and attentive yet so passionate, so heady that we immerse ourselves in one another wholeheartedly. Time stops. It's as if nothing else exists except for our lips, our tongues, and Gabe's hands on my face.

When Gabe stops kissing me, his lips resting against mine, it takes a moment for me to come back to the present and open my eyes. I feel his lips quirk into a smile, his cheeks rising as well. He's so freaking adorable.

"I better go get my shower now," I tell him.

Gabe moves away as I start putting my gifts back into the bag. A glance at the clock tells me I have to seriously put a move on it if I don't want to be late. Being late is nothing new, so I'm not that concerned about it. Still, I make my shower quick because if I'm running late, then Gabe will be too. Once I shower and get ready, about to leave, Gabe asks if he can see me Thursday night.

Smirking, I say, "Sorry, Gabe. A damn cop gave me a ticket, and I have to go to a four hour defensive driving class to avoid getting points on my license."

He laughs. "All right. I'll talk to you later. Go before you're late."

I leave him behind to drive to school. There are a couple of texts from my parents on my phone when I look, but they can wait until later. I scurry across campus, knowing that Viv is waiting for me. When I spot her, I practically run to her.

"We need girl time, stat," I rush.

Her brows raise. "Why? What happened? You look... frenzied," she finishes.

Immediately, I smooth my wavy hair, trying to tame my now obvious frayed nerves. The past twenty-four hours, Gabe, and my crazy realization have me all over the place. I don't like it. Normally, I would consider myself confident without a care in the world. Gabe has, in a way, shattered that for me. At least until I figure out what I'm supposed to do with what I'm feeling.

"Let's get these classes over with and then we're going for a massage. I'm long overdue for one anyway."

"Is everything okay?"

"Yeah, I think so." Love isn't a bad thing, right? It's massively scary with a huge potential for pain, but it's supposed to be better to love than to never experience it. At least, that's how that old saying goes. I should be just fine either way then. If I could only stop feeling out of place and crazy.

Viv nods, satisfied with my answer, and in the moments before class, I manage to get us appointments for later today.

* * *

Even though I feel a bit greasy from the massage oil, my mind and body are in much better states after our massages. Viv and I are now getting a mani/pedi.

"Okay, Ryan. What the hell is going on?" She asks curiously, waiting for me to explain things.

I don't look at her because for some reason, I feel weak for admitting this. Not because of it, but more because I'm scared. The more I think about it, the more terrified I feel. Gabe does have the power here, he always has, and even though he doesn't know it, he has the capacity to ruin me. To damage me more so than I already am.

"It's Gabe," I mumble, watching the woman work on my feet. In between classes, I already told her about what he did for my birthday, so she's rooting for Gabe. From the corner of my eye, I can see Viv perk up, eager to hear what else I have to say. But it won't happen that easily. So I do what I do best.

Ramble.

"I've never met a guy like him. One that wants me for more than what my body can offer. I mean, even I never wanted more than that. Not at this point in my life anyway. I was happy with that and more than happy to offer it. It's not like it was a one way street, you know? I wanted to give it as much as they wanted it, but Gabe," I shake my head, "he makes me think about the possibility of more, to want more." I pause to take a deep breath, still occupied with the woman's work on my feet. "It's weird," I chuckle in disbelief.

It *is* weird. I've never wanted more than sex. Never really thought about it. And now, it's all I can think about. What does more even mean? Do we keep going as we are now? How would things change with love involved? Will everything go down in a disaster like with my parents? I pause my inner thoughts and continue talking to Viv.

"Sex has always been my go-to and all I

wanted from boys. Anything more could wait until after college at least. Then Gabe waltzed right in, and I'm fumbling to figure out what the hell I'm doing. He's sweet, thoughtful, *good*. He's throwing me off my game, Viv. I want to know everything to the last detail about him. I stupidly want to meet his parents and have them like me, which is already nearly hopeless. I want to give him every part of me to the fullest.

"He makes me feel like I can openly voice my opinions without blatantly being turned down. This is new territory for me, and I don't know how to operate. I feel like I'm walking through a minefield and to make matters worse," I stop, taking a moment to recollect myself. "I think I'm in love with him, Viv." Finally, I cut my eyes over to her, and she's grinning.

"Does he know?"

"Hell no!" I screech, causing heads to glance at us. Calmly, I add, "Do you really think I would tell him this until I can get myself under control? Besides, aren't guys supposed to say it first or something?"

Viv laughs. "There are no rules, Ryan. Love has its own set of secret rules. I'm happy for you, though. This means you'll stop sleeping with all the guys on campus." I can't help my giggle. "In all seriousness, Gabe at the very least cares for you. I think you should tell him, find out how he feels, and then go from there."

"And if he doesn't feel the same? Won't he feel

206

pressured to say it to me?" I grimace at the thought. "Or he'll stop seeing me completely, thinking I'm fucking crazy."

"No, he won't. If Gabe is the kind of guy he sounds like he is, then he'll appreciate your honesty and won't freak out. Hopefully."

"Hopefully," I grumble.

"Wait a little longer though. You need to be sure of yourself."

So over the next few days, I do a lot of thinking, trying to make sure that I'm sure. All it does is confuse me. What does Gabe expect from me? That's what I need to know. It all comes down to that one question, and I want an answer. He's never told me his expectations. If I knew that, then I would feel a hell of a lot better about us. Whatever we are. I would know how to move forward and whether I bury my feelings or go with the program to let the pieces fall where they may.

My stomach sinks because whatever Gabe is hoping to gain from me, I'm sure this will end up like everything else. I won't be good enough. Not for a relationship, not for him, and certainly not for his love. Everyone expects certain things from me, expectations I've never been able to reach. The odds have been against us from the start. His parents don't think he should be seeing me. My parents don't think so either because he's too old. Could something last between us if we're doomed to fail from the start according to those around us?

Damn it. I need to stop. This is getting

ridiculous, and my rambling train is flying off the tracks. The fire painting and what I felt when I saw it comes to mind. Maybe I should make a trip back. It couldn't hurt, and a chance to see everything again would be fun. I could go tomorrow.

First, I have to get home from my class for my ticket. This week has been full of homework, texting Gabe, thinking too much, and classes. I haven't been to a party since that one after I met Gabe, and it feels odd. Only because it's a change in routine, though. Instead of going out, getting drunk, dancing, and sleeping with a random guy, I've been hanging out with Gabe. I don't miss it though. Not really. If I'm honest, I would even go as far as to say that I like things better this way.

I'm enjoying learning Gabe's body and what he likes. I like that he's learning those same things about me. We've developed an intimacy between us, something more than simple touches that don't mean a thing, and I think that's my favorite part. He's sweet and thoughtful, and I hope he'll let me stick around for a long time.

Once I park and get out of my car, I wrap my jacket tighter around me as I walk up the stairs to my apartment, keeping my eyes down at the ground to watch my step. When I look up after the last step, Gabe is leaning against my door with his arms folded over his chest, his focus on his crossed ankles. He looks so good like that.

"Gabe? What are you doing here?"

He lifts his head with a smile. "I wanted to see

you."

"How long have you been waiting in the cold?" I ask as he steps aside, so I can unlock my door.

"Not long. I knew about what time you would be here, so I came over."

Hm. He didn't text me first or anything to tell me he was here. We step inside, and I'm slammed with worry over his surprise visit. Is he here to break up with me? Or does he just want sex? What couldn't be said over the phone or wait until tomorrow? I really hope he's here for sex. That I can easily deal with, and I could go for some sex. Why am I freaking out? I never freak out. See what has happened to me?! This is what my thinking does to me. I need to know what he wants from me, from us. Sooner rather than later.

"Are you going to keep trying to figure out why I'm here or are you going to let me tell you?" By Gabe's tone, he's obviously trying not to laugh.

I send a glare his way before going into the kitchen to grab something to drink. "Do you want anything?" I ask sweetly.

"No, thanks."

Removing the bottle cap and leaning against the kitchen counter, I finally ask, "Okay. Tell me why you're here." I watch him as I take a big swallow of drink.

Gabe walks over, rests his hands lightly over my hips, and I gulp. "Do you have any plans this weekend?"

"No. Why?"

"Want to make a trip to Raleigh?" His eyes light up, thinking about the art museum. I'm surprised when I feel a surge of excitement to see more art, and I squeal a yes. This is perfect timing, especially since I was just thinking about going to see the painting again. Gabe laughs, kissing me quickly. "You don't know how excited it makes me that you are just as thrilled as I am about this," he says.

"I can't help it. What time do we leave?" I wish we could leave right now, but I doubt the museum is open tonight. That place is supposed to be huge, three stories high according to their website. I was curious about it and since I was thinking about the fire painting during my class and was bored, I looked up the Raleigh museum. I can just imagine all the fantastic pieces that will be there.

"Around one. We can hang out in Raleigh tomorrow and then go to the museum on Saturday, coming home Sunday morning. Does that sound good?"

I nod. "Do you know what would sound even better?" Gabe raises an eyebrow, waiting for me to continue. "If you stayed here tonight." Now that he's here, I don't want him to go, even though I'll see him tomorrow and spend the next two days with him.

Gabe grins. "I was hoping you would say that." He laughs and adds, "I took the liberty of packing my bags already because if you didn't ask me to stay, I was going to ask if I could. If you said no, I would be a very sad man having to drive back home."

Laughing, I shake my head at him. "Well, I don't know about you, but I've had a super long day, and I'm tired. Go get your things. I'm going to take a shower."

He nods, gives me another quick kiss, and then heads to his car while I head to the bathroom. It feels like this is quite a step forward for us. I'm not sure why, but it seems like since we're taking a trip, even if it's only a couple hours away, that our relationship is getting more serious. It shouldn't be too different, though, I wouldn't think. I mean, we have spent weekends together before. This time we're going to be away from home and in a hotel. At least no one will be able to barge in on us.

When I get out of the shower, all ready for bed, Gabe is already laying down. The blankets stop at his hips, leaving his chest bare and yummy with his hands behind his head. I took extra time to dry my hair, so I half expected him to be asleep already. Wearing shorts and a cami, I slide into bed next to him. I scoot closer, laying on top of him, returning his smile, and wanting nothing more than to kiss Gabe. So I do.

Gabe pushes my shirt up a bit to lay his fingers flat on my back. For minutes, we kiss before he playfully bites my lower lip and then kisses me fully again. I can't help my sigh. Gabe pulls away a bit, grinning.

"What?" I ask, my lips feeling a bit swollen.

"I love when you do that."

"Kiss you?" I question, confused as to why he would interrupt our make-out session to tell me that.

Gabe laughs. "Yes, but that's not what I meant. I was talking about that little happy sigh of yours."

Oh. Anchoring my arms on either side of his head, I bend my hands so I can play in his hair. "This one?" I sigh breathlessly, but end up laughing at how ridiculous it sounds. Gabe grins, but he nods anyway. "Good to know." I kiss him once. "We should get some sleep, right?" Before he can answer, I give him another kiss, parting his mouth with my tongue.

"Mhm," he hums.

Reluctantly, I pull away, sliding off to lay next to him. I rest my head on his chest and attempt to fall asleep, but it's impossible. Why did Gabe pick this weekend to go? Or what made him decide earlier tonight that he wanted to go?

"Hey, why are we going this weekend? It's kind of last minute. Not that I don't want to go, but I'm just wondering."

"I need a break, and I wanted to leave here for a bit. Work has been stressing me out, so with two days off back-to-back, I figured I better make the most of it. I booked the hotel this afternoon. You going with me was the only thing I wasn't sure would happen. And just so you know, I expect at least one bubble bath while we're gone."

"We can make that happen." I smile. "Let's go to bed for real this time," I add, closing my eyes and falling asleep much quicker than I expected.

* * *

It's Friday and once we got to Raleigh, we pretty much just loafed around. We walked around, did some shopping, and held hands all day. I truly felt like Gabe's girlfriend. We were a couple. It sounds weird to me. I almost don't recognize myself. I'm still me, sure, but something is different. The thought nags in the back of my mind as we walk around the museum.

We've already been here for an hour and haven't even made it to the second floor yet. Each painting grabs my attention, begging me to look at the texture the brush strokes made, to examine every piece, and to appreciate the beauty each one offers. This place is much larger than the one back home. I can't absorb everything in one day! But I'm trying. Who knows when I'll be here again. None of the paintings captivate me quite like the fire one, but I do find a few more favorites.

Some are landscapes, which turns out to be Gabe's favorite kind. I love listening to him tell me bits of information about either the paintings or the artists, but it's not much. Just things that he's learned along the way. There are a few particularly haunting paintings that I see and love immediately. One is set in a living room, quite bare with a lack of items. There's one table and three people are sitting at it. A man, a woman, and an elderly man. All of them are wearing smiles, looking happy. But on the opposite side, there is a girl in a long, poofy dress. She's looking longingly out the window, and her stance allows me to see her face just enough to know what she's feeling. The girl is sad, not nearly as happy as the others seem to be. She's lonely. Her gaze outside makes me think that if she had the chance, she would run away. My mind starts to build a story for each of them. What is hidden beneath the ordinary faces of adults to make the girl want to run from them? Or maybe there is something on the other side that we can't see, something to make her want to leave and give up her family.

I stand for a long time looking at that painting before Gabe drags me to see more. The next two I find are drawings and are opposite copies of one another. They are set up the same, but done with different colors. They both focus on a couple in the center of the canvas. The couple is holding hands, standing as if they were at the alter about to be married, only they are dressed plainly and are alone. They are surrounded by a semi-circle of trees and birds, butterflies, and even a doe are mixed in the background as well.

The drawing on the left is done in varying shades of black, gray, and white with bursts of color here and there. One of the butterflies is drawn in perfect detail in brown, blue, and yellow. A leaf in each one of the trees is a bright green. A single piece of grass stands out near their feet. The faces of the couple are done in color too, and they are smiling with love. Next, I notice that a gold ring as been drawn on their hands. It's easy to see on the woman's hand, but the color just is noticeable on the man's left hand.

The other one is the complete opposite. It has lots of colors with voids here and there. There are black leaves randomly hanging in the trees. A patch of black grass, a blackbird, a black butterfly, and then, there is the couple's faces. A black oval. These two don't make sense to me, but I have the nagging urge to figure them out.

Why does one highlight random places, their rings, and their faces with color while the other is so colorful, but has those dreary black voids? What was the artist trying to say? What does it all mean? If there is a meaning behind it. In the first one, simple, ordinary things are in color. A blade of grass, the butterfly, leaves, the rings, and their faces. Why those things? And with the other, the black takes up more space in comparison to the color in the first. I think I like the one with bursts of color than one with black tainting the overall feel.

I see hope in the colors against the bland background. There is hope in the couple's faces. With the other, I feel like the blackness is going to grow until it sucks away all the colors completely. There. I've figured it out. One holds promise while the other is beginning to lose the battle.

"What do you see, Ryan?" Gabe asks quietly. We've been standing here too long, I know. I don't think I can explain what I see though. It probably won't make a lot of sense out loud.

"I'm not sure," I lie before I move us on to the next one.

The more I see, the more I want to see another and then another and another. Honestly, I love them all. I can appreciate some of the sculptures on display, but the paintings, drawings, and photographs lure me in, hypnotizing me. I soak it up, greedy for more. Hours pass as we walk through this place.

Even after we leave and Gabe heads to eat at a modern, cozy restaurant, I'm still thinking about the art, replaying them in my mind, searching for an absolute favorite. One that I can compare to the fire painting. It has to be the drawings. I'm still mulling over those more than any of the others.

"This weekend almost doesn't seem real. Does it feel that way to you too?" I ask after our waiter walks away with our orders.

"What do you mean?" Gabe tilts his head, and I feel his fingers drawing patterns on my knee underneath the table.

"It's been like the most laid-back weekend ever. I guess that's why it feels that way. Or the calm before the storm. Thanksgiving is in two weeks." I frown at the thought. Things haven't been peachy lately, which means the holidays are going to suck. Maybe I'll just stay here this year.

"Ryan." He waits until I look up at him, I didn't even realize I was staring at my glass. "We aren't thinking about that stuff today. Tell me which painting was your favorite," he says to effectively change the subject.

And just like that my mind is lost in all the art we saw today. For some reason, I don't want to tell him that my favorites were the drawings, so our conversation turns into idle chit-chat. Gabe starts telling me some story as we eat, but I barely pay attention. Walking around that museum, seeing all the art, felt so good. This is twice that I've loved coming to a place like this, and I want to come back again and again.

What if every day could be like today? Wouldn't it be so cool to be surrounded by art like that all the time? That would be awesome. As we head back to the hotel, I wonder what other art museums we have in the state. Thoughts like these swirl around my mind as we go back to the hotel and then change for the night.

Gabe retreats into the bathroom, and I sit at the foot of the bed, still thinking. Suddenly, everything clears, and it hits me. I *can* have days like this all the time. I would love to have a job as a dealer, an art historian, or an appraiser. Something in that area. That's what my major should be. I can get an art degree and do any of those things.

"Ryan," Gabe interrupts my thoughts, sounding exasperated.

"What?" I question when he walks over and

sits next to me, placing a hand on my thigh.

He examines me carefully and says, "I've been trying to get your attention. What are you thinking about? Is everything okay? You've been pretty quiet for the past few hours."

My heart swells, feeling too large for my chest. There are so many things that I want to tell him, and I'm not sure where to start or if I should tell him everything that's happening in my head right now. With a deep breath, the words flow from my lips, my eyes focused on his.

"Gabe, you've somehow managed to come in and completely change my life. You have reorganized, thrown things away, and unearthed things I didn't even know I had. I found my passion today, and you were the one to lead me to it. For the first time in my life, something seriously appeals to me. It's all thanks to you. I want to major in art. Realizing that, I feel at peace almost, but then again, I feel off kilter. Life for me feels calmer but chaotic at the same time. I don't know what to do about it."

The words I said about loving Gabe repeat themselves once more. In reality, I probably shouldn't actually do anything, but I feel like I should. Like something has to be done to acknowledge what has happened here. I don't think I've even cussed today. What the hell?

Whew. That felt good.

Gabe reaches over, takes my hand, and silences my inner dialogue. "Nothing."

"What?"

"You said that you don't know what to do. Nothing. If you're happy, then nothing needs to be done. Leave it alone and let it be."

Nothing? Is that even possible?

"Don't start thinking, Ryan," he playfully chides.

I grin, the sudden urge to kiss him and tell him I love him overwhelms me. The words refuse to leave my mouth, so I lean over to let my lips talk for me. Does Gabe feel the atmospheric change around us too? Pulling away from our kiss, I gaze at him. Everything seems to be falling into place for me. I couldn't complain about my life in this exact moment even if I wanted to do so.

"We haven't taken our bath yet, you know," I say.

Gabe smiles, wordlessly stands as he takes my hand and leads me into the bathroom. He booked a bigger room for just this reason. The white tub is large and round, inviting two people to relax inside. While Gabe turns on the water, allowing it to run over his fingers as he tests the temperature, I grab my bottle from the sink. The tub starts filling with hot water once Gabe is satisfied. I pour in a bunch of the bubble bath liquid. Steam rises from the tub, and I wonder if it will be too hot.

When it's halfway full, Gabe stands upright and pulls his shirt off. My eyes travel over his torso, the black chest hair standing out against his tan skin. Not to mention the line of hair that disappears beneath his pajama pants. I lick my lips intentionally, and Gabe laughs, a wide grin showing off his teeth.

"Now, Gabe, how am I supposed to get naked and get in a tub with you when you're laughing at me?"

The jerk has the nerve to laugh harder. "I'm sorry," he lies once his laughter dies down. Gabe steps over to me, lifting his hand to run his thumb over my lower lip. "The way you looked when you ran your tongue over these? You just seemed so turned on with a little skin showing and," he starts to chuckle, "I found it funny."

I playfully push him away and turn off the water before the tub gets too full. "You're a jackass." Trying my best to not look at him, I quickly undress, slowly stepping into our bubble bath. The water is like two degrees away from being too hot. Once I've lowered myself completely, I bring my knees to my chest and finally look at Gabe.

Mmm. He's completely undressed now. I could look at his body all day. Unfortunately for me, he steps in behind me. With his legs on either side of me, he pulls me backwards to rest against his chest. The quiet around us reminds me that we don't have any music.

"We forgot the music," I tell him as he kisses the top of my shoulder.

"We don't need it, do we?"

"No." And we don't. We can sit here in total

silence.

Gabe tucks my hair behind my ears, so he can kiss my neck. With his lips against my skin, he murmurs, "Are we taking a relaxing bubble bath?"

His lets his fingers drum from my knees down my thighs. We've had sex three times since yesterday already. I don't know what the hell is wrong with me or why I answer the way I do.

"Yes, we are."

Gabe lays his hands over my stomach, not even going to try to change my mind. Like the last time, I lean my head back on his shoulder and close my eyes. As we soak, I soon get lost in my thoughts. This weekend seems too perfect. I'm here with Gabe, we went to the art museum, and I found my passion. What will my parents think of this? They weren't happy with a language degree, so I doubt they'll be happy with an art degree. Will this world as I'm currently experiencing it crash around me when I get back home?

It's not like I can completely go against my parents. Not right now anyway. I'm one hundred percent dependent on their money. If they wanted, they could force me into making a decision that they want just so they will keep paying for everything. Maybe I should go get a job and start saving money because I have a feeling that that day will come before I finish college. And with Thanksgiving coming up, I really hope my parents will find something else to do so I can stay here instead.

"What are you thinking about?" Gabe's voice interrupts my thoughts.

"A little bit of everything. You?"

"I was wondering about something important."

"And that would be?" I question, noticing that the water is slowly starting to chill, and the bubbles are disappearing one by one.

"If you're willing, I'd like for you to officially meet my mother. You didn't seem excited about going home for Thanksgiving, so you could have dinner with us. If you want."

My stomach drops. I open my eyes and sit up, focusing my attention on my knees. Is he fucking crazy? Knowing I need to say something, I try to sound calm. "You want me to meet your mother at Thanksgiving when your entire family will be present?" Then what it means for him to ask hits me. "*You* want *me* to meet your *mother*?" I repeat with a small smile to celebrate Gabe's question as I turn around to face him, my knees still tucked against my chest.

"Yes, I do," he answers with a grin of his own.

Gabe wants his mother to meet me because he likes me that much. He's ready to show them what he sees in me, and he's confident that they'll see it too. But the fact that his whole family will be there slams into me, slapping away any previous good feelings. His father doesn't approve, and neither did his mother from our brief encounter. That will be amplified, I'm sure, with everyone else there. I want them to like me so much. My gut tells me it's a bad idea. A really, gigantic, fucking bad idea.

"I don't know, Gabe," I say quietly with loads of apprehension tucked into the words. "You want them to like me and I want that too, I do. Do you honestly think that's possible though? Based on their reactions to me so far. Not to mention that you want to do this on a damn holiday. I don't want to be the reason your family has a less than happy Thanksgiving."

He reaches out, takes my hand and holds it up, intertwining our fingers. "Ryan, it will happen. Maybe not right away, but they are going to love you. Gramps will be there and he definitely loves you. You'll for sure have Gramps, Owen, and me on your side. I want you to go, Ryan. If you rather not or rather wait until a different time, just tell me. I want you to be as comfortable as possible."

That's not going to happen no matter what. His parents are scary as hell. None of that really matters. At least, I hope not. Gabe wants to take me on this next step for him, and I can't say no.

"Are you sure you want this?" I need him to say it out loud one more time.

"I'm absolutely sure."

Relenting against my better judgment, I nod.

Chapter Eleven
Gabe

I love that Ryan obviously doesn't seem sure about this, but she's determined to do it anyway. If Gramps can like her, then my parents can too. Her age seems to be the biggest concern for them. That doesn't matter to me. All they need to see is that Ryan is a good person, and a good person for me. The water is cold now and I'm ready to get out.

"C'mon. Let's take a hot shower and go to bed." Ryan nods, turning to drain the water from the tub. As we step out to move to the shower, turning on the water, I add, "We can do a test run of sorts, if you want. Owen has another home game next week. My parents, Gramps, and Grandma will be there. Do you want to go with me?"

"You sure are asking a lot of me, Gabe."

I laugh and drag her into the stall with me. "Nothing I wouldn't do for you."

She smiles, wrapping her arms around my

neck as the water showers over us. "I'd love to go."

"Good."

Ryan steps around me and reaches for the soap and a rag. We quickly wash ourselves, my eyes glued to her body. It's on display just for me until she wraps a towel around it once she gets out of the shower. I reach out, grab the white fabric, and tug.

"I don't think so."

Ryan props her hands on her hips, her long, red hair attempting to cover her breasts, but failing. "Gabe, I need to dry off." As if to prove her point, water drips from the tips of her hair. But all I can focus on is the path the droplets take. Ryan snaps her fingers to get my attention. "I shouldn't go to bed with wet hair."

I brought something with me this weekend for us to try and now is definitely the time to do so. "Do you want to take time to dry your hair or do we want to find out if handcuffs really do have a better use?" Her jaw drops, shock clearly written on her face. Uh, oh. "Wait, you weren't serious about that, were you?" I ask, feeling like an idiot.

She throws her hands up in the air. "No! I was trying to distract you, so you wouldn't arrest me!" God, I'm so dumb. Her voice comes down a couple notches as she curiously adds, "Did you really bring them?"

I hand her back her towel and she wraps it around her. Wordlessly, I nod and wrap my own towel around my waist. All of a sudden, Ryan bursts into a fit of laughter. She takes my hand, leading me out of the bathroom, still laughing.

"You can stop laughing at me any time now," I tell her. She giggles harder. "What are you doing?" I ask when she grabs my luggage and places it on the bed. I stand next to her and she grins at me.

"Get them. Let's find out."

"What?" I'm confused. She just said that she wasn't serious.

"All hilariousness of this situation aside, if you want to try it, then I'm up for it. Get them, Gabe," she repeats.

I stare at her, still unsure if she's serious.

Ryan takes my hand. "I'm going to be honest with you, okay? I've never done anything like this before and I'm a little nervous. I trust you, though. As long as you don't go overboard or anything, I'm sure it'll be fun. If it isn't, I'll tell you without any hesitation. Have you ever restrained someone during sex?"

I shake my head. "No, I haven't. Your comment has been on my mind lately, so that's why I thought of it. Are you sure? Because you being nervous is making me nervous."

"I'm excited too." She smiles to reassure me. "It's not like you're going to chain me to the bed and leave me here. It's only handcuffs. You're starting to over think this like I am. Get the handcuffs, Gabe."

Ryan lets go of my hand and pushes my luggage closer to me. I flick my eyes to her towel. "Take it off and lay down."

She grins, knowing that I'm going to do it. While she does that, I open the front pocket and retrieve the cuffs before putting my bag back in its place. When I turn around, Ryan is laying on her back, looking relaxed.

"Are those the ones you use for work?" She asks, glancing at the silver pair in my hand.

"No," I answer as I walk back to the bed, stripping my own towel off. "These are an extra pair." I arrange the pillows to sit against the headboard on the left side of the bed. "Scoot over here and lift your arms up with your wrists together."

She glances up, watching as I place one cuff around her wrist. I put it near the headboard where I want it and reach for her other wrist. I make it so the links connecting them go around the bedpost to keep her hands there. The bedpost isn't much higher than the headboard and the pillows are supporting Ryan. Her elbows are slightly bent, which is perfect in case she wants to stop and remove her hands from their place.

"If you want to take them down, just push your wrists backwards and lift. You should be able to do it, even though it's as big and as round as it is. Try it for me, just to make sure." Her elbows lock up as she straightens her arms and lift. "Good," I nod, gently pushing her wrists back in place. "Unless you don't like it, don't move them until I say so."

Satisfied, I climb into the bed, settling myself

between her legs. Excitement sparkles in Ryan's eyes. I trail my fingers from her wrist, slowly down her arm, as I press my lips to hers. She greets me eagerly. My fingertips dance downward to graze her breast and I leave her mouth behind. I kiss her collarbone, her sternum between her breasts, and her stomach. One final kiss over her dandelion tattoo before I spread her legs wide.

She's expecting my mouth. Not quite yet. I lightly blow over her sensitive skin. Her arms jerk and I glance up at her. Ryan's watching me though. I smirk before lowering my mouth onto her. That happy sigh I love to hear escapes as I lick and suck. Ryan moves her legs over my shoulders when I push a finger inside her. I hear a scrape of the metal against the bedpost again.

"Gabe," Ryan breathes when I look up at her. She lets her legs fall to the side, a silent gesture that she's ready for me. I grab the last of our stash of condoms from the top of the nightstand.

"Legs over my shoulders again," I order as I put on the condom. When she does, I place one foot on the floor to half stand and give myself a better leverage. I slide her hips over just a bit before guiding myself inside her.

My right hand steadies me on the bed as I begin to move. My free hand reaches out to play with her breast. The moment my fingers tug on her nipple, her arms pull forward a bit. I love being able to see that she wants to touch me so much, but I need to make sure she's fine.

"Doing okay, Ryan?" I pinch her nipple and her back arches, pushing her breast further into my hand.

"Mhm," she hums. I pull out until just the tip off me is inside her. "Gabe," she breathes.

"Yeah?"

"None of that tonight. I can't touch you, so you can't tease me. Just fuck me hard."

A second after she finishes talking, I slam into her and she yells out. I do it again twice. "Like that?"

"Mhm," she hums again, her eyes closed as I begin to repeatedly thrust into her hard and deep.

"Look at me."

Those green eyes flash open in a hurry. Ryan watches me as my movements quicken until I feel her tighten around me. My hand glides down her torso, reaching between her legs as my thumb begins to rub the spot that will push her higher and over the edge. Ryan screams, her eyes closing, as she arches her back, the heels of her feet digging into my shoulders. She unravels beneath me, pulsing around my cock.

My release hits me hard. I push her legs aside and fall on her. The girl takes every ounce of my energy.

"Gabe," she mutters, her voice strained.

"Yeah?"

"Get off me, please. These handcuffs are biting into my wrists and I can't really move like this."

Her words stir me into action. I get up, pull out

of her, and lift her arms for her. Quickly, I go to the bathroom to clean myself up and slip on my boxer briefs. When I come back, she's sitting up on the bed with her wrists in her lap. She puts them in my lap for me to help her remove the handcuffs when I sit back down.

"Oh, Ryan," I say softly with remorse. There are bright red lines around her wrists. My thumb runs over them lightly.

"It's fine, Gabe. I tugged harder than I thought, I guess. Be right back." She gets up, disappearing into the bathroom. A minute later, her voice carries to me, "It was fun and really good." Ryan walks out, dressed in pajamas, and comes to straddle my lap. She makes a show over running her hands over my bare chest. "But I much rather be able to touch you whenever I want."

"I do love your touch."

"Good." She kisses me softly and then smiles. "Let's watch a movie."

We rearrange ourselves on the bed. I grab the remote, turning on the TV, as Ryan snuggles up to me. This has been a wonderful mini-trip and I can't wait to take Ryan to see more artwork.

* * *

Ryan is having to meet me at the game because I wouldn't have time to pick her up and make it to the game before it started. And good thing I'm meeting her because I got off a few minutes later than I was supposed to, so I'm still partially in work clothes. Getting to the game as quickly as possible is my first priority. Instead of changing completely, I kept my pants on and changed my shirt and such. My navy slacks are paired with just a white t-shirt and a jacket to keep me warm. The November air is extra vicious tonight, it seems. Ryan told me roughly where she and my family are sitting, but I've already missed kick off.

Quickly, I walk up the ramp to the bleachers, walking down to the other end, where Ryan is laughing next to Gramps. God, she's beautiful. She's wearing dark jeans, a red shirt, which makes her hair look brighter than usual, and a black leather jacket with a white scarf wrapped around her neck. She grins when she sees me. My eyes flicker to everyone else. They seem to be watching with scrutinizing eyes, except for Gramps. There's an empty spot next to Ryan, and I take it.

"Hey," she greets.

"Hey," I reply, not being able to help myself as I squeeze her knee, lean over, and give her a little, worthy-in-front-of-my-mother kiss. Ryan's already pink cheeks grow a little darker with a blush. Looking past her, I say hello to my family, asking how they've been. My grandfather is the last to answer.

He proudly puts an arm around Ryan with a grin. "This girl knows her football and can shoot. Better keep her, Gabriel."

Ryan lets out a girly giggle. "You have Gabe to

thank for both of those things, Gramps." She looks at me with a sly smile. "He taught me everything I needed to know."

A call on the field distracts everyone, the conversation ending as Gramps' arm falls from her shoulders, but Ryan is still watching me, as if her words have more meaning to them and she wants me to catch on. Her green eyes seem to be a stark contrast against her skin tonight, holding my gaze captive. I can't resist any longer as I lean over to whisper in her ear.

"You are gorgeous. I am so very excited to get you home."

Then I pull away and look onto the field to find my little brother. From the corner of my eye, I can see Ryan turn to the same direction, but she glances at me after a few seconds. I smirk, see her shake her head, and then she hooks her arm through my elbow before sticking her hand back into her pocket.

My family loves football, so with the game in full swing, there isn't a lot of talking going on that isn't football related. Gramps includes Ryan in his comments. She seems to be enjoying herself, but I notice her teeth are chattering a little. Is she that cold? I mean, there's a bite in the air, but she should be warm enough.

"Hey," I catch her attention. "Do you want some hot chocolate?"

Ryan grins. "Yes, I would."

"Do y'all need anything?" Everyone shakes

their heads. "We'll be right back then," I say to the rest of my family, noticing my mother paying extra attention to us now. Ryan slips her hand into mine as we stand, and I lead her down the steps. Once we are down the ramp, there are less people around. I swivel, causing Ryan to run into me as she laughs with embarrassment. I don't give her a chance to apologize. Instead, my hands dive through her hair to grasp her neck, bringing her to me for a kiss. Ryan's icy fingers chill my skin over my beard.

Needing to taste her, I swipe my tongue over her lips, and they part quickly at my demand. She sighs, leaning into me as she fervently kisses me back with the same eagerness. Reluctantly, I pull away, her lips already forming a smile.

"Is that why you dragged me out here?" She asks.

"Partly. I've wanted to do that since the moment I saw you. But your mouth was moving like one of those chattering teeth toys, so I figured you might want something to warm you up."

"C'mon then," she laughs, taking my hand and tugging me towards the concession stands. While we wait in line, she adds, "The cold is bitter tonight. If I had known, I would have brought a thicker jacket or something."

"You didn't watch the weather?" I tease, remembering what she said the morning after her birthday.

Ryan seems to be full of laughter tonight. "No,

I didn't, smart ass."

We step forward, and I order her drink before she can. When asked if she would like whipped cream, Ryan shakes her head. I go to reach into my wallet, but Ryan waves her hand at me, pulling money from her pocket.

"Don't even think about it," I protest.

She shoves the money at the woman before I can stop her. When she turns to face me, she rolls her eyes. "Relax. It's only hot chocolate, Gabe. C'mon, we're in the way." We step to the side, Ryan taking a moment to sip her drink before we head back to my family. "Mmm," she mumbles heavenly.

I laugh at her. "Ready now?"

Ryan holds out her hand, so I take it and lead her back to our seats. Gramps smiles when he sees us.

"About time you two got back. I was startin' to think y'all escaped."

Ryan giggles, taking her seat next to him. "Now why would we do that?"

I wrap my arm around her shoulders, tugging her closer to me in hopes to keep her warm, and Gramps gives a hearty laugh.

"Darlin', I remember how I was when I was young and in love with my sweetie." At this, he pats my grandmother on the knee affectionately as the horn sounds to alert us of halftime.

I expect Ryan to tense, and she does for a moment, but then she smiles sweetly at Gramps. "I bet you do, Gramps. It couldn't have been that long ago," she says.

He laughs. "You are a charmer, darlin'."

Just then, my mother drags him into a conversation with her and Dad. Ryan drains what's left of her drink and looks at me as the players start to file back onto the field.

Quietly, so no one will hear her, she mutters, "Oops. I didn't offer you any." She holds up her empty cup and intentionally licks her lips. "You can still taste it though, if you want." Ryan gives me a wicked grin.

With my forefinger under her chin, I keep her in place, pressing my lips against hers for just a moment.

"You're terrible," I chuckle. "Pay attention to the game. You may have Gramps convinced, but I want to see if you remembered anything."

Once the game resumes, I start questioning her, and she answers correctly each time. Sometimes, it takes a moment before she can think of the right answer. It's adorable because she'll look up at me expectantly, waiting for me to nod in approval. We do this into the fourth quarter.

"Okay, what was that?"

"A fumble." Ryan turns to me, and I nod that she's right once more. She smiles, satisfied, before turning her attention back to the game. "Did you doubt your teaching abilities, Gabe?" She teases, without looking away from the current play.

"No. Just checking to see how well I did."

She chuckles, but doesn't say anything more. We watch the rest of the game with only a few comments here and there. As expected, we win. Owen's team held a good lead throughout the game. My family follows Ryan and I as we walk over to the field goal posts, waiting for his coach to finish talking to them. Ryan stands close to me, much as before, and I keep my arm around her.

Owen grins big at Ryan when he makes his way over. His hair is sweaty and matted down on his head from his helmet. Owen holds up his hand and Ryan high fives it.

"Good game," she tells him.

"Thanks. I'm excited that you're joining us for Thanksgiving next week." I told my family soon after we came back from Raleigh.

"Owen," my mother sternly interrupts. "We should go."

"Yes, ma'am. See y'all later," he mumbles. Owen gives me a fist pump, hugs Ryan, and then hugs my grandparents.

We all say our goodbyes, Gramps hugging Ryan, and then we go our separate ways. I was able to park near Ryan and as we walk towards our cars, she looks over at me.

"I guess your mother isn't thrilled about me joining y'all?"

"That's not it. Owen was caught sneaking in this week, so he's in trouble. That's all," I reassure her.

Ryan nods, goes over to open the little door to

the gas cap, and grabs her keys. She unlocks her doors, and I open it for her.

"I'll see you at your place?"

"Yes, you will." I give her a kiss before she gets in, and I go to my own car. I'm so happy I told her she should pack ahead of time and come stay with me tonight.

My stomach growls loudly. It hits me that I haven't eaten supper yet. Ryan pulls up right behind me and once inside the house, I go straight to the fridge while Ryan goes and puts her things in my bedroom. I decide to fix a grilled ham and cheese and while I'm standing at the stove, Ryan comes up behind me, burying her face in between my shoulder blades.

"Your parents still hate me, you know," she whispers into my back.

"They do not," I object.

"Oh really?" she says sarcastically. "That's why they all talked to me like Gramps or even Owen did." Ryan sighs, and I realize she's right. Not one of them really spoke to her. "But it's not me who has to get used to that, Gabe. I mean, what I'm trying to say is that there is a serious possibility that your parents aren't ever going to like me and that Thanksgiving is going to be shot all to hell. So if you plan on keeping me around, you are the one who has to get used to it."

I scoop my sandwich onto the small plate, turn off the stove, and face Ryan. Cupping her cheeks, I tell her, "They do not hate you. They just don't know you yet."

She rolls her eyes. "They tried so hard to fix that."

"Did you try to talk to them?" I question, raising an eyebrow at her.

Ryan frowns. "I said, 'Hello, how are you.' Does that count?"

"How about we forget my parents for tonight? How does that sound?"

"Perfect."

I give her a kiss and ask if she would like a sandwich as well. She shakes her head. Ryan grabs me a drink from the fridge, grinning when she sees that there are some Sunkists in there.

"So you do plan on keeping me around?" She says as we go into my living room.

"Absolutely."

We sit down and turn on the TV, but Ryan still wants to talk. "I declared my major this week."

I smile. "You did? How do you feel about that?"

"Liberated. Although, I haven't told my parents yet. They actually haven't even tried calling me at all this week. Not since I texted my mom to let them know that I wouldn't be going home. But I'm really excited about it. I've even looked up other museums and galleries in the state."

Ryan is thrilled about choosing a major, one that she wants without a doubt. That is clearly written all over her face, and I love seeing it. I especially love having her in my house, watching how comfortable she is here. My family needs to like her. Or at least respect that I want her in my life. Their opinion matters to me so much, even though I have ignored some of it since seeing Ryan. I've ignored theirs and my own reservations about her age, which actually no longer concerns me. I've definitely chosen to ignore the comments about her tattoos, because I love those.

"Hey, did you ever decide on your next tattoo?" I ask, having finished my sandwich.

"Yeah, I did. There's not really a reason for me to get this particular one, though. I was just searching the internet for inspiration, came across this one, and knew I needed it. Just a matter of going to get it."

"Want to do it tonight?" For some reason, I really want to watch this happen. Ryan's eyebrows rise, so I add. "I would like to go with you. We're already here together, so why not?"

"I usually set up an appointment, but if you really want to go with, then let's go." Ryan grins.

We lock up the house, and Ryan drives to the tattoo parlor she likes downtown. She holds my hand as we walk inside, the sound of the needles buzzing immediately making me queasy. The guy behind the desk grins at her, and his stupid eyes rake over her body.

"Ryan! It's good to see you again." He glances at our hands, but ignores me. "We weren't expecting you, but I'm happy you're here. Which part of your body will we be privileged to see tonight?"

She laughs. "My side. Where's Max?" Ryan turns to me to let me know who she's talking about. "I didn't get my tats until I moved here for school, and Max has done them all."

I nod, and the guy tells her, "He's not in tonight unfortunately. All our other artists are busy. You can wait for one of them or I could do it. I'm only filling in here until Sally finishes smoking her cigarette."

Please say you'll wait, I think. It didn't occur to me that someone else would be touching her, especially not this guy who would love to do it.

"I don't know," she says, but there's a playful tone in her voice. "I love Max's work the best. However, this is a simple tat, so I guess you can do it. It was a last minute decision to do this tonight. Can I borrow the computer to show you what I want?"

"Sure thing."

Ryan leaves my side to walk behind the desk, next to him. She doesn't seem to pay him any attention as he looks over her once more. Which is why I'm completely surprised when she says, "If you expect to tattoo me, quit looking at me like that." Without taking her eyes off the computer, she tilts her head towards me and adds, "I don't appreciate it, and I doubt he does either."

He looks over at me. "And who is he? You've never come here with a guy before." His entire attitude has changed now that Ryan has forced him to be aware of my presence. Thankfully, he's stopped looking at her like he wants to fuck her.

"That is Gabe, and he's a cop. Future warning, Pete, if he ever pulls you over, don't be a smart ass."

He laughs, and I smile at her comment. "I told you that mouth of yours would get you in trouble," he says. "That's what you want?" He adds, apparently seeing the tattoo on the screen.

"Yes, and I want it right here." Ryan lifts her shirt on her left side and points to a spot just a little bit away from the side of her breast, but down a little to sit more on her ribcage. She's going to have to unhook her bra, so it won't get in the way. Great.

"All right. Have a seat, and I'll draw up a copy. Do you want it exactly like that? Black too?"

"No," Ryan tilts her head at the screen. "I want red instead."

"Okay."

Ryan walks back around, takes my hand, and we sit down on a couch as we wait for him to do his job. "Sorry about that," she says softly. "He's a huge flirt, and I've always flirted back."

"It's fine. What are you getting?"

"A heart. I fell in love with how it looked," is her only explanation.

Before I can question her further, a girl comes from the back, plopping into the seat that Pete vacated. The hum of the needles is threatening to make me sick, and I don't understand how just the sound doesn't bother her. Pete returns and calls us back. We pass a burly, shirtless man, who is getting work on his arm, a woman in her thirties getting something on her foot, and another girl getting someone on her lower back. Pete leads us to the very back. I watch and listen as Pete tells Ryan to lay down on the table and lift her shirt. He tells me where I can sit, so I take a seat.

"Been doing good, Ryan?" he asks as he unhooks her bra, making sure that won't be in his way. I hate that his hands are on her at all. Ryan takes her arm out of her sleeve and that side of her bra before lifting her left arm over her shoulder while the other holds her shirt in place. A small swell of the side of her breast can still be seen though. Then Pete applies a piece of paper with the outline of the heart on it.

"Better than ever." She smiles at me, and I return it. "Is everything good with Max? I don't think I've ever known him not to be here on a Friday night."

"He's been sick all week, and we sure as hell don't want him here like that. I'll make sure he knows that he missed you though."

"Thanks. This will be my last one for a while, I think."

"Why is that? You've let Max work on you three times. I think I deserve two more times to make us even. He did a good job, especially on this seahorse." Pete runs his fingers over it, looking just like I'm sure I did when I did the same thing. "Why the hell did you get a big ass, pink seahorse anyway?"

"And this is why I love Max. He doesn't ask questions. Are we ready to get started or what?" Ryan rolls her eyes, and I laugh.

"Are you ready?" He asks her.

"Yep."

My eyes focus completely on where he's working. But after he does one line, I have to look away, finding Ryan's face a picture of perfection.

"You okay, Gabe?" She questions.

I shift in my seat. "Yeah, but now I know why I never wanted a tattoo. The sound for one and then to see it happen?" I shake my head, resisting the urge to shudder.

Ryan grins, and she's dying to laugh. "Glad to know it's not because you are a goody-two shoes who is scared of his-"

"Don't even say it, Ryan."

"Fine. I won't. But you have to admit that it's hilarious that a measly tattoo scares the big bad cop."

Leaning forward to rest my elbows on my knees, I tell her in a low voice, "Thanks for finding me so hilarious all the time."

Ryan's smile widens, obviously thinking of the handcuffs incident. "You're welcome."

* * *

The easy, laid back banter between us continues throughout the weekend. I love her new tattoo so much too. The red ink sticks out against her skin when she's naked and her arm moves. I love catching sight of it. Like right now as she reaches over to grab the remote from my end table, turning off the TV. She lies back down and pulls the comforter up to cover her breasts, careful not to let it touch under her arm where the tattoo is because of the cream she has to keep on it. I love spending Sundays with her. Especially when our day starts with a little bit of morning sex.

"How is this Thanksgiving ordeal going to work?" She asks, and I can hear a bit of worry hidden in her words.

"We usually get together around noon, eat around one or two, and hang out all day. You can stay with me Wednesday night or I can pick you up from your place Thursday. And you are more than welcome to stay with me Thursday night. I have to go in Friday evening, though."

"Viv and I are going shopping Friday, so I'll just go home afterwards. She's supposed to come over and stay with me that night. Are you nervous about this at all?" She turns her head to look at me.

"No. Not one bit and you shouldn't be either."

Chapter Twelve
Ryan

All week, when I'm not in school, I'm vigorously cleaning my apartment. Gabe might not be worried, might not think I should be, but I am. And I hate it. Gabe and my feelings for him have me feeling vulnerable. Not to mention my new tattoo.

Love.

Love, love, love, love, love, love, love.

That's *all* I've been able to think about. A new four letter word that takes up too much of my thinking. When I saw the heart online, I craved it. That little tat seemed just as mesmerizing as my favorite paintings. I *needed* it on my body. I needed the perfect, pretty heart tattoo on my side near my own, not so pretty, not so perfect heart.

My nervous, scared to death heart.

I have no idea what's going to happen if his parents don't accept me. Will Gabe stand up for me

245

again or will he succumb to his family? I may mean something to Gabe, and I say it that way for a reason, but if he has to choose between them or me, he would choose them.

Right?

That is his family, who he loves and cares about more than anything. Surely, he wouldn't risk his relationship with them just for a relationship with me. To avoid thinking about this all the time as Thursday loomed closer and closer, I've been cleaning like crazy. This place is spotless. Every inch of it. But the day is here. I can't clean anymore. A knock sounds at my door, and I go to answer it. I couldn't even manage to run late like usual. I'm too nervous.

Gabe stands on the other side with a big smile. At least someone is excited about this. I'm not excited, but my nerves disappear at seeing him. Instead, they are replaced with determination. I will do my best to make them like me. I want this so badly. Being in love with Gabe without him knowing is hard enough. I don't need his parents to reject me and make this harder.

"You're ready?" He says with surprise, stepping forward to kiss me sweetly.

"Crazy, I know."

"Well, let's get this show on the road." Gabe holds out his elbow, and I loop my arm through his. On the ride over, Gabe tells me about work and how he and his partner are working well together. He's in the middle of a sentence when we pull up to a house, the driveway and curb full of parked cars, when I interrupt him.

"You are not allowed to leave me alone with anyone other than Gramps or Owen, okay?"

He smiles. "I don't plan on leaving your side, Ryan. It'll be great and fun."

I nod because that is the plan. We get out of his car and head inside. The men are gathered in the living room, and I can hear the bustling of the women in the kitchen. Gramps seems to be the only one missing from the men.

"Hey y'all," Gabe says as we walk further into the house. Heads swivel to look at us and voices all tell us hello. There is only one guy I haven't met. "I'm sure y'all remember Ryan."

"With an aim like that, how could we forget her?" Gabe's cousin, Frank Jr., smiles.

"It's nice to see you guys again," I tell them honestly, noticing that Gabe's father actually smiles at me. What changed his mind about me?

Gabe leads me over to the guy I haven't met yet, and he stands. "Keith, this is Ryan Kavanaugh. Ryan, this is my older brother, Keith."

Keith shakes my hand with a friendly smile. He definitely fits my image of an FBI agent with the exception of his casual clothes. "Nice to meet you, Ryan."

"It's about time you got here, darlin'," I hear behind me before I can respond to Keith. I turn at the sound of Gramps' voice. He comes over and gives me a bear hug. "We're thrilled that you could join us."

I can't help but smile. "Thanks for having me."

"You can come sit with me," Owen says from the couch.

I turn to Gabe, and he smiles in reassurance. "I'm going to say hey to the girls and then I'll be back, if you want to stay in here."

I nod, moving over to sit with Owen. It's better to be in here than with the women. On one side is Owen, and Gramps takes the spot on the other side of me. Gabe's father, Larry, starts talking with Keith about football and then all the men are talking about it. I listen, paying attention to what they say, in case I can learn something new about the sport. Gabe returns to the room, but I have no idea where he's going to sit. He walks in front of Gramps and motions with his hand for me to stand.

Oh, no. Please tell me he isn't going to have me sit in his lap. He's trying to get his parents to hate me even more! Sure enough, Gabe takes my seat before tugging me down, joining in the conversation as if I'm not in his lap. Larry doesn't seem fazed by it, so that's good. But I feel awkward sitting here in a room full of men. Gabe grabs my hips and squeezes lightly as he talks.

"Keith, are you staying for the weekend? Are we still going shooting?" he asks, redirecting his question to everyone else. They all nod and murmur confirmation.

"Darlin', are you going to join us?" Gramps

asks me.

"Oh, I already intruded on y'alls men's day once. I-"

"Nonsense. You have to come. Keith needs to see what you can do," he interrupts.

"Yeah," Keith chirps. "All I've heard about is how you showed up Dad after only shooting for an hour."

Great. I glance at Larry, and I'm shocked when he grins at me. "I'll admit that I wasn't so sure about you that day, but you earned my respect regardless. I could easily see why Gabe would give you a ticket after you asked for it. How exactly did that happen?"

I turn to look at Gabe, but he doesn't say anything. His father did ask me, so I should answer him. "I was having a bad morning. So much so that it irked me when he called me ma'am. I said a few things and then told him to give me my ticket already. He said okay and did just that. Can't blame him either because I deserved it, especially for some of the things I said."

The guys laugh, and Keith speaks up. "How in the world did that turn into you two dating?"

"Ryan is trouble, plain and simple," Gabe says, his thumbs moving up and down over my lower back while keeping his hands on my hips. "And it's very hard to say no when she catches you off guard."

"Hey," I start defensively, turning a bit in his lap to look at him. "Have I had to use my card yet?

No, so I'm not that much trouble."

He laughs. "Good point."

"Let's eat," his mother calls from the dining room, halting the conversation.

Everyone stands simultaneously and heads into the other room. This time, Gabe is on one side and Keith is on the other as we take a seat at the large table. I stay quiet as we all hold hands, and Larry says prayer. Once food gets distributed to everyone, his mother, Camilla, decides to start talking to me. Or should I say, interrogate me.

"So you're in college?" She asks.

"Yes, ma'am." It's best to be as polite as possible. "I'm in my second year, and my major is art, thanks to Gabe," I finish.

"Thanks to Gabriel?" Camilla frowns in confusion.

"Yes, he was the one who helped me figure out what I wanted to major in, Mrs. O'Connor."

She's still frowning, but she continues her interrogation anyway. She should have been an interrogator for the police because she's fucking intimidating. "And do you work as well?"

"No, ma'am. My parents want me to put all my focus on school, so they pay for my expenses." That should be a good thing to say, right? Because it means I'm concentrating all my efforts on my education.

"Your parents have lots of money then?"

"Mom," Gabe protests. "Why does that matter?"

"I only want to make sure that she's not a young, rich, spoiled brat looking for someone to take care of her when her parents decide to stop doing it for her. You're my son, Gabriel, and you often fall for girls who aren't any good for you. I only want what's best for you."

Is she serious? This is fucking ridiculous. Gabe doesn't say a word as he stares at his mother, his mouth closed. He isn't going to say anything. The moment has come, and he's not going to mutter a damn word. I decide then and there that I'm done. The table rattles as I slam my napkin down.

"I think Gabriel," he flinches next to me as the rage courses through me, "is old enough, as you love to point out to me, and smart enough to handle himself. I'm sorry that you have to be rude with the most ridiculous fucking questions that don't have a damn thing to do with who I am as a person." I turn to Gabe. "And Gabe, thanks a lot for standing up for me. I can clearly see how much I mean to you. Now, if you'll excuse me, I have my own fucking problems to deal with instead of your family."

The sound of my chair scraping back is deafening in the room, and I stalk out of there as fast as I can.

"Ryan, wait," Gabe pleads from behind me as I swing the front door open and keep walking.

"Don't even," I call over my shoulder. I was right. Damn it, I was right. He's not even going to stand up for me, and I guess I shouldn't have expected him to do it. See what happens when I have stupid expectations? People fail me. At least now I know how my parents feel.

"Let me take you home."

"No!" I yell, turning to face him.

"Ryan, I didn't say anything because-" he attempts to explain, but I don't want to hear any of it.

"Because you're a goody-two shoes who can't go up against his mother. Viv will come get me. Go enjoy your day with your family."

"Don't be ridiculous. I'm taking you home." He grabs my elbow and pulls me to his car. "And you're going to calm down, so I can talk to you," he says, ushering me into the passenger seat before slamming the door.

I don't want to be around him, but if he needs closure, then he can have it. Let him say whatever he wants. It doesn't matter because this was a terrible idea. Another massive mistake. Gabe backs out, putting more force on the gas than necessary. Once we're on the road, he starts talking.

"Look, I didn't say anything because I was shocked by what my mom said. I've never seen her be so critical before, so I couldn't believe it. You don't need to be pissed at me because I was five seconds away from defending you before you went and made a fool of yourself."

"You've got to be kidding me! Standing up for myself was me being a fool? What the hell did you expect to happen, Gabe? Look at me! Do you not remember what she said when she came over? Do you not remember what my own damn parents are like? I told you from the start that I am not meet-the-parents material, and there's your proof. I want to believe you, I really do, but I don't think you would have said anything to her. That's your mother, and you said so yourself that her opinion matters to you. There's her stupid, fucking opinion from hell. I don't think for a second that you would go against your *family*."

My rant lasted all the way to my apartment, and I couldn't be happier to be here. I quickly get out of the car, briskly walking towards the building.

"She's being overprotective," Gabe tries to defend from behind me.

"You're twenty-five! Do you seriously need your mother to look out for you? To protect you from *me*? Because that's what you're saying." I shove the key into my door and find that it's not locked. Oh, hell no. Not today. Sure enough, my parents are inside, dragging an annoyed and frustrated groan from me. "Why the hell are y'all here? Can't y'all ever call before you come?"

"Quit being so dramatic, Ryan. It's Thanksgiving. You told us you were staying here, so we came to tell you that we've picked a degree for you," her mother says. "We didn't know that you would be out with him."

"I'm seriously not in the mood for this, Mom. Please come back another day."

"Ryan," my dad speaks up. "This is our last day in town. We rather not waste time with your silly, girly tantrums."

What an ass! I walk in front of where they are sitting on my couch, fold my arms over my chest, and glare at them. "Well, waste no more time, because I'm majoring in art."

Mom's mouth hangs open. "Where did that even come from? You can't be serious, Ryan. That's a terrible decision. We should have never left you here alone because you obviously can't make good, reasonable decisions. Although, I guess we should have expected as much."

"Stop! Just stop!" I erupt with long overdue fury, finally letting it loose. This is not the day for them to rain down their shit on me after what I just went through with Gabe. "I'm so tired of hearing how nothing I do is good enough. What the hell do you expect me to do, Mom? I have been the best I can possibly be for you, and that bit of fucking effort means nothing to neither of you!" I point back and forth between my parents. "Because of you, I don't have a fucking clue about what I want to do with *my* life because I've been busy trying to please *you* and make *you* proud. It's pointless because you don't give a damn. You set me up for failure with your ridiculous expectations.

"I'm sorry I'm not a boy. I'm sorry I don't play football and baseball or any other boy sport. I'm sorry I can't walk in Dad's footsteps. I'm sorry I don't wear suits and care about business. I'm sorry

254

I didn't ask for a sports car. I'm sorry I like shopping. I'm sorry tradition says you'll pay for a wedding. I'm sorry father-daughter dances sound so fucking horrible. I'm sorry pink disgusts you. I'm sorry that you think I'm a quitter because nothing I liked growing up was worth 'wasting' your precious money on or because you insisted I do the impossible. I'm sorry that because of the stupid fact I'm a damn girl that I can't do anything right. I'm sorry my absolute *best* is shit to you, and that I can't do what's expected of me because you expect *more*, which isn't even possible! I'm sorry that all your dreams died with me.

"But you know what? I don't care anymore! Fuck you both." I take a deep breath, noticing the stunned faces in the room. "Fuck you too, Gabe. Now, if you don't mind, all of you can go to hell and get out of my apartment!"

The pure rage runs through me, and my hands are aching to do something. I walk into my kitchen, ignoring them and hoping they'll just leave. My hip bumps into the counter, and I scream in frustration, yanking open the dishwasher. Yes. Breaking something will release some of this from me. I grab a glass plate, hold it over my head, and then throw it down on the floor. A frantic energy buzzes through me with a touch of excitement. God, that felt good.

I pull out the top rack, picking up the first glass thing I find. A bowl. It crashes to the floor, shattering to pieces, and mixing with the remnants of the plate. Faintly, I hear my mother shouting for me to stop, but the sound of her voice fuels me to do it again, but with a cup this time. When I lift a bowl above my head, hands grab my wrists.

"Stop it, Ryan," Gabe says quietly from behind me.

"Let me go!" I try to twist my wrists free, but his grip is too strong.

"No. You need to stop."

His soft tone breaks through my anger. "Fine," I mutter. He takes the bowl from my hands. "Everyone needs to leave. Now." I turn to face my parents, but I'm speaking to Gabe as well. "Either y'all leave or I will."

My parents actually look terrified by my outburst and fit of rage. They nod solemnly before walking out, leaving only Gabe for me to get rid of.

"Ryan," he starts.

"No, Gabe," I interrupt quietly, facing him completely now. With as much strength as I can muster, I continue, "I've been worrying about letting you down and not meeting your and your family's expectations. Not once did I consider that our roles would reverse, and you would be the one to let me down." His mouth parts to speak, but nothing comes and I finish, "Just go home. I don't want to deal with anything yet, and I need to clean up. Please go."

He closes this mouth, nods reluctantly, and then he's gone too. Part of me wishes Gabe wouldn't listen to me. That he would make me listen, but I can't blame him for leaving when I asked him to go. It wouldn't be right to expect two opposite behaviors from him, and in the end, I'm more grateful that he is giving me space than staying. I stare at what remains of my dishes. This day has gone to hell in a hand basket, that's for sure. I leave the mess of broken glass on my floor. Once I lock my door, I go to my room, texting Viv that I've gotten terribly sick and can't go shopping tomorrow. She's with her family, so I know it may be awhile before she responds. I hook my phone up to the speakers, turning on my rock playlist, and flop onto my bed.

I can't believe that I completely broke down, not only in front of my parents, but Gabe too. I don't know why I care though. He doesn't. He couldn't even defend me to his mother. This has to be the worst day of my life. While I lay, listening to "Crazy Bitch", I realize that staying here probably isn't a good idea. Viv has a key, my parents have a key, and Gabe knows that he can find me here if he decides to come back to talk to me.

Getting up, I start packing some bags. I don't want to see anyone and the only way to make sure that happens is to go stay somewhere else. So I shove some clothes and other necessities into a bag, grab my other things, and leave for a hotel downtown. It takes a couple stops to find a hotel with a vacancy, but I do. A few calls from Gabe and texts from Viv filter in, so I turn off my phone.

The relentless thoughts continue to plague my

mind. I stuff my face with desserts from room service while I think. I probably ruined things with Gabe if he was telling the truth about how he would have defended me to his mother. The fiasco with my parents doesn't even bother me. Not in comparison to things with Gabe. My parents aren't ever going anywhere. There is no guarantee that I'm going to have Gabe in my life at all, much less for forever. Not that I can say I want that. Picking a major freaked me out. I doubt I could say I knew for sure that I wanted Gabe.

Once again, I find myself being pulled in a million different directions, it seems. The art museum and that fire painting come to mind. I look up their hours online and find that they are open tomorrow. Maybe that will make all this shit go away for a little while.

Chapter Thirteen
Gabe

I storm back to my parents' house after leaving Ryan's. Leaving her alone was the last thing I wanted to do, but I didn't want to make things worse. If she needs time, I'll give her some. But not for long because now, I do need to swoop in like Prince Charming and fix this mess. When Ryan told me that I let her down, I couldn't find words to defend myself. As soon as the words left her mouth, I realized that was my fear with Ryan, and that it had come true. I let her down and in the worst way possible. I disappointed her. I failed to meet her expectations. A couple seconds of silence and my mother made me hurt her. She expected more, and that's exactly what she deserved.

Right now, I need to find out what my mother was thinking when she opened her mouth. If she was thinking at all. Things appear to have continued relatively normally. The guys are in the living room, watching TV, and the girls are cleaning up in the kitchen. The door slams loudly behind me, causing them to look at me.

"Gabriel," my father starts with a small warning in his voice.

I ignore him and burst through the swinging door to the kitchen. Everything halts as the women turn to look at me. My eyes find my mother's. I wasn't lying when I told Ryan that I was shocked by what she said. She's never been so hard on a girl before. That wasn't how the day was supposed to go. Not in the least. I have to find out what in the world happened.

"I would like to speak with you," I say calmly.

Mom nods, and wordlessly the others leave the room. "Gabriel," she begins.

"What *was* that?" I harshly ask, my hands clenching in fists at my sides. Now that I'm back here, I'm pissed.

"I'm sorry-"

"You should be! Ryan has been worrying ever since I asked her to come here. I told her she had nothing to worry about, and you go and say that she's a rich brat wanting me to take care of her?! Where did you even get that impression, Mom? When have I ever said something like that about Ryan?"

She wrings her hands together. I've never spoken to my mother this way, but then again, I've never had a reason. "You didn't. I was out of line, I know, but I was worried about you overlooking signs that show she's no good for you. You've done it before, and she's young-"

"I don't care, Mom!" I interrupt, irritated that she's still on that. "There's nothing wrong with Ryan! Not her age, her tattoos, or her personality." I take a deep breath to calm my anger. "She is amazing, and there's a lot you don't know about her because I haven't told you. There's no way for me to explain how beautiful a person Ryan is without telling you everything about her, but I shouldn't have to do that. I asked you not to judge, Mom. I asked you to ignore what you saw and get to know *her*. You went into that dinner with the intentions to grill her until you found a reason to doubt me. And now, she doesn't want me near her.

"I love you, Mom, but you have to stop. You care and want to protect me, and I get that. But I learned from my mistakes, and I'm twenty-five! I can take care of myself. You can't ruin my relationship just because you have this absurd idea that Ryan isn't a good person. *I'm* in a relationship with her, not you! An open mind, so you could get to know her is all I asked for, Mom. Instead, you completely overstepped, jumped to conclusions, and didn't treat Ryan anywhere near to how she deserved to be treated."

"Gabriel," my father says from behind me, interrupting my rant.

With another deep breath, I try to tone down my words one last time. "Ryan isn't like anyone I've ever dated before. You should have trusted my

261

judgment. Even if you didn't, you still shouldn't have said those things because now, I have to go fix what you've broken."

Turning around, I brush past my father and leave before anything else could be said. I'm not in the mood to be around everyone any longer or hear an apology from Mom. What I really want is to go check on Ryan, but I go on to my house. She probably needs more time to cool down, and I most definitely do not want to interrupt and cause her to need even more time. When I get home, I shower and then lay down on the couch to watch TV.

I do call Ryan twice. She doesn't answer, so I leave a simple voicemail, asking her to call me back. She doesn't. Just in case she calls at a late hour, deciding she does want to talk, I try to stay up. My eyes start to get heavy during a late night talk show, and before long, I drift to sleep.

* * *

My phone blares loudly as my eyes squint open. A pain shoots through my neck thanks to falling asleep on the couch. I sit up, look around for my phone, and find it on the floor under the coffee table. It must have fallen while I was sleeping. My hope is that it's Ryan, but one look at the unfamiliar number diminishes my hopes.

"Hello?" I answer.

"Gabe? It's Vivian. Is Ryan with you?" She sounds a bit panicked, which immediately brings me to attention.

"No, she isn't. She's not with you?" I'm positive she told me that they were going shopping today.

"No. I just got to her apartment to check on her because she cancelled on me yesterday and her phone keeps going to voicemail. She's not here, and I wondered if she might be with you. Oh, God!" She screams.

"What is it?" My body tenses waiting to hear what's going on.

"There's broken glass all over the kitchen floor! What-"

"Ryan did that yesterday while I was there. It wasn't a good day," I sigh, remembering it all. "You don't know where she might have gone?"

"No. She's never disappeared before."

"I'm sure she's fine, but I'll try to get up with her, okay?"

That soothes her as she demands I call her the moment I hear from Ryan. As I get dressed, I wonder where Ryan is. She didn't clean up, like she told me she needed to do. Instead, she left. Where would she have gone? I'm not sure what I should do, so I drive around, looking for her car, and feeling a bit on the stalker-ish side. But then I spot it in the parking lot of the art museum. It's kind of hard to miss because there aren't many cars there in the first place.

She was fascinated with the fire painting, and I bet that's where she is. That's my first stop. Sure enough, she's standing before the wall, staring at the flames. Quietly, I walk up behind her and clear my throat.

Ryan glances back, her eyes watery before they harden at the sight of me. She faces the painting again and in a harsh whisper, she tells me, "Go away."

"Ryan," I try. It kills me that she won't even look at me. I reach out, my fingers brushing her hips to bring her closer to me. The need to touch her and feel her is overwhelming now that she's right here. As soon as the tips of my fingers are on her, Ryan steps away to be out of my reach. The message is clear. She doesn't want me here with her. "I'm sorry. I should have-"

"It doesn't matter," she interrupts. "I don't want to hear whatever you have to say. Leave me alone, Gabe." With that last sentence, she doesn't sound angry anymore. It reminds me of when she asked me to leave before, and she only sounded tired.

"Will you let me-"

"No," she curtly cuts me off, the anger flaring again with my attempt.

"Okay," I relent as a terrible feeling of despair grasps me. "I'll go." That's the last thing I want to do, but I won't force her to talk to me. Her shoulders relax slightly, just enough to make me realize that they were tense. "If you change your mind-"

"I won't."

I ignore her and continue, "Call me. I'll be working, but we could talk when I get off. We need to talk, Ryan. I need you to talk to me."

She doesn't acknowledge me anymore, and it breaks my heart. It hurts even worse to know that she loves me, I've inadvertently hurt her, and she doesn't know how I feel. She's not in the mood to talk to me. I have to respect that as much as I don't want to do so. Turning on my heels, I leave her behind, wondering how long I'm going to have to wait before she'll hear me out.

Chapter Fourteen
Ryan

There aren't many people here, thank goodness. Two lone tears, one on each side, run down my face. Just as I'm about to turn around, to give in to the plea in his voice, I hear Gabe walking away. Too late now. I'm not going to chase him, even if I'm dying to talk to him. He's leaving, and I'll let him go. I told him to anyway. This is okay, I think as I stare at the painting.

The bleak, black background is a stark contrast to the orange-reddish flames. I feel the battle between the flames as they try to stretch upwards, each lick of fire trying to reach farther than the other. The longer I look, the more I can feel the same battle against oneself inside me. This sucks. It's not making me feel better, so I turn to leave.

I can and will be fine without him. Part of me wants to fight to hold on to him, but I can't. I won't. My damn mind keeps replaying Gabe's silence.

266

Over and over. If he had even an inkling of love for me, he would have immediately said something.

He didn't.

So, he doesn't.

Besides, I should be more focused on the disaster I call family. My parents call the following Sunday. The conversation is much longer than I wanted, but I get my way in the end. I can still hear the skepticism in their voices after I calmly explained why I wanted to major in art. My mother was thoroughly confused why I picked that. I'm pretty sure I scared them with my outburst, and she was genuinely trying to understand my decision.

After I told her, she seemed to accept it. Mostly. Their displeasure was apparent, but it all came down to one thing. If I was going to fail, then it might as well be because of me and only me. Then she said that if I changed my mind or if my grades slipped, they were cutting me off. They weren't going to waste money on my indecisiveness or laziness. Overall, the conversation was bullshit.

Nothing has changed. I don't even know if I want things to ever change. The way our relationship is right now is all I've ever known. It's a sucky one, but it doesn't have to change because it would either be for the better or for the worst. Hell, talking to my mom like normal was new, and I kind of hated it. Explaining it to her was torture because all it reminded me of was Gabe. He led me to the decision after all. Damn it. I miss him.

    None of that matters, though. The only person I'm talking to is Viv. I told my parents I needed some space, so they've stopped calling for the mean time. And I'm still ignoring Gabe. He calls, leaves messages, but I don't listen to them. I can't. If I do, I'm scared it'll wear me down and I'll call him. My grudge against him is still there, and I'm still mad as hell over it. Right now, it's easier for me to stay pissed off than to face the music and listen to Gabe.

    If I stop being angry, then it'll hit me that I bitched at Gabe and he might have been telling the truth. He could have been seconds away from standing up to his mother. I'll never really know because I spoke up first. He should have beaten me to it, but he didn't. Even if he was going to, I don't want to become a wedge between him and his family. His mother aside, Gabe has a wonderful family. They love each other to no end. I don't want to interfere with that.

    No matter how many times Gabe calls, I don't answer. He calls at least once every day, and even a call to Viv here and there. I was with her the first time he called. She didn't tell him much, and after she hung up, I told her that if he calls again, she better not say anything more than I'm fine. Gabe doesn't get to know those things anymore. I almost want to give in because he calls her to check on me, but then again, that pisses me off too. If I wanted him to know, I would answer him myself.

    For now, Viv is all I need, and I'm happy with

that. Finals are coming up in a few weeks. Part of me wants to go party, get fucked, and forget about everything. I don't really want to do that, though. Besides, I need to make all A's, so the only thing I have time for is studying. I don't need my parents, Gabe, or that stupid four letter L-word on my mind to distract me.

Chapter Fifteen
Gabe

I never went shooting with the guys, and I've immersed myself in my work. My boss gets sick of seeing me at the station, finding paperwork to do. If my brain is numb with writing stuff down, then it'll be too tired to think about Ryan and her silence. I've tried calling Ryan multiple times, but she never answers. I don't even get to hear her phone ring and ring because she hits ignore, sending me straight to her voicemail. Maybe she just needs time to figure things out for herself. She's probably having to deal with lashing out at her parents too. Ryan doesn't need me adding to her problems.

Every day, I think about the night of her birthday. When she told me in false confidence that she loved me. I know that I have feelings for her, and I know the extent of those feelings. Not once did I tell her before Thanksgiving. I should have because now, she's dealing with what happened with us as well as her parents, and she doesn't know. What's worse is that she probably doesn't think I have feelings for her at all. I've tried to speak with her, but I have to wait until she's ready to talk to me. Whenever that will be. Every time she sends me to her automated voicemail, I want to run over there and demand she listen to me. I can't. So I'll keep calling, keep leaving messages, and wait until I can't wait anymore.

I make sure to work every Sunday to get out of going to dinner at my parents. I'm still not happy about Thanksgiving, and I haven't been talking to my mom that much. Of course, I'll be back soon enough, but for now, I just want to work as much as possible. Anything to keep me from being at home. Because when I'm at home, the thoughts of Ryan are so much worse. The memories of her birthday party, of the night it stormed and she didn't want to come inside, of the night we had sex in every room of my house, and of her smile when she saw I bought Sunkist for her.

She's everywhere.

When I patrol downtown and pass where we saw her on Halloween, I think about her stumbling down the street and me taking her home. Any time Fredrick says something inappropriate, I remember that night. I think about her every time I wash dishes. It's crazy! I'll end up washing the same dish for ten minutes because Thanksgiving replays in my mind as I picture her breaking down and throwing the glassware onto the floor. I saw her relax bit by bit with each thing she destroyed, but I stopped her anyway. All my memories of her play on a loop in my mind.

I want to see her and force her to talk to me. The main reason why I haven't is because I don't know what's going on with her parents. If things aren't going well, I want to be there for her, but I don't want to make things worse either. I've even called Viv a few times to check on Ryan. She only says that Ryan is fine, and she'll let her know that I called. I've done everything short of stalking over there.

"You're here early," Fredrick says, taking a seat in the empty chair at the table in the break room, pulling me from my memories.

"There was some paperwork I needed to do."

"You've been doing a lot of paperwork lately."

"Are we going to work or not?" I snap.

He holds his hands up in surrender as I mutter an apology, and we head outside to leave. I don't know why she continues to ignore me, but I think it's time I stop doing as she wishes. Tomorrow, Ryan is going to talk to me because I can't let this go on any longer.

* * *

The sound of a gunshot rings loud in the air.

"You good?" I call out to Fredrick.

"Yeah," he yells back.

The idiot shooting at us takes off running

down the street. We got a call about a burglary in progress and came onto the scene while he was still here. I move from my spot behind the car and take off after him. I yell out for him to stop, but it's pointless. He rounds a corner about ten seconds before I do.

Two shots ring out, burning pain hitting me in the shoulder and knocking me down with surprise. His footsteps take off again and moments later, Fredrick is next to me. God, this hurts. The next few hours pass in a blur as I'm shipped off to the hospital, and they go to work on my shoulder.

When I wake up in a hospital room, I think about Ryan. I haven't spoken to her in two weeks. I miss her, and I want to talk to her. I want her. It's that simple. My shoulder aches, and I turn my head to see my mother asleep in the chair. A nurse enters the room, dragging my attention to her. She smiles when she sees I'm awake.

"How are you doing, Officer O'Connor?" She asks quietly.

"You tell me."

"You're doing well. After some time to recover, you'll be good as new," she tells me as she looks at the numbers on the monitor.

"What time is it?" I question.

"Almost four in the morning."

"Gabriel?" At the sound of my mother's voice, I turn my head. She's sitting up in the chair with a blanket covering her lower body and a pillow has fallen behind her back.

"You didn't have to stay the night, Mom," I tell her as the nurse leaves.

She gets up and walks over to me. "You're my son. Of course, I did. I, uh," she hesitates. "I didn't know if I should get Fredrick to tell Ryan or not, so I told him not to until I talked to you to see what you wanted. I don't know what's been going." A guilty look passes over her face, even though I'm the one who hasn't been talking to her.

"It's fine, Mom. I haven't spoken to her since Thanksgiving, so it's not like she's expecting to hear from me or anything."

She nods. "You should get some rest."

"Yeah, I guess so."

Mom goes back to the chair, and I close my eyes, knowing I'm going to have to see my father and Owen in the morning. Mom probably sent everyone home. Her mentioning Ryan has me thinking about her again. All this time, I've known how she feels, or felt, about me, and I never told her my own feelings. Whether she wants to or not, she's going to talk to me. As soon as I can get out of here.

Chapter Sixteen
Ryan

A pounding lulls me out of sleep, and I realize someone is at my door. I glance at the clock and see that it's seven in the morning. Who the hell is here? Groaning, I roll over, get out of bed, and grab a scrunchie on my way to the door. I throw my hair up, the pounding louder now, and yank open the door.

"What the fuck do-" The words clog my throat as I see Camilla, Gabe's mother, standing outside my door. I stare at her, my heart frozen mid-beat. Why is she here? What does she want? Did Gabe send her to apologize or something?

"Morning, Ryan," she says. "I'm sorry that it's so early. May I come inside?"

"Why?" I question with confusion. The words she said to me reappear in my mind full force, sparking my anger. "Would you like to look at all the things my parents have provided for their little, spoiled brat? I'm sorry, but it's way too early in the morning for personal tours."

As I start to close my door, her hand shoots out to stop me. "Ryan, wait."

Huffing, I open it again. "Honestly, Mrs. O'Connor, I don't want to hear what you have to say."

"I think you do," she says quietly, her eyes never wavering from my own. "May I come inside?" she repeats. Something about the way she said it makes me step aside.

I lead her to the kitchen table, thankful that during my study breaks, I've been in a cleaning frenzy. Camilla sits down and places her hands in her lap. For a moment, she doesn't say anything at all.

"Gabriel told me that you haven't been talking to him."

Narrowing my eyes, I interrupt, "No, I haven't spoken to *Gabriel*." It pisses me off that she says his first name like that, which is ridiculous.

"And it's no wonder. You're a hard person to apologize to." My mouth opens, but she holds up her hand to stop me and keeps going. "I'm sorry, Ryan. Sometimes, I worry too much. Gabriel's relationships always end because he's too compliant, too willing to trust. He dated a girl once who was a few years younger than him, and she took advantage of him and his hard earned money.

"I made assumptions about you because of that, and I shouldn't have. My son told me to trust

276

him, and I didn't. So I'm sorry about what happened. And so you know, after he brought you home, Gabriel came back and let me know how angry he was over I what I said. He did stand up for you."

"He did? Right after he left here?" I question, and she nods.

Camilla lets that sink in. Gabe stood up for me. Before I can fully process this, she continues, "I didn't know until last night that Gabriel hasn't heard from you. You've been ignoring him, and he's been ignoring me." Gabe hasn't been talking to his mother? "I came over to apologize and to let you know that he got hurt last night."

"What?" I breathe what little air I have. Her final words steal all my breath from me. "He's been hurt? Is he okay? Where is he? What happened?"

She gives me a reassuring smile. "Gabriel will be fine. He was shot twice in the shoulder, and he'll need some time to heal, but he's okay. He's still at the hospital. Would you like to go back with me to see him?"

Gabe was shot? Oh, my God. My heart rams into my chest furiously. She said he was okay. That's what I keep repeating in my head as I nod to let her know I want to see him and I go change. I'm a wreck, and I'm rambling at an all time high as I worry. Two sentences are a calming mantra in my head.

He's okay. He's going to be fine.

I'll be fine once I see it for myself.

Chapter Seventeen
Gabe

I've just finished eating breakfast. My boss and Fredrick have already stopped by to see me as well as some others from the station. Mom peeks from around the door. Dad and Owen must be here now. I try to sit up a little more.

"Are you up for some company?" She asks.

"Absolutely."

Mom disappears instead of walking in with my dad and Owen behind her, like I expect. Instead, Ryan hesitantly enters the room.

"Hey," I greet. A smile instantly appears on my face. To say I'm thrilled that she's here in the same room as me doesn't even begin to cover it.

"Hey. Your mom came to my apartment this morning and told me you were hurt," she explains, still standing by the door. Ryan clasps her hands together in front of her, and I realize that she's nervous.

"My mom went to your place?"

Ryan nods. "You didn't know?"

"No, I didn't." Wow. I can't believe my mom personally went to Ryan's. But I'm so happy she did. Ryan is standing too far away from me, so I add, "You don't have to stand way over there, you know."

She seemed to be waiting to me to give her a sign that I wanted her here because she rushes over, the words spilling from her mouth.

"I'm so sorry, Gabe. I shouldn't have been so angry not to listen to you, to let you explain. With your parents and then my parents, I wanted some time to clear my head. I'm so sorry."

"I love you," I interrupt. I just want her to know, but it doesn't faze her rambling. By the faraway look of terror in her eyes, she didn't even hear me.

"You have to understand that I was just upset. Ever since I met you, you opened my eyes to better things, to the possibility that I can have more, should have more, and I haven't been able to completely figure out what to do about that. Or how to fix things with you."

"I love you," I try again. She still doesn't hear my words.

"I've never wanted someone like this in my entire life. That scared me more than anything, and I'm so sorry. I-"

"Ryan," I say as sternly as I can. She blinks, her eyes finally focusing on me. "Did you hear me?"

Ryan shakes her head. "I told you, twice," I add, laughter hinting in my tone. "That I love you," I finally finish, grateful to have her undivided attention.

Confusion flits across her face for a moment before it's replaced with relief. "You do?" The corners of her mouth tilts up slightly.

"Absolutely." I squeeze her hand. "I love you, Ryan." My words are soft, but the love in my voice is unmistakable. She leans forward to kiss me, accidentally leaning on my shoulder. "Ow," I flinch in pain.

"Shit! Sorry!" Ryan moves to the other side of the bed, carefully hovering above me and kisses me. "I love you too. I'm so happy you're okay, Gabe."

"It's nothing serious. I'm fine. I'm more happy to see you."

"You were shot," she frowns at my dismissive tone towards what happen.

"Trust me, I know. I'm even thankful I was."

"What the hell are you talking about, Gabe?" Ryan is thoroughly confused now.

"Well, I wouldn't choose for it to happen, but it did. My *mom*," I emphasize so she'll understand my point, "went to tell you what happened when she found out we weren't talking." I lace my fingers with hers. "You're here. I've missed you so much."

"I missed you too." She smiles.

"I've been worried about you."

Ryan frowns. "Worried? Why were you

worried?"

"I didn't know how things were with you and with your parents."

"Oh. Well, I told them how badly I wanted to major in art and why I picked it. They told me they would support my decision under a few conditions. Other than that, we haven't really talked much. I think blowing up like I did really caught their attention. There's still a long way to go before things are better." She sounds hopeful, and that makes me hopeful for her.

"It's a start, right?" She nods. "C'mere." I keep saying, "Closer," until she's close enough for me to kiss her. Ryan's grinning when I press my lips to hers. I kiss her slowly, but fiercely until I hear that happy sigh of hers. "Are you going to take care of me when I go home?" I mumble against her lips.

She laughs. "Yes, I will."

"Thank you."

Her green eyes pierce me. "You've taught me so much more than football or shooting, Gabe. Thank you for that."

I smile because she's taught me so much too. Not only that, but I've finally met the person I can love with everything I am and who will love me just the same. Just as Ryan is about to give me another kiss, the door creaks open to reveal my mother, causing Ryan to stand upright again.

"Is everything okay in here?" She asks.

"Yeah, Mom. We're good." I squeeze Ryan's hand, and she smiles down at me.

"Great. Your father and brother are here if you want to see them." She glances between us, almost as if she's intruding.

I open my mouth, but Ryan beats me to it. Her eyes find me, and she gives me a small smile. "I'm going to go, but I'll be back, okay?"

"You don't have-"

"Your mom woke me up and then we came straight here. I haven't eaten anything yet, so I'm going to find some food in this place. I'll be back," she repeats as she finishes.

I don't want her to go. I just got her back. But she needs to eat, so I nod reluctantly. Ryan carefully leans down to give me a quick kiss before leaving the room as my family reenters. Mom, Dad, and Owen spend some time with me, talking to me, but I'm barely paying attention. For the first time in weeks, Ryan is in the same building as me, and we need to make up for lost time.

When she finally comes back, I grin at her. "You missed all the action, Ryan," I say.

"I did? What happened?" She asks as she comes to stand to my right.

I move my left hand over my stomach, palm up, and she reaches out to hold it like I was hoping she would. "I'm being discharged. Are you ready to take care of me?"

Ryan laughs. "Of course, Gabe."

"Good. Dad and Owen are going to take me home. Mom can take you back to your place so you can get your things and then you can come over."

"Sounds like you have everything planned out," she says.

"I do."

"We should go; you'll be discharged soon," Mom inputs.

She and Ryan leave, and I'm once again playing the waiting game. At least the next time I see her, we'll be alone. My arm goes into a sling, which I can already tell is going to be a pain, and soon I'm being dropped off at home to wait for Ryan. I go into my bedroom to attempt to change into more comfortable clothes. What I really want is a shower.

"Gabe?" Ryan calls out.

"In here."

"Who's pants-less now?" She laughs as she walks in, sees me in boxers and a t-shirt, and sets her things down at the foot of my bed.

Chuckling, I wiggle my fingers for her to come over. "Help me with my shirt, please." Ryan carefully helps me remove my shirt, her eyes traveling over my body. "Miss me?"

Her eyes snap up to mine. "So much." Ryan rests her forehead over my heart as she wraps her arms tightly around me like I might disappear at any second.

With my hand on the back of her neck, I softly say, "Hey, what's the matter?"

"Nothing," she answers, her warm breath hitting my skin. "I was pissy with your mom when she came to my door. Then she told me you were hurt, and I felt like I couldn't breathe. You scared me to death, Gabe. It could have been so much worse and then I wouldn't have ever told you I loved you because I was too damn stubborn to answer your calls. I just-"

I move my hand to her chin, a tear falling onto my hand. "Look at me," I interrupt. Ryan lifts her head, and my thumb wipes away her tear-streaked cheeks. "I'm okay, Ryan." Cupping her cheek as she leans her head into it, I add, "I'm right here with you. I'm fine, so don't worry about the 'what could have been'. Besides, I already knew you loved me. All I was worried about was making sure you knew I loved you too."

Ryan frowns. "How did you know? I never told you, unless..." Her eyes widen. "You heard me? You've known all this time?" She doesn't sound angry, but she does seem a bit upset.

Nodding, I explain. "I was nearly asleep, but when you started talking, it woke me up. I'm sorry. It wasn't until you left me that I realized exactly how I felt about you. You not knowing killed me as much as you ignoring me. I didn't want to be just another person in your life who has let you down. You deserved better than that, and I wanted to make sure I could be what you deserved, someone worthy of you."

Another tear falls, and I swipe it away, waiting for her to speak. "I love you, Gabe." It seems like she can't find more words than that. Ryan smiles and adds, "I brought dinner. We should go eat before it gets cold. And just so you know, I expect a kiss every time I do something to take care of you." Ryan smiles.

"Oh yeah? I may end up being a little helpless then." She gives me one of her sexy laughs that I've missed so much. "Thank you for being here," I add.

"There's nowhere else I'd rather be." Ryan tilts her head, watching me for a moment. I wait to see if she's going to say something else. "You owe me a kiss, Officer."

Without waiting even a second longer, I lean forward to press my lips against hers. That happy sigh comes immediately as I part her lips, slowly exploring her mouth as if I've never been there before. It's as passionate and heady as before, but this time it's infused with care and love. Ryan digs her fingers into my hair, nibbles on my lower lip, before deepening our kiss one more time.

When I pull away, my favorite sight is before me. Ryan's eyes are closed as she tries to savor what she felt for a few more moments. Her eyes open, and I grin.

"Let's go eat."

We go to my kitchen and while Ryan is taking the burgers out of the bag from the fast food restaurant, a hint of a red heart tattoo can be seen through her thin white shirt. I reach out and run my fingers over the spot. Ryan stops, looks down at my hand, and then back to me.

"Why did you get this? All your tats mean something to you, but you never said anything other than you found it online and loved how it looked." The more I think about it, the more curious I am. Ryan doesn't just get inked. There's always a meaning with each one, but I don't know what this heart means.

"I know I told you that if you were to get one, I didn't want you to get anything related to me because it should mean something to you, but you were a reason I got it and you do mean something to me." I still don't understand, but Ryan continues in a ramble, something I've undoubtedly missed. "When I saw the heart, I was feeling vulnerable over you, and all I could think about was love. Love this and love that. It was annoying as hell, Gabe.

"But I needed this heart. At first, I thought it was because I needed a pretty and perfect heart next to my own not so pretty, not so perfect heart. Now though, I think I wanted it because I love you. You are the one person who I can tell anything to without worrying about expectations and even if it scared me, I could put my heart out there for you to see because I knew you would take care of it. It's a symbol of how I am with and because of you," she finishes.

I smile. "You were always that way, Ryan. You just didn't know it yet."

Epilogue
Ryan
Three Months Later...

I took care of Gabe, just as I said I would, until he was completely healthy again. He kissed me every time I helped him and even when I refused. He started asking for ridiculous or impossible things, cracking me up with his creativity, and every time I said no, he kissed me. It kind of sucked when he got better and didn't need me there as an excuse to help anymore. I stayed with him the entire time and with him healthy, I went back to staying at my apartment.

My parents and I remain at a standstill, but that's okay. I've started working at a convenience store with an awesome boss who works with me being in school. Earning my own money and spending that is such an awesome feeling. I try to spend my parents' money instead of my own. This way I can save it for whatever I do after college, and I can officially stop being dependent on my parents.

When I'm not working or in class, I find time to spend with Gabe. We've visited three more museums and a few galleries. I've been shooting with them too, and Gramps has become my biggest fan. Larry, Gabe's father, has even given me pointers on how to shoot better when Gabe was talking to one of the guys. Owen still harmlessly flirts here and there, which really irritates Gabe. Turns out he's a bit possessive over me, even with his own baby brother. It cracks me up sometimes. Owen has found a confidant in me, texting me with questions about girls. It's sweet that he thinks I give good advice.

Best of all, his mother loves me. We've had lunch together a few times, which she insisted upon. She wanted to know me like her son does. Camilla is almost a mother figure to me now. It's kind of weird if I think about too much, so I don't. His entire family has become family, really. They've accepted me as one of them, and that has been a wonderful experience.

"Are you coming or not, Ryan?" Gabe calls from my bathroom where he's waiting for me in our bubble bath.

"We're not taking a relaxed bath, so I guess the answer is only if you can make me," I yell back, pressing play on my love playlist. When I turn, intending on going to join Gabe, he's walking toward me, dripping wet with suds sliding down his hard body. He picks me up in his arms, causing me to squeal. "You're getting me wet," I laugh, feeling my clothes dampen thanks to him.

"That's the point," he smirks.

"You're staying tonight," I inform him as he begins stripping me down. It's been two weeks since he's stayed over because we've both been busy.

Gabe's hands still with the hem of my shirt bunched in his hands, his fingers brushing my side just below my bra. "I'm staying a lot longer than that, Ryan."

"Promise?" I ask, not minding that he went from playful to serious so fast. I love when does. He tells me all the time what he's feeling and thinking. He never wants me to doubt it, and I never do.

"Absolutely."

About the Author

Lindsay Paige is the author of the Bold as Love series, *Don't Panic*, and *You Before Me*. She is also the coauthor of The Penalty Kill Trilogy.

She has three passions in life: reading, writing, and watching hockey, especially the Pittsburgh Penguins. Among the pile of books to read, stories to write, and games to watch, Lindsay is also focused on completing college.

Lindsay resides in North Carolina and is inspired by world around her and the people in it. Many of the aspects in her books stem from her love for hockey and her struggles in life and with anxiety, as evident in *Don't Panic*.

She is currently working on numerous solo works and a couple of projects with coauthor Mary Smith as well.

For more information about the author, visit authorlindsaypaige.blogspot.com/

Coming Soon

Be on the lookout for a New Adult Hockey Romance featuring new characters, Neil, Grant, and Winston. They are friends and teammates on a college hockey team, each having vastly different relationships with girls.

Lindsay Paige and Mary Smith are teaming up once again to bring you a new standalone series titled:
Oh Captain, My Captain.

Books by Lindsay Paige

Bold as Love series
Don't Panic
You Before Me
The Penalty Kill Trilogy with Mary Smith